Also available from Sandra Owens and Carina Press

Operation K-9 Brothers
Keeping Guard
Mountain Rescue

Coming Soon

Her Delta Force Protector

Also available from Sandra Owens

Blue Ridge Valley Series

Just Jenny
All Autumn
Still Savannah
Caitlyn's Christmas Wish

Dark Falls Series

Dark Terror
Dark Memories

Aces & Eights Series

Jack of Hearts
King of Clubs
Ace of Spades
Queen of Diamonds

K2 Team Series

Crazy for Her
Someone Like Her
Falling for Her
Lost in Her
Only Her

The Duke's Obsession
The Training of a Marquess
The Letter

IN HIS PROTECTION

SANDRA OWENS

carina
press

carina press®

Recycling programs for this product may not exist in your area.

ISBN-13: 978-1-335-47398-1

In His Protection

Copyright © 2022 by Sandra Owens

For questions and comments about the quality of this book, please contact us at CustomerService@Harlequin.com.

Carina Press
22 Adelaide St. West, 41st Floor
Toronto, Ontario M5H 4E3, Canada
www.CarinaPress.com

Printed in U.S.A.

This book is dedicated to Brianna.
You were loved so hard, sweet butterfly girl,
and you will forever be missed so hard.

IN HIS
PROTECTION

Chapter One

"Damn, you shot the sheriff."

Tristan Church glared at his brother while considering putting his ass on the ground. For one, stating the obvious while Tristan tried to convince himself that he was having a nightmare. That he had not, in fact, shot the sheriff. For another, he seriously wanted to wipe that smirk off his brother's face.

But he'd have to take Kade down some other time. At the moment, he had to accept that he wasn't in the middle of a nightmare, that he actually had shot the sheriff. He was never going to hear the end of it. Even his dog was giving him the side-eye. Fuzz cozied up to the sheriff as if too embarrassed by his person to be seen with him. *Traitor.*

"The hell, Chief. You shot me," Sheriff Skylar Morgan yelled, glaring at him as red paint dripped down her arm. "You can't tell the difference between me and the bad guy? You have your eyes checked lately?"

He narrowed said eyes. "I had the bank robber in my sights, *Sheriff.* You jumped in front of him." Skye was the bane of his existence. She was their county sheriff, and he was the city police chief. They bashed heads over everything, mostly because she was more stubborn than Old Man Earl's goat. He wanted her out of his life, and he wanted to lock his lips on hers and kiss that sass right out of her mouth. He wasn't sure which he wanted more, but he was sure about one thing. He'd go to his grave before admitting he liked her sass.

"If a hostage jumps in front of the bad guy, you gonna shoot him, too?" She poked a finger into his chest, leaving a red fingerprint on his T-shirt.

She had him there, and that chafed. He leaned down, putting his face inches from hers. "No, I only like shooting sheriffs."

And as hard as he'd tried to forget he knew her intimately, knew her soft sighs and the feel of her fingernails scraping down his back, he hadn't been able to. A year later, he still had erotic dreams of her. Not as many as he used to, but they still happened. He shook his head to rid it of images of a naked Skye under him.

"Let's try this again," Kade said, then smirked at Tristan with entirely too much amusement in his eyes. "Try not to shoot the sheriff this time, brother."

"When did you say your leave was up? Tomorrow, right?" His brother was Delta Force, stationed at Fort Bragg. He was also downright annoying.

"You trying to get rid of me?" Kade slapped him on the back. "If I didn't know you loved me, my feelings would be hurt."

"Since when do you have feelings?" he muttered, turning his back on Kade's laughter so his brother wouldn't see his grin.

Kade gave a sharp whistle. "All right, people, let's give this drill another go."

"Don't shoot me this time," Skye said as she passed him.

Tristan wondered if the only way to shut her up *was* to kiss her.

"I'd never shoot you, even accidently, beautiful Skylar." Kade winked at her, then monkeyed his way up the ladder to his tower.

Tristan lost his grin. Kade was the only person in the world besides him and Skye who knew about that night. His brother also knew how to annoy him, and since that was one of Kade's favorite things to do, he flirted with Skye whenever Tristan was around.

The law enforcement officers—some Skye's people and some his—took their places. A few years ago, Tristan had talked Kade into conducting training drills with his officers. After the drill was over, they'd have target practice. Five months ago, Skye had showed up with her deputies and crashed the party. Tristan still didn't know how she'd learned of the drills.

Since Marsville's squirrely mayor considered himself an expert with a weapon, and since Luther would love playing cops and robbers, and since he was as likely to shoot himself in the foot, or God help them, one of them, the drills and especially target practice were top secret. Every one of Tristan's officers had been sworn to secrecy, and the location was out in the boondocks on two acres he had bought for next to nothing.

No one was supposed to know about this place outside of his police force and his brothers, but Tristan had a sneaking suspicion Kade was the one who'd tipped Skye off. It would be just like him to do that, then sit back and enjoy the hell out of the fireworks that exploded anytime Tristan and Skye were within spitting distance of each other. His brother denied it, of course, but Kade loved stirring shit up.

From his lookout tower, enabling him to see everything going on below, Kade blew his whistle, signaling the drill was starting. Tristan kept eyes on Skye as they moved through the obstacle course he, Kade, and their baby brother, Parker, had built to simulate a few of Marsville's downtown buildings.

Parker, being an artist, had insisted on accuracy, thus all the storefronts looked just like the real ones, the only difference being there weren't any roofs. That had been Kade's idea, so he could see what was going on inside the businesses from his "boss tower" when they drilled.

Tristan let Skye take the lead. He inwardly snorted. *Let her* his ass. She'd taken the lead, no *let her* about it, but he was enjoying the view. Skylar Morgan was easy on the eyes from her front and her back. She was tall, but still a head shorter than him, a body he could drool over if he allowed himself—and he had once—light brown hair that she kept in a tight bun low on her neck when in uniform, and blue eyes that had a hint of violet in them. Funny, though, how those eyes turned icy blue when they landed on him. But stored in his memory bank was how dark they'd turned when he was buried deep inside her and she'd screamed his name.

He could almost hate her for that night because she'd slipped right inside his mind and stolen any interest he might have had for any other woman after her. He wasn't a manwhore, but he wasn't a monk either. Or, he hadn't been before Skye. He wasn't liking his new monk status so much.

If he'd known who she was the night he'd met "first names only" Skye at Beam Me Up, Marsville's honky-tonk bar, he would have steered clear of her. Hell, if he'd known how miserable she'd make him, he'd have run far, far away.

Who was he kidding? He'd have done exactly what he had…followed her to her motel room. A man in a trance. Over the past year, he'd decided that Skylar Morgan was a witch and had slipped enchantment powder in his drink when he wasn't paying attention to what her sneaky hand was doing. He wanted her to unchant him.

The only reason he'd been at Beam Me Up that night was because the Watters brothers had been causing more trouble than usual. He'd stopped in to see if they were at the bar, and if so, put a stop to their shenanigans before things got out of hand, as often happened with those boys. They hadn't been there, but the beautiful woman sitting at the bar had drawn his attention, and since he knew every living soul in Marsville but had never seen her before, he thought she was just passing through. Why not join her, see if she was interested in a little playtime, and then she'd be gone the next day.

After a bit of small talk and a lot of chemistry sizzling in the air between them, "first names only" Skye let him know she was interested. Only one problem, she was back a month later. The new sheriff in town. And when Luther introduced her to the existing chief of police, Tristan got his first glimpse of how icy blue her eyes could turn. He tried not to take it personally when she acted like they'd never met, but he had.

Then there was her name. She preferred Skylar, and that was what everyone called her. But she'd told him that night her name was Skye, so she'd forever be Skye to him. Added fun…fire flamed to life, melting some of that ice in her eyes, every time he called her Skye, and he knew why. His calling her Skye was a reminder of the night they'd spent together, and try as she might to hide it, he saw desire in those flames. He just didn't know what to do about it.

"Much better, people," Kade called from his tower. "Except for you, Chief. You daydreaming over there?"

Tristan blinked, then scowled at Skye when she

snorted. When he was satisfied she'd seen his scowl, he turned it on his asswipe brother. "No, I am not. I was observing."

"Uh-huh," Kade said, the laughter in his voice downright annoying. "That's enough training for today, people. You did good. Trade your paintball guns for real ones and let's annihilate some targets."

When they'd built their fake town, they'd included a changing room with lockers for their weapons. Because Tristan had one female officer and hoped to have more eventually, they'd added a wall between the two dressing rooms, giving any women training with them privacy. Skye and Vee, his officer, disappeared behind the wall. Tristan tried not to imagine Skye peeling off her paint-splattered T-shirt. He failed.

"She's really gotten under your skin, brother," Kade said, coming up next to him.

Tristan didn't have to ask who *she* was. "You're seeing things that aren't there."

"Right, keep on lying to yourself."

He glared at his brother, then stomped away. If he wanted to lie to himself, that was his business. He was halfway to his car when he realized Fuzz wasn't following. His dog was in love with Skye and would jump ship to the sheriff's department given half a chance. Tristan gave a sharp whistle, and a minute later, the German shepherd trotted his way.

"I know she's pretty, but you need to remember who feeds you, bud." Not that he blamed Fuzz for his fascination with the sheriff. At all.

Chapter Two

Skye drove her cruiser up Marsville's Main Street. Horace County, of which she was the sheriff, was only three hundred and fifty-three square miles in the North Carolina foothills. Not the smallest county in the country, but certainly not the biggest. The county government was located in Marsville, and she had a meeting with the city mayor in an hour. She was early because there was no better way to start her day than breakfast at Katie's Corner Kitchen.

Spying a parking spot one door down from the restaurant, she aimed for it. An ancient turquoise Cadillac cut her off, stealing her space. Skye banged her hand on the steering wheel. "One day, Miss Mabel, I'm going to write your scrawny butt another ticket." She'd tried that once after clocking the old bat going fifteen miles over the speed limit. Miss Mabel had laughed, handed the ticket back to her, and told her to give it to Luther, Luther being Marsville's mayor and Mabel Mackel's nephew.

Skye found a spot on the other side of the street. Her mouth already watering, she headed for the restaurant. The Kitchen, as it was referred to by locals, had the best ham, egg, and cheese omelet in the world. And the buttermilk biscuits, so melt-in-your-mouth good.

She couldn't eat here every morning or she'd have to order larger uniforms, but she tried to start her week off with breakfast at Katie's on Monday mornings. And yes, there really was a Katie.

"Good morning, Sheriff," Katie said as Skye slipped onto a bar stool at the counter. "The usual?"

"Morning, Katie. Always the usual."

Katie stepped to the back counter, picked up a coffeepot and a plate of steaming hot biscuits. She set the plate down in front of Skye and filled her coffee cup. "One usual coming right up."

"Thanks," Skye said around a mouthful of buttery biscuit. She liked sitting at the counter since it gave her a chance to talk to people, and she glanced to her left. "Morning, Earl."

He grunted, which was about all the greeting she'd get out of him. It was all he gave anyone, so she didn't take it personally. "You keeping Billy out of trouble?" Billy being his goat, and that Earl had named his goat Billy amused her.

The goat was a terror, though. At the moment, he'd be waiting in Earl's fifty-something-year-old pickup, eating more of the seats. There wasn't much left except for metal now, so maybe Billy was starting on the dash. Didn't seem to bother Earl that his goat was eating him out of a truck from the inside out. The old man loved that creature.

"Billy ain't no trouble, Sheriff."

She begged to differ but wisely kept her opinion to herself. Nothing could get Earl fired up more than dissing his goat.

The bell over the door chimed, and she glanced over

to see who was entering. The coffee she was swallowing went down the wrong way, causing a coughing fit.

"You okay, Skylar?" Parker Church said, walking straight to her and patting her on the back. That was just like Parker. He was the sweet, quiet brother. He was also the one who'd tipped her off about Tristan's drills. Tristan would never suspect Parker, and she'd never tattle. He was sure it had been Kade, which was the kind of thing Kade would have done if he'd thought of it.

Kade stepped next to him, devilment in his eyes. "Need mouth to mouth, Sheriff?"

She rolled her eyes. Kade was the brother always up for shenanigans. Standing behind his brothers, Tristan glared at Kade, then slid his gaze over her. She willed herself not to react. How did he do that? Make her goose bumpy with a mere skim of his eyes? However he did it, he needed to stop. She'd never responded to a man the way she did him, and it was downright annoying.

"I'm okay, Parker, and no, Kade, I don't need mouth to mouth." She dipped her chin in Tristan's general direction. "Chief."

He bumped Kade, forcing his brother to step away. "Morning, Sheriff." He flicked the corner of her mouth with his finger. "Had a biscuit crumb there."

"Uh…thanks." He'd only done that because he knew it would irritate her, and it did, but no way she'd let him see that. He softly chuckled as if he could read her mind. And did he have to smell so good? Like the forest on a crisp autumn day. All woodsy and fresh.

Seeing one Church brother at a time was enough to turn a woman's head, but seeing the three together? Every woman, single and not single, young and old, inside the Kitchen was sighing into her coffee. But really, only one of those brothers did it for her, and had she said how annoying that was?

All three were tall, an inch or two over six feet, and had similar features: eyes the color of dark chocolate, strong jaws, and full pillowy lips. The biggest difference between them was their hair. Parker had long, brown hair that he kept pulled back in a ponytail that matched his artsy self. Kade's was almost black and scraggly, and he sported a beard. He'd never said exactly what his role in the military was, but she suspected he was Special Forces. Then there was Tristan. His short hair was caramel colored with blond highlights in the sunshine. Women paid a lot of money to get that color and those highlights. It wasn't fair.

The brothers moved to a booth, and Skye poured half the ice water down her throat that Katie pushed her way with a chuckle. It was useless to deny she was hot and bothered, because what woman in the room wasn't, but at least Katie thought it was just from seeing the Church brothers en masse.

Her breakfast arrived, and Skye tried to concentrate on her omelet and not think of the night she'd spent with Tristan last year, but her mind refused to obey. He'd cast some kind of spell over her, and she hadn't even considered the consequences of sleeping with a local. That wasn't like her. She always considered the consequences of her actions, especially after Danny. But that night, the hot-as-sin man in the bar had crooked his finger, and she'd followed him like a lovesick puppy. Well, he'd actually followed her back to her motel room, but semantics.

Most sheriffs were elected by the voters, but a few counties like Horace appointed their sheriff. More than ready to get out of Central Florida, she'd been watching for law enforcement openings in states north of Florida when she'd seen that Horace County was looking for a sheriff. As the chief deputy sheriff, reporting directly to the sheriff in her county, she was qualified for the job and had applied. As a female, she hadn't been sure she'd even get an interview, but she had.

Because she'd wanted to get the lay of the land before her interview, she'd come up a few days early so she could look around. She'd only gone to Beam Me Up to check out the bar, having identified it as a place she would likely get called to when trouble started. If she got the job, that was. One drink to justify hanging out for a while and getting a feel for the people had led to a night of the best sex she'd ever had. How was she supposed to know the man was Marsville's police chief?

That was her fault, so she couldn't hold that against him. She was the one who had insisted on first names only and no sharing of personal details. It was stupid really to think she'd never see him again, considering how small the county was, but thinking hadn't been her strong point that night. That—her inability to think— *was* his fault. He'd bedazzled her. Yeah, that was a good word for what he'd done to her.

Two days later she was interviewed by the county commissioners, and a week later, offered the job. A month after her best ever sex night, she reported for duty and was introduced to Marsville's police chief. His eyes had lit up at seeing her. She'd panicked and pretended like she'd never seen him before, and the light in his eyes had died. But what did he expect? For her to tell him in front of the people in the room that she'd dreamed about him and their night together? Uh…no.

Later, when her brain was working again, she realized she could have told him it was nice to see him again and explained to the others that they'd met when she was exploring the town or something like that. No one had to know sex was involved. But the damage was done, and she stubbornly doubled down on her lie. Since then, their relationship was filled with tension, not of the good kind, and she didn't know how to fix it.

Even though her back was to him, she could feel Tristan's eyes on her. She needed to finish her breakfast and go. Usually, she'd take her time and enjoy her omelet, but not today. Five minutes after the Church brothers arrived, she was done. She left enough money to pay for her breakfast and a tip under her plate. "See you next Monday, Earl."

He grunted.

"Skylar."

Well, rats. She'd made it to the door. So close to escaping. At least, it was Kade. Hopefully, Tristan wasn't with him. She turned. "Yeah?" Just Kade, so that was good.

"Wanted to say adios. I'm heading back to base as soon as we finish breakfast."

"Oh, okay. You stay safe out there catching bad guys."

"Always." He grinned. "I'm appointing you to keep my brothers on their toes while I'm gone."

She gave him a hug. "You better come back to us in one piece, you hear?"

"Hear you loud and clear." Surprising her, he kissed her cheek, then put his mouth next to her ear. "That was for big brother's benefit. I don't even have to look at him to know he's shooting daggers at me with his eyes." He laughed. "He's so easy to rile."

"You're a very bad boy, Kade Church."

"Can't deny it." He winked, then headed back to his brothers.

She told herself not to look at Tristan. Her eyes refused to obey. He was scowling, but it was impossible to tell whether at Kade or her. Not that it really mattered.

Outside, she stopped to greet Fuzz. Tristan's dog was the sweetest, best-behaved dog she'd ever been around.

"Hey, Fuzz. How's my favorite boy today?" She gave him a scratch under his chin, chuckling when his eyes rolled back in his head. Fuzz considered everyone in Marsville a friend until Tristan said otherwise. The residents were allowed to pet him, and everyone did. He wore a vest that said Police on it, but that was for the benefit of tourists. It worked to keep strangers' hands off him.

He snapped up his rubber KONG—a toy he carried everywhere with him—and she played tug with him for a few minutes. "I know you could do this all day, sweet boy, but I don't want to be here when your daddy comes out." She gave him one last scratch, ignored his big brown eyes begging her to play some more, and headed for her meeting with the mayor.

Marsville was a charming town. The road was only two lanes through downtown with mature trees lining the road on both sides. The shade was great in the summer, and at Christmas the trees were wrapped in white lights. The storefronts were all brick with colorful awnings, each a different color. She didn't know whose idea that was, but it was striking. The pots filled with flowers hanging from the awnings added to the charm.

Her new town and job would be perfect if not for the night that was now the reason for the tension between her and Tristan. She was never one to lie to herself, and the truth was…she wanted a man she couldn't have. Not if she wanted to keep her job.

Chapter Three

Tristan and Parker saw Kade off, then Tristan walked with Parker to the next block, where his brother veered off in the direction of the firehouse. Baby brother was not only the artist known as Park C but was also Marsville's fire chief. Tristan, with Fuzz at his side, headed over to the mayor's office for a meeting about who knew what? With Luther, it could be anything from his aunt complaining that kids were running across her lawn to Earl's goat getting loose again and wandering into town, terrorizing everyone.

"Morning, Rebecca," he said, greeting Luther's assistant.

Fuzz, knowing that a Milk-Bone and a bowl of water awaited him behind Rebecca's desk, dropped his KONG toy at Tristan's feet, then headed straight for the treat.

"Good morning, Chief. Luther's running late as usual. He's on his way, though."

"You know what he wants to meet about?"

"I never have any idea what that man's up to," she grumbled. "You want a cup of coffee while you wait?"

"Thanks, but I just came from the Kitchen, so I've had my morning cup." After taking a seat, he pulled out his phone to check his messages. He was frowning over a text from Eric, one of his officers, saying he was sick and wouldn't be in, when the door leading to the hallway opened. In walked the woman he couldn't stop dreaming about.

"Sheriff." He was still irked from watching her let Kade kiss her on the cheek earlier, so his greeting came out harsh. Yeah, he knew his bonehead brother did it just to mess with him, but it still put him in a sour mood.

"Chief." She frowned at him, then turned a smile on Rebecca. "I have a meeting with Luther this morning."

"He's running late," Tristan said before Rebecca could answer. "You'll have to hang tight until I finish my meeting with him."

"Why should you get to go first?"

"Because I was here first?" Yep, there went her eyes, going icy blue. Little did she know seeing them turn to ice only made him want to nibble on that soft spot below her ear that he knew from experience would heat her blood, melting those icicles in her eyes.

"I have an appointment, so you'll have to be the one to hang tight, Chief."

"Don't think so, Skye."

She flinched when he said her name, drawing the four-letter word out as much as possible. He hated that since learning who he was, she refused to say his name. Not once since then had she called him anything but Chief. The night he'd spent with her, she'd moaned his name, cried out his name more than once, and still did in his dreams. He wanted to hear her say it again.

"Ah, Tristan, Skylar, y'all are meeting with Luther together," Rebecca said, her gaze bouncing between the two of them.

Skye must have realized they were giving Rebecca

a show because her cheeks pinked. He chuckled, which earned him a glare. He smiled at Rebecca, then kept the smile on his face for Skye. "See, no problem."

She muttered something that sounded a lot like, "Says you."

He cupped a hand around his ear. "Sorry, I didn't catch that."

Her mouth opened, but he'd never know what she was about to say as Luther walked in with his aunt Mabel at his side. Tristan's gaze shot to Skye's and they both groaned. It was never good when Mabel Mackel was involved in anything. On this one thing, they were both united. As was Fuzz. He snatched up his toy, then disappeared behind Rebecca's desk.

"Good morning, Miss Mabel, Luther," Tristan said.

"What's good about it?" Miss Mabel replied.

He and Skye wisely kept their mouths shut as they followed Miss Mabel and Luther into his office. There were only two chairs in front of Luther's desk, so letting the ladies have them, he walked to the window and perched on the sill.

Luther, who stood to inherit everything Miss Mabel owned—and it was half the town—smiled at his aunt. "Auntie, would you like me to explain things, or do you wish to?"

Personally, Tristan thought Miss Mabel was too ornery to ever kick the bucket, so Luther always kissing her ass was a waste of time, but whatever. Get a few whiskeys down Luther's throat, and you got his true feelings. His aunt drove him bonkers with her demands.

"I reckon you'll muck it up, so I'll take over." She glanced over her shoulder. "I can't see you back there, Tristan."

"Sorry, ma'am." He moved to the next window, which was in her line of sight, getting a nod of approval.

"I'll get right to it then. We're reopening the museum."

Say what now? Luther beamed as if this was the best news in the world. It was not. The Marsville UFO Museum was a joke. The damn thing had been closed for fifteen years now, and it needed to stay closed. The story behind it was an embarrassment to the town.

"Museum?" Skye said.

Luther nodded, that ridiculous smile still on his face. "Yes, the Marsville UFO Museum."

"UFO?" Skye glanced at Tristan as if confirming her ears were working right.

He shrugged. "Later," he mouthed.

Ignoring Skye's question, Miss Mabel said, "Since that fancy resort opened on the lake, we have more tourists visiting Marsville, and we need to offer them entertainment, things to spend their money on. That will mean more jobs for our residents, so everyone will be happy."

He doubted anyone would be happy hearing the museum was reopening, but one question now burned in his mind that he didn't want to ask but might as well get it over with. Opening the museum up again had nothing to do with him and Skye, so… "Why are you telling the sheriff and me this now?" When Miss Mabel gave him a smug grin, he eyed the door, wondering how fast he could get out it.

"You and Skylar are on the planning committee. You will need to plan for the extra traffic, parking, if we have adequate motel rooms, should we install parking meters, all those sorts of things."

Just kill him now. "Who else is on this committee?"

"Are you saying the two of you can't handle the job?" Luther said.

Tristan glanced at Skye, who seemed to be in shock. Whether it was learning there was a UFO museum or that she'd have to work with him, he didn't know. Probably both. Although…he almost grinned. She'd have to work with him. He wanted to gleefully rub his hands. This could be fun.

Miss Mabel excused them, and he walked out with Skye. "Let's go, Fuzz," he said as they passed Rebecca's desk. His dog raced ahead of them. Tristan chuckled. "He's afraid Miss Mabel will show up again."

"Smart dog." She stopped on the sidewalk outside the municipal building. "I have questions. Lots and lots of questions."

He laughed. "I'm sure you do. Let's head back to the Kitchen. I could use a drink after that, but since it's still morning, I guess a cup of coffee will have to do." Fuzz settled in his usual place outside the restaurant door. Like Rebecca did, Katie kept a bowl of water for him.

"Back already?" Katie said when they walked in.

"We are. Just some coffee this time." The breakfast rush was over, and there were only a few people still eating. Tristan reached out to put his hand on Skye's back as they headed for an empty booth but jerked it back. She'd bite his head off if he touched her. At the moment they had something of a truce going, and he didn't want to remind her that they were…what? Not exactly enemies, but certainly not friends.

Katie was right behind them with their coffees.

"Thanks, Katie." He waited for her to leave. "Okay, shoot," he said when they were alone.

"I don't even know where to start." She lifted her

gaze from her coffee to him. "UFOs? Really? And Marsville, I thought it was just a name with no meaning behind it. It's not, is it?"

"No, it's not. The town used to be called Foothills because obviously, we're in the foothills of the mountains." To the west of them were the Blue Ridge Mountains. He'd much rather live in Foothills than Marsville.

"And it changed to Marsville when and why?"

"Okay, here's the story. Some fifty or so years ago Mavis Mackel, Mabel's seventeen-year-old twin sister, disappeared. Mabel swore a UFO had landed in the field behind their house, and an alien snatched Mavis away."

"People believed her?"

"You have to remember that everyone knew about Roswell, that the government supposedly had a UFO. There were also numerous UFO sightings during those years. It helped that Jim Bob Ketchen, dead some years now, claimed to have seen a UFO a few weeks prior to Mavis disappearing. That's probably what gave the twins the idea. Also, the Mackel family pretty much owned the town, so yeah, people believed her. If they wanted to keep their jobs, they did."

"What really happened to Mavis?"

He sat back in the booth and grinned. "Not a believer, yeah?"

"If you tell me you are, I'm walking right out of here."

"No need for that. The story was as phony as they come. Two years later, Mavis showed up with a baby boy in tow, and they gave him their last name. The two of them claimed, and Miss Mabel still does to this day, that the baby was half alien, which means as his son,

Luther is what? One fourth alien?" He outright laughed when she spewed her coffee. "True story."

After wiping her chin clean, she looked at him with laughter still lighting up her eyes. "Well, that explains a lot."

He chuckled. "Never thought about it that way."

"The girls' parents had to know that was a bunch of malarkey."

"Hard to say." He tapped his head. "The family was a little off. Still are."

"No kidding. So, what's the real story?"

"Mavis ran away with the town's baddest bad boy. Typical rich girl falls in love with the forbidden bad boy from the other side of the tracks. Since that version was mortifying to the family, they were more than willing to go with Mabel's story, which she came up with to keep her parents from blaming her for helping Mavis steal away with her lover. Too bad it didn't last. The dude abandoned her as soon as she got pregnant."

"What happened to her?"

"That's the saddest part of the story. About a week after she came home, she turned her son over to her twin, then went out to the lake and swam until her arms and legs didn't work anymore. They found her body the next day."

"Oh, that really is sad. How do you know all this? The real story?"

"Much of it I've heard from various people over the years. Also, my aunt loved to gossip, and I'd sometimes hear her tell her friends things." This was the most Skye was talking to him since their unforgettable night, and he didn't want it to end.

"Okay, that answers a lot of my questions, but what's in the museum?"

"To answer that, I'll have to show you." And that was going to be fun.

"I've lived here a year, and I don't even know where this museum is."

"It's been right in front of your face the entire time. What are you doing tonight?"

Chapter Four

Tristan had told her that they'd be sneaking into the museum and to wear dark-colored clothes. Skye thought he was being ridiculous since they were the top two law enforcement officers in the county, and if they wanted to check out a museum, what of it? She'd been tempted to wear white jeans and a bright yellow shirt, but all black it was. All she needed was a black cowboy hat, and she'd look like the villain in a Western.

Why hadn't she insisted on meeting him wherever this UFO museum was? Being in a car with him, especially at night, was a bad idea. It was too intimate. She'd have to talk to him, something she avoided as much as possible because she enjoyed it too much. And in a closed car, she'd smell him, and he smelled entirely too good. But the only way he'd agreed to show her the museum was if she rode with him, and she was too curious to see it to refuse.

She snorted. UFOs? A UFO museum? Really? It was strange that she hadn't heard a word about it or the story behind it in the year she'd been here. She supposed it was what Tristan had said, that the incident was an embarrassment to the town, a story best put behind them.

Tristan would be here in ten minutes, and she made

a quick tour of her one-bedroom apartment. She tended to not put things away until her once-a-week cleaning frenzy on her day off. Although she didn't want him in her home and wouldn't invite him inside, Tristan had a way of getting her to do things she didn't want to. Like riding in a car with him. Or spending a night with him. Well, in all fairness, she had wanted to do that at the time.

If he wasn't the police chief, say he was a Realtor or farmer, anything but what he was, she would have been happy to see him again. Okay, excited. But dating a man in law enforcement…a big no. Not going to happen. Been there, done that, and it had been the biggest mistake of her life. She liked to think she learned from her mistakes, so Tristan was off-limits.

When Danny Peterson had started paying attention to her, he'd seemed almost perfect. Kind, funny, and easy on the eyes. They were both in law enforcement, her a chief deputy sheriff and him a police officer. They'd had so much in common, understood each other's dedication to the job, could sympathize when one of them had a difficult day.

Danny had been all smoke and mirrors, though. He'd asked her to marry him, and as soon as his engagement ring was on her finger, he'd shown his true colors—manipulative, controlling, selfish. When she'd ended their relationship, he'd started rumors about her, and she'd felt she had no choice but to resign from her job as chief deputy sheriff.

She'd learned her lesson. No law enforcement boyfriends. Not now. Not ever. Not even a certain police chief who woke up the butterflies in her stomach.

"This is it?" she said when Tristan stopped his car at the abandoned mill. She'd passed the place hundreds of times in the past year, never once thinking it was more than what it looked like, a mill that hadn't been operational for many years. Vines grew up the side of the stone walls, the waterwheel was rotted, half the wood missing, and she had her doubts about how safe the roof was.

"Yep. Started out as a grist mill sometime in the nineteen twenties."

"And then it morphed into a UFO museum?"

He laughed. "For a while, a pretty successful one. Everyone wanted to hear the story about the girl who was abducted by an alien and had his baby."

"What all was in it?"

"From what I remember, a lot of junk. Fake outer space stuff, rocks supposedly from other planets, those kinds of things."

"You actually saw it when it was open?"

"When I was a kid. My aunt took me and my brothers." He glanced at her. "Ready to go in?"

She eyed the building. It looked creepy. "Is it safe?"

"The roof worried me, so I came out this afternoon and took a look at it. It's going to need to be replaced if Miss Mabel does actually reopen the place, but it's safe enough for now."

"How do we get in?"

"With these." He dangled a set of keys from his fingers.

"Okay. Show me some space rock."

"Awesome." He reached to the back seat and grabbed a canvas tote bag. He pulled out two heavy-duty flashlights, gave her one, then handed her a ball cap. "It'll keep the spiderwebs out of your hair."

"There's spiders?" She shuddered.

"Bound to be with how long it's been closed up." He stuck a cap on his head. "Ready?"

She was having second thoughts about this, but if she backed out, he'd probably never let her hear the end of it. "Let's do this."

"Hold this while I get the door open." He handed her his flashlight, and she shined it on the lock.

The door creaked like something right out of a horror movie when he pushed it open. He walked ahead of her, and she impulsively reached up and lightly brushed her fingers over the back of his neck.

"Shit," he yelled as he swatted at his neck while doing a pitiful imitation of a jig.

Laughter burst out of her. Suddenly, there was a bright light shining in her eyes, and she squinted.

"That was you?"

She nodded.

His eyes narrowed. "You're going to pay for that, Sheriff. I don't know how or when, but it will happen."

"Oooh, I'm shaking in my boots."

"Game on," he said with a smirk that made her uneasy.

She had the feeling she'd just poked the bear.

Chapter Five

Tristan swallowed a smile at the flash of interest on Skye's face before she hid it. So, she liked games. She'd gotten him good, so kudos to her. But he had two younger brothers who'd loved to terrorize him growing up. He had a bag full of tricks thanks to them, and he would pay her back. Not right away, though. She needed to stew a bit, wondering what he might do to retaliate.

He flashed his light on the ten-foot-tall green replica of an alien at the entrance. The damn thing had scared the bejesus out of him as a kid. "No one could agree back then if this guy here was Luther's father's taxidermic body. Some said it was, but those were mostly the people employed by the Mackels."

She leaned toward the spaceman, shining her flashlight over it, stopping the light on his groin. "Can a plaster man even get his dick up enough to beget a child?"

Tristan snorted a laugh. "If so, it would be something of a miracle." As they went from display to display—moon rocks, precious metals from other planets, pictures of spaceships, and other ridiculous space items—he found himself laughing at her opinions of everything.

"That's pretty much it," he said when they'd circled the room.

She shined her flashlight around. "This place is so hokey that it's hilarious. I'd pay at least five dollars to come here for the laughs if nothing else. What's that in the back there?"

"That's where they sold outer space ice cream and moon rock candy."

"Did you have any?"

"Absolutely. The ice cream was green and mint flavored, and the candy looked like ice crystals. I don't remember what it tasted like." She was actually being nice to him, and he'd enjoyed the past hour with her. He wasn't ready to take her back home. "Now I have a craving for ice cream. What say you that we make a stop at the Purple Cow?"

After a hesitation that stretched long enough for him to believe she was going to refuse, she shrugged. "Sure, why not?"

"Your excitement overwhelms me."

She rolled her eyes. "You need to calm down, Tristan. Obviously, you're too easy to excite."

"I'll do my best, but ice cream, you know. Exhilarating stuff." It was the first time she'd said his name in a year, and he considered it a victory. A small one, but one all the same.

"You're not wearing all black," she said on the way to the Purple Cow. "Why did I have to?"

"I wanted to see if I could get you to do it." He laughed when she poked him. She was sexy in those black jeans that hugged her hips and legs, and the black sweater with a V-neck that showed just enough cleavage to make a man want to see more. Instead of her usual bun, her hair was pulled back in a ponytail. He'd only seen it down once, and that had been the night he'd met her. He wanted to see that again, run his hands through those long silky strands, have it form a curtain around them while she was riding him and had her mouth on his. He shifted uncomfortably in his seat.

"Then that counts as getting me back."

"Oh, no, Sheriff. Not even close." He parked at the Purple Cow, then glanced at her as he opened his door. "When you least expect it."

She met him at the front of his car. "Don't start something you can't finish, Chief."

"Hmm." He leaned his mouth close to her ear, intending to remind her how capable he was of finishing and she damn well knew it, but thought better of it. She'd been relaxed and fun tonight. A reminder of their night together would send her right back to shutting him out. "Sounds like a challenge," he said instead.

"Take it however you want."

Didn't he wish. Just thinking of taking her however he wanted had him aroused, but it was not the time or place, so he turned his attention to deciding what flavor ice cream he wanted. Deciding to go with the theme of the night, he asked for two scoops of the mint.

"For you, ma'am?" the teenage girl behind the counter asked.

"I'll have a scoop of bubble gum, one of red velvet cake, and a scoop of the coffee and doughnuts. Fudge sauce and whipped cream on top. Oh, and throw a few cherries on it, please."

He stared at her.

Her brows shot up. "What?"

"You're a very interesting woman, Skye Morgan." If

asked, he would have pegged her for something plain like chocolate or vanilla. The woman had depths he wanted to peel away, layer by tantalizing layer.

"Nothing interesting about me."

He begged to differ.

"Uncle Tris," Everly yelled when he returned home. His five-year-old niece shouted everything lately.

"What can I do for you, Miss Everly?"

She giggled. "Tell Daddy I don't have to have a bath tonight."

"I don't know." He wrinkled his nose. "Is that stinky you I smell?"

It was a good thing she was already sitting on the floor because she fell over, laughing so hard that she scared her cat. Jellybean shot out of the room. Tristan didn't blame him. The kid was loud, hyper, and a handful, but he wouldn't have her any other way.

He wanted to go to his room and think about tonight. It was the first time in a year that he let himself have hope that he could penetrate Skye's defenses. He'd need to be subtle about it. If he went in guns blazing, she'd shut him down so fast he wouldn't have time to blink. He hadn't missed how her eyes had lit up when he'd sworn to pay her back for her spider joke. She liked to play, so they would play.

But first he had his favorite—okay, only, but still favorite—niece to entertain. "Where's your daddy?"

"In the bathroom making a bath. He's going to make me take a bath. I don't want to." All of that was screamed at the top of her lungs.

Parker walked into the living room. "Come on, kiddo. When you're all sweet smelling and in bed,

Uncle Tristan will read you however many stories you want him to."

Uncle Tristan narrowed his eyes at his brother. "Says you."

"Please," Parker said, glancing back as he carried Everly down the hall.

Parker's favorite time with his daughter was her bedtime and reading her stories, so if he was begging Tristan to take over tonight, that meant inspiration had struck and he was anxious to get back to his studio. It also meant he'd lose track of time and be up all night, and Tristan would have to get Everly up, dressed, fed breakfast, and dropped off at school. That was okay. He'd learned long ago that having an artist in the family meant odd hours, and sometimes stepping up and taking care of that artist when he forgot to take care of himself.

When Parker had returned from France with a two-week-old baby in tow, it had been a surprise. He hadn't told them in any of their phone calls that he had a baby on the way. Kade helped out when he was home on leave, but mostly it was Parker and Tristan raising her. Neither one of them knew a thing about taking care of a baby, and Tristan had been sure she'd be damaged for life, but they'd muddled through. In spite of their incompetence, Everly was a happy and delightful child.

"I don't know why she fights taking a bath," Parker said later, walking into the kitchen. "Once she's in there, she doesn't want to get out. She's waiting for you to come read to her."

"Who knows why a kid does anything." Parker headed for his studio, and Tristan went to read a bedtime story to his favorite niece. He eased off the bed after she fell asleep, turned off the lamp, and left her snuggled up to Jellybean.

Fuzz followed him upstairs, went to his dog bed, and after making several circles, curled up with his stuffed bear, a toy he'd stolen from Everly when she was a baby. Tristan showered, slipped on a pair of pajama bottoms—something he'd had to start doing after Everly learned to walk and had no respect for a man's privacy—and settled in bed on top of the covers. Usually, he read for a while until he got sleepy, but tonight, his mind was on a certain sheriff. He thought about her for a while, then came to a decision. It was time to make her think about him.

If she wasn't interested in him, he'd move on. But she was. He could see it in her eyes, and in the way he'd catch her watching him. Something was holding her back, but he didn't have a guess what the issue was. He'd make sure she was thinking about him, though.

He picked up his phone, typed a text, and sent it to her. "Let's see what you do with that, Sheriff."

Chapter Six

Why are aliens messy tea drinkers?

Skye stared at the text from Tristan. They had each other's numbers in their phones in case there was an emergency of some kind. In the year she'd been sheriff, he had never once called or texted her for anything personal. She should ignore him. But she didn't want to. If she responded, though, she'd only be encouraging him. Not a smart thing to do.

She set her phone face down on the nightstand. For thirty minutes she tried to go to sleep, but after tossing and turning, huffing and puffing, she grabbed her phone. She was going to regret this.

I'll bite. Why?

Dots danced on the screen, disappeared, appeared again, then went away before starting up again.

I'll hold my thoughts on biting for now. The answer is with flying saucers, it's hard not to spill it.

She snorted at the answer, but her gaze snapped back

to his comment on biting. What comments had he deleted before deciding on that one? Had one of them been a reminder that she *had* bitten his shoulder when she was coming apart in his arms? He'd responded to that with a low growl of pleasure, and just remembering that night sent heat spiraling through her. As if the phone was burning her hand, she dropped it to the bed.

Damn him for making her remember. Her phone chimed with an incoming text. She would not look. Five minutes later, she sighed, berating herself as she gave in and looked.

Goodnight Skye

She chewed on her thumbnail for a good minute, then shrugged.

Goodnight chief

Two minutes later, she fell asleep with a smile on her face.

"Sheriff, Tom Gibbons wasn't home, and his wife claims she has no idea where he is," Johnny Cooper said from the doorway of her office.

"Of course she doesn't." She eyed the two cups of coffee her deputy held. "One of those for me?"

He grinned. "Yes, ma'am." He walked into the room, handing her one of the cups. "I put a BOLO out on Tom. He'll turn up drunk somewhere."

"No doubt." The man had failed to show up for his court hearing. Again. This was the fourth time in the year she'd been here that Gibbons had done a disappearing act and they'd had to track him down. She tapped her cup. "Thanks for the coffee. Much appreciated."

"No prob. I'm going to go hit up some of Tom's favorite hiding spots."

"Good luck." She had a great team. Well, except for one problem child. Mason Culpepper, her oldest deputy and longest on the force, thought he should have gotten her job and resented the hell out of her. He wasn't shy about letting her know, either. Mason was lazy, had a bad attitude, and wasn't liked by the other deputies.

The sheriff's department was half the size of Tristan's police department, not an unusual thing even though her people had the entire county to cover, and Tristan's officers only patrolled inside the city limits. Those thoughts led her to thinking of Tristan, which soured her mood.

Four days had passed since their UFO museum night and the texts. She hadn't seen or heard from him since. Not that she wanted to. *Liar.* "Shut up, voice in my head."

"You got voices in your head talking to you? Not a good endorsement for a sheriff." Mason laughed as he walked into her office.

Of course Mason would be the one to hear her. "Why aren't you out on patrol?"

He threw his hands up. "Chill, boss lady. I'm going, okay? Just thought I'd stop in and say hello."

No, he thought he could mess around a little, cut time off being on patrol. After he stomped out, she tried to work on the budgets for next year, but her mind kept drifting to Tristan. Since she'd come to Marsville, her life had revolved around her job. She hadn't met anyone she wanted to date.

Liar. Damn voice. Fine. She'd very much like to date Tristan. There. She'd admitted it.

Sneaking into the museum and going for ice cream with him had been the highlight of her year. The night had reminded her how much she liked him. When he took her back home, he'd walked her to her door. She'd thought for a second that he was going to kiss her. She would have let him. But he hadn't, and although disappointed, she was glad because she probably would have forgotten her no-cops rule, grabbed his hand, and dragged him straight to her bed.

Finishing these budgets wasn't going to happen today. She shut down her computer. An hour or two out of the office was what her brain needed. Despite not having any intention of going near the Marsville Police Department, she somehow ended up parked in front of it.

The police building was next to Marsville's municipal building and two times the size of hers. The sheriff's department was located outside the city limits. Tristan's people could walk outside their door and have a variety of places to eat lunch. The only businesses near her were a tire store, a clothing consignment shop, and a strip mall that housed a tattoo artist, an insurance agent, and a few other places that did not offer food.

She yelped at the sharp raps on her window. At seeing Tristan peering in and grinning, she wanted to punch him in the nose. It was, after all, his fault she hadn't been herself since she'd fallen asleep thinking about him, then hadn't heard another word from him. She powered down her window.

"Can I help you, Chief?"

"Now that's a loaded question, Sheriff." He comically waggled his eyebrows. "I was going to call you today, but surprise, here you are. You coming to see me?"

"Um, no, I have to..." What? She wasn't about to admit he was the reason she was staring at his building, trying to think of a reason to stop by his office. She glanced at the municipal building. "I have to pick up some paperwork from the courthouse."

"After you do that, stop and see me. Miss Mabel asked me this morning what we'd accomplished so far. I almost told her we'd come up with some good UFO jokes but thought better of it."

"Yeah, probably not a good idea."

He tapped the roof of her car. "See you in a few." With Fuzz at his side, he walked into the police building.

Great, now she had to go to the courthouse and scrounge up some kind of paperwork. Fifteen minutes later, having conned a court clerk out of some blank pages and a manila folder, she stopped in the doorway of Tristan's office. He was on the phone, but he waved her in.

Fuzz rose from his bed and came to her. She slid a Milk-Bone from her pocket and gave it to him. He put his paw on her knee as if to thank her, then returned to his bed. Half the town carried treats for Fuzz in their pockets or purse.

"Earl, he followed someone into Fanny's shop and ate half of a fifty-dollar dress. Fanny's demanding you reimburse her." Tristan looked at her and rolled his eyes. "Since the dress is ruined, I'm sure Fanny will give you the rest of it if you pay up."

Skye chuckled. A definite bonus of her job was that she didn't have to deal with Earl and his goat.

"Great, I'll tell her. You really need to put a stop to Billy escaping." After disconnecting, he shook his head. "Earl said if he has to pay for the dress that it's only fair Billy gets to eat the rest of it."

"Can't argue with that." She really wished he wouldn't grin like that. It did funny things to her stomach. "So, what are we going to do about Miss Mabel?"

"We're going to do what she wants. Have meetings and write up a plan addressing the extra traffic she's sure we'll have after the museum opens."

"You really think the town's going to be overwhelmed with tourists because of a hokey UFO museum?" The idea of a horde of tourists swarming into Marsville like locusts to see green men made out of plaster and fake moon rocks was ridiculous.

"No, but it's easier to humor her than to try to make her see the light. I've jotted down some thoughts, which I'll email to you. You read through them. Add any suggestions or thoughts you have, send them back to me, then we'll sit down together and write up a plan."

"Okay." That was perfect. Meant spending less time around him. So, why was she disappointed? "Well, I need to get back."

"Skye."

She paused at the door and turned. "Yes?"

"You're still going to pay for your spider prank."

"Like I told you, don't start something you can't finish."

His grin was positively wicked. "When you least expect it, Sheriff."

"Game on, Chief." She walked out to his laughter.

Chapter Seven

For a week after throwing down his challenge, Tristan had steered clear of Skye. She'd replied to his email the day after getting it, and he'd been impressed with her suggestions. She'd asked when he wanted to meet, and he'd put her off, telling her sometime next week. By now, she likely thought he'd forgotten he'd promised to get her back for the spider scare. She would be wrong. Everyone knew revenge was best served cold.

She'd about given him a heart attack, making him think he had spiders crawling down his neck, and she needed to pay. He'd considered and discarded several practical jokes to play on her and had finally come up with the perfect one. Tomorrow she'd learn he was a man of his word.

Matt Butler, his captain, poked his head around the doorjamb. "Chief, Miss Bauman is here, demanding a word with you."

"Tell her I'm in Tahiti and won't be back until next year."

"You should be ashamed of yourself, Tristan Church, for lying to one of your citizens," Miss Bauman said, marching into his office.

At hearing her voice, Fuzz dashed under Tristan's

desk. There were two people he avoided at all costs—
the Misses Bauman and Mackel. Tristan wished he
could join his dog under the desk. He inwardly sighed
as she settled herself in a chair, then fussed with the
hem of her dress, making sure it properly covered her
knees. He waited for her to take her list of complaints
out of her purse. There was always a list. On the plus
side, this one was only one page long. Sometimes, there
were multiple pages.

Why had he wanted to be the police chief? He must
have had a good reason.

As she made her way down her list, his mind wandered to Skye. For a year he'd tried to forget the night
they'd spent together. Not at first. When she turned out
to be the county's new sheriff, he'd surprised himself
with how happy he was to see her again. Their chemistry had been off the chart, and he'd thought they had a
connection. Still thought so, but something was keeping
her from exploring a relationship with him.

They were both single, and there wasn't any rule or
regulation against their dating, so that wasn't the problem. As far as he knew, she hadn't shown an interest in
another man since she'd moved to Marsville. So, what
was her reason for shutting him down? There had to be
one. It could be his ego talking, but she was attracted
to him. He was sure of it.

How could he find out why she had thick walls built
around her? If he knew the answer, he would know how
to tear them down. Because she definitely had them,
and he didn't like being on the outside of those walls.

"And I must insist you do something about those kids
riding their bikes and skateboards on my street, Chief."

He sighed as he tuned back into Miss Bauman's
complaints. He'd addressed this one in the past. Several

times. "They live on that street, so it's as much theirs as yours, Miss Bauman. They aren't hurting you in any way. Would you rather they be out stirring up real trouble?"

Had she ever been a kid? He thought about it and decided probably not. She'd never married and didn't have many friends as far as he knew. She wasn't a happy person and not enjoyable to be around. He was sure she was lonely, and he felt sorry for her, which was why he tolerated these visits of hers, but she was exhausting.

She huffed. "I would rather you did your job and kept those delinquents off my street."

"They aren't breaking any law, and they have as much right to the street as you do. There's nothing I can do. You know that." She lived on a street that ended in a cul-de-sac, so the only traffic was the people who lived there, and they knew to watch for children. It was a good road for kids to ride their bikes and skateboards on.

"I know nothing of the kind. Perhaps we should find a police chief who will do his job."

Right this minute, he was all for that. "Let me see your list." They played this game each time she arrived with her list of wrongs. There was usually at least one thing on it he could do something about or pretend to, and she'd leave feeling she'd won.

He scanned the page. There it was, the bone he'd throw her. She would have already voiced her complaint, but he hadn't been listening. If he had, he could have stopped her right then, and she'd be gone by now. "Did you personally see Melissa put earrings in her purse without paying?"

"Of course I did. I wouldn't be telling you about it if I hadn't. That girl is going down the wrong road, and her mama needs to be taking her in hand before she ends up in prison."

Melissa's mother worked two jobs, the school cafeteria during the day and cleaning offices at night, to keep food on the table for her three children. At fifteen, Melissa was the oldest, and Tristan had already had a few run-ins with the girl. Miss Bauman was right. Melissa was headed down the wrong road.

"I'll talk to her," he said.

"See that you do."

He chuckled as the biggest pain in his rear end marched out with her nose high in the air. Then inspiration struck. He stood, debated the wisdom of his idea, decided the hell with it, and caught Miss Bauman on the sidewalk. He was going to regret this, but...

"Miss Bauman, a few more minutes of your time."

"What is it? I'm a busy woman."

Busy his ass. She had nothing better to do than to spy on people and make her complaints lists. But maybe he could change that. "You know Mary Beth works two jobs to keep a roof over her children's heads and food on the table."

Miss Bauman nodded. "Commendable, but that doesn't excuse her not keeping that girl—"

"You can help," he said, cutting her off before she could get started on a tirade.

"Help? Why would I want to?"

Because you're a lonely old woman who needs a kid in her life to brighten her days even if you don't know it. And here's a kid who is going down the wrong road, and maybe we can change her life. "Because I'm asking you to."

"Asking me to do what?"

She was trying to be her snotty self, but he saw the interest in her eyes. *Gotcha, lady.* "I'm going to talk to Melissa about her stealing. That can't be condoned. But the girl needs guidance. Her mother is doing the best she can, but we should offer help when we can, no?"

"I don't see what I can do."

"You can give Melissa a job so she'll have money to buy earrings instead of stealing them."

"Give her a job?" Miss Bauman looked at him as if one of Miss Mabel's aliens had invaded his body.

"Right. Think how much easier Melissa can make your life, Miss Bauman. She can clean your house, cook your meals, and whatever else you want her to do for you. Maybe read your books to you." The woman loved her books and spent half her days at the library as a volunteer. "But you'll need to pay her. Not much, but enough for her to have a little spending money."

"Why should I give her money?"

"Because you're a nice woman," he replied. She wasn't, but he thought she could be with the right motivation, and just maybe this woman and that girl needed each other. "Besides, you can't expect her to work for free."

"I suppose not, but I don't want a thief in my house."

"How about I talk to Melissa, and then I'll bring her by to talk to you? You can tell her what you're expecting from her, and if she's interested, the two of you can come to an agreement." He'd make sure Melissa understood she didn't have a choice in this.

She sighed, sounding as if he was setting the weight of the world on her shoulders, then gave him a perfect royal wave. "You may do that."

He was tempted to bow and say, "Thank you, Your Majesty."

The city wasn't paying him enough.

"What are you doing?" his niece said, coming into the kitchen.

"Nothing." Tristan pushed the bakery bag to the back

of the counter, hoping he didn't have a guilty look on his face.

"What's in the bag?" She stood on her tiptoes, trying to see above the counter.

"Nothing you need to worry about. Did you lose your soft voice again?" Did all kids go through a shouting stage?

She giggled. "Yes! I lost it."

"Well, do my ears a favor and try to find it again. How's grilled cheese and fruit sound for dinner?"

"And pickles?"

"Yes, and pickles."

"Okay."

"Go tell your dad to come in for dinner. And don't you start painting, or you'll be eating a cold cheese sandwich, and you won't get a pickle." He tapped her nose. "Got it?"

"Got it." She took off running.

It would take Parker a good twenty minutes to clean his brushes unless Everly forgot to tell him dinner was ready and decided to paint. The two of them would forget to eat, and paint all night if he wasn't around to make sure they got fed.

Before he got dinner ready, he took the bakery bag upstairs to his room to keep it out of Everly's nosy little hands. He chuckled as he set it on his dresser.

"Let the games begin."

Chapter Eight

Skye had come in early to work on next week's assignments for her deputies. It was usually quiet during the early morning hours, and she was able to get paperwork done without interruptions. It was Mason's turn for jail duty, and he wasn't going to be happy. Too bad, so sad. He had to take a turn just like the other deputies.

Randal Parsons, her chief deputy sheriff, was retiring next month, and Mason was expecting to get his job. It wasn't going to happen. She hoped that when he was passed over for the promotion, he'd get mad enough to resign. He probably wouldn't, though. Out of spite, he'd stick around for the sole purpose of making her life miserable.

At some point she was going to have to deal with him, and she had started keeping a record of the problems he caused. The only reason she hadn't fired him already was because he'd told another deputy that he'd file an age discrimination complaint if she did. The last thing she needed as a new sheriff was a legal battle with one of her deputies.

She was a year in now, more secure in her job, and Mason's days were numbered, no matter his threats.

He didn't have any friends on the force, so if it came to that, every one of her deputies would support her.

Her stomach was growling by the time she finished the assignments for next week. She printed the schedule out for herself, then emailed a copy to Jackie, the sheriff's office administrative coordinator, to post. Since it wasn't a Monday, her omelet day at the Kitchen, yogurt it was.

Tristan and Fuzz, carrying his toy, walked into her office. "Good morning, Sheriff."

She was going to have to have a serious talk with her heart about its fluttering whenever he made an appearance. "Chief, what can I do for you?" Was that a pastry from Sweet Tooth Bakery he was eating? Her stomach rumbled.

He grinned. "Now that's a loaded question if there ever was one."

Note to self: Don't give him an opening like that. Also, he was just too damn adorable when he smiled and amusement danced in his eyes. She was not immune to his charms, and that aggravated her. "I'll rephrase that. What brings you to my side of town this morning?"

"I have a teenager to deal with. Thought maybe you'd be agreeable to coming with me this afternoon to talk to her. You being a girl and all, she might listen to you better than me."

She would not laugh, but she sure wanted to. "Me being a girl and all? You really have a way with words." Her gaze narrowed on the white bag he held. Did he have more goodies in there?

"What can I say? I'm a silver-tongued devil." He glanced down at the bag she was staring at. "Tell you what. I'll give you my last pastry if you'll come with me. And you should know I really wanted to eat it."

"What are you talking to the girl about?"

After he explained the situation, she couldn't refuse to help. "Deal." She held her hand out. "Give me."

He set the bag in her hand. "I'll pick you up at three. By the time we get to Melissa's house, she should be home from school."

"I'll meet you there." Being in a car with him was not good for her resolve to avoid spending time with him.

"Negative, Sheriff. We need to plan our approach. We can do that on the way over." He walked to the door, then glanced back at her. "Enjoy my pastry."

She stared at the empty doorway for long moments after he was gone. What was that flash of mischief about that she'd seen in his eyes? She took out the pastry and studied it. Cream filled, one of her favorites. Yet… She flattened the bag, then set the pastry on it. Studied it some more. Her stomach said, "Eat it," but he'd promised retribution for her spider joke. Could this be it? She couldn't see anything wrong with it, though.

"Morning, Sheriff," Bradley Burns said as he walked into her office. "All was quiet last night." He was coming off the night shift and was in the habit of checking in with her before heading home to sleep.

"That's always good."

His gaze landed on the pastry she'd pushed to the edge of her desk. "You gonna eat that?"

"No. You're welcome to it." She hoped it didn't have a laxative in it.

"Thanks." He picked it up. "See ya in the morning." As he walked out, he took a big bite of the pastry. "Urgh." He spit the bite into his hand, then marched back to her desk, dropped the pastry back onto the bag, and glared at her.

"What? There's something wrong with it?" She knew it!

"Yeah, it's filled with mayonnaise."

She couldn't help it, she burst into laughter. *Good one, Tristan.*

"Not funny," her deputy said.

Oh, it was. It really was.

"How do you think Melissa's going to react to your idea?" Skye asked Tristan as they drove to the girl's house.

"Your guess is as good as mine, but she probably won't like it. What do you think of me giving her a choice between working for Miss Bauman or sending her to juvie?"

"You would do that?"

"No, but she doesn't need to know that."

"Do we need to talk to her mother first?" She tried not to find things sexy about him, such as the way he drove with one hand on the steering wheel and his other one resting on the console, his fingers tapping to a beat only he could hear. She tried not to imagine that hand on her, but she had an excellent memory, and those long fingers of his had expertly toyed with her in the most magical of ways.

"I talked to her mother yesterday. She's worried about her daughter and said she'll support whatever I think is best for Melissa."

"Sorry, what?"

"Where's your mind, Sheriff?" He glanced at her and smirked as if he knew exactly where her mind had wandered off to.

On your fingers and how much I want them on me again. "My mind is right here." Well, it wasn't. It was stuck on their night together. Why couldn't she put that time with him right where it belonged? A one-time thing, never to be repeated. No matter how much she wanted a repeat.

"Thanks for coming with me," he said, interrupting her thoughts of him, of them together, again. "Even if it cost me a pastry I really wanted."

She barely held in a snort and almost laughed at his frustrated expression. "You're welcome." He was dying for her to call him out for his joke. Not going to happen. She wasn't about to give him the satisfaction of telling him how funny she'd found it.

"So, you liked my pastry?"

"It was delicious." His expression was priceless. She was immensely enjoying this and had to turn her face to the window so he wouldn't see her grin. Also, she was definitely going to retaliate, as soon as she thought of the perfect practical joke.

"Here we are." He stopped in front of a small cottage.

Although the house could use a coat of paint, the yard was well maintained. "I don't think I've ever met the family."

"There are three children. Melissa's fifteen and the oldest. Mary Beth Compton is a single mother, working two jobs to support her family."

"Okay. Let's do this."

Chapter Nine

Tristan walked to the door next to Skye. He was puzzled. She couldn't possibly have thought a mayonnaise-filled pastry was delicious. He'd been fully prepared to get his ears blistered for his joke. Had looked forward to it. He was annoyed that she'd taken his fun away.

The front door opened before they reached it, and Mary Beth walked out. "Melissa should be home in a few minutes, Chief."

Every resident of Marsville called him Chief. He wasn't sure anyone even remembered his name. "Mary Beth, this is Sheriff Morgan. Sheriff, Mary Beth Compton."

"Pleased to meet you, Ms. Compton," Skye said. "I do wish it was for a better reason."

"Just Mary Beth, and believe me, so do I. I don't know what to do with that girl." She glanced at his car. "You can bring Fuzz in."

"Thank you, but he's good." The windows were down, and he wouldn't leave the car without permission.

She stepped back. "Please, come in."

As he and Skye took seats on the sofa, he glanced around. Although there was a bare minimum of furniture, the place was clean and neat. He guessed Mary

Beth to be in her late thirties, not old by any means, but the way her shoulders slumped and with the bags under her eyes, she looked as if she carried the weight of the world on her back. He supposed working two jobs and worry about a child could do that to you.

"Would you like something to drink? I have sweet tea, or I could make a pot of coffee if you prefer."

"No, thank you."

"A glass of water would be lovely," Skye said.

Mary Beth seemed pleased by the request as she dashed away, and he glanced at Skye to see a soft smile on her face. "What's that look for?"

She shrugged. "She needed to feel useful."

This was why he was glad she'd agreed to come with him. Women picked up on stuff that went right over a man's head. He had a suspicion that was going to prove useful in dealing with Melissa.

Mary Beth returned, carrying a tray with two glasses of water and a small plate of Oreo cookies. She set it on the coffee table, then sat in the chair closest to Skye. "I'm going to apologize in advance for my daughter's attitude."

Skye reached over and put her hand on Mary Beth's arm. "You're doing the right thing, Mary Beth. Sometimes children need a little tough love. The chief here said he talked to you about the choices we're going to give her."

"Yes, but I don't want her to go to juvie."

"And she won't, but that option is only to encourage her to make the right choice. She doesn't need to know that, okay?"

It occurred to him that he and Skye were going to

play good cop, bad cop, and she was going to get to be the good cop. He didn't like being a bad cop.

The front door slammed open, and Melissa walked in, wearing jeans that had to be a size too small, a deep red blouse with too many buttons undone, too much makeup for her age, and large silver hoop earrings that matched the description Mrs. Bauman had given him. Her long blond hair had blue streaks running through it.

She came to a full stop at seeing her mother had company. Her gaze slid from Skye to him, and her eyes widened, fear flashing in them. So, she probably guessed why he was here. She reached up and pulled her hair over one ear, then did the same to her other ear, hiding the earrings. She definitely knew why a police officer was sitting in her living room.

"Have a seat, Melissa," he said.

She spun and headed for the door.

"If you walk away, I will arrest you." Yep, bad cop here. But she needed to be afraid. He wouldn't arrest her over a pair of ten-dollar earrings, but it was best if she thought he would. He'd also bet serious money on this not being the first thing she'd shoplifted, only the first time she was caught.

Melissa froze but didn't turn around. Skye stood and went to her. She put her arm around the girl's shoulder. "Come sit down, honey."

Next time they had to deal with a teenager, he got to be the good cop.

Melissa broke away from Skye and went to her mother, squeezing onto the chair with her.

"You know who I am," he said once she was seated. He lifted his chin toward Skye. "This is Sheriff Morgan. You know why we're here, Melissa?"

The girl shook her head, and he wanted to sigh. She knew exactly the reason two police officers were in her home.

"Where did you get the earrings you're wearing, Melissa?" Skye said, keeping her voice soft.

"A friend gave them to me." She kept her gaze down as she picked at invisible lint on her jeans.

Bad cop Tristan shook his head. "Lying to the police doesn't score you any points. You want to try the truth now?"

When she didn't answer, Mary Beth said, "Did you steal the earrings, Mel?"

Melissa opened her mouth, then snapped it shut as a mulish expression crossed her face.

Tristan took out his phone and brought up the video he wanted. He handed the phone to Mary Beth. After Miss Bauman left his office, he'd gone to the pharmacy where the supposed theft had occurred. There was a small jewelry and makeup section, and he'd reviewed the security feed for that area. Sure enough, there was Melissa, slipping the earrings into her purse.

He kept his attention on Melissa as she watched the video with her mother. The blood drained from her face, then she eyed the door. She was going to run. He moved to block her escape.

"Why, Mel?" her mother said as tears streamed down her face.

"Because I wanted them." She shrugged as if wanting a pair of earrings meant it was okay to steal them.

"Then ask me for them."

Melissa rolled her eyes. "Like I'm going to ask you for money. You already work two jobs and still have trouble keeping the lights on."

Standing in front of the door, Tristan pulled his handcuffs from their pouch. Fear filled Melissa's eyes as she stared at them. "I'm going to give you two choices, Melissa. The first is a trip to the Juvenile Detention Center where you'll wait for a judge to pass down your sentence. The second is that you'll spend two hours a day after school working for Miss Bauman. Do you know who she is?"

"She's that old woman from the library. Why would I want to work for her? She hates kids."

"Two reasons. The most important one, if you agree, it will mean you won't be making a trip to the detention center today. The other reason, she's going to pay you. That means you'll have money to buy the things you want instead of stealing them."

"I have to help mom with my brothers after school."

"You come home from school, close yourself up in your room, and don't lift a finger to help, so that excuse doesn't fly," Mary Beth said. She glanced between him and Skye. "She does have to be home at night to watch her brothers, but in between my two jobs, I'm here in the afternoons. She's free to work for Mrs. Bauman." She put her arm around her daughter. "Do you want to go to juvie?"

Melissa shook her head.

"I guess you only have one choice then," her mother said.

When they stood to leave, Skye whispered something in Melissa's ear.

"Thanks for coming with me," Tristan said as they drove away.

"No problem. I'm glad I could help."

"What did you whisper to her?"

"I told her I really liked the earrings on her, but that she'd feel a lot better wearing them if she went back to the store and paid for them."

"Did you ever steal anything when you were a kid?"

He hadn't because he knew if he got caught, his aunt would skin his hide. She'd also threatened to stand him and his brothers in front of any store they stole from with a sign around their neck announcing their thievery. He hadn't doubted for one minute that she meant it.

"I almost did once. David Rhodes was my first crush, and he liked me back. A few weeks before Christmas he hinted that he'd gotten me something. When I told my mother I wanted to get him a present, she refused. She didn't think a thirteen-year-old girl had any business giving a boy a Christmas present. Can you imagine how embarrassing it would be for him to give me something and he got nothing from me?"

"Horribly embarrassing," he said, thoroughly amused by her story. "So you tried to steal him a present?"

"I did, a pocketknife. And I could have gotten away with it, even had the little knife hidden in my hand, no one the wiser."

"What stopped you?"

"I was halfway to the exit when it hit me that if I walked out those doors, I would officially be a thief. I didn't like the idea of that, so I put it back."

"What did your David Rhodes give you?"

She laughed. "Nothing. A week before Christmas, he decided he liked Emily Henderson better. He gave her a bottle of perfume."

"Your perfume?"

"No doubt."

"If I ever buy you perfume, I promise not to give it to another girl."

She turned her face to the window, but he didn't miss her smile.

Chapter Ten

"Well, well, what have we here?"

Skye froze as she clutched the roll of aluminum foil against her chest. Ten more rolls were on the floor next to her feet, the evidence of her crime overwhelming. "Kade?"

His gaze roamed over Tristan's classic Mustang, which she was wrapping in foil. "Should I call the police, Sheriff?"

Okay, that was amusement in his voice. That was good. "I thought you were back at the base."

"Just home for the night to spend a little time with my brothers and Everly since I'm shipping out tomorrow afternoon."

"It's three in the morning. Shouldn't you be sleeping?" Not standing here in their garage.

"Don't sleep much. Thought I heard something and came to investigate. What's with the foil?"

No use denying what was in front of his eyes. "It's supposed to look like a spaceship."

"Skylar, I hate to be the one to tell you this, but that does not look like a spaceship. However, I have an idea." He rubbed his hands together. "Okay, let's get this done before we get caught."

She grinned at her new coconspirator. "All righty then."

"Just be careful to not scratch the paint," Kade said. "We do that, and the police chief won't hesitate to put us behind bars and throw away the key."

"If he doesn't shoot me first."

He laughed. "Yeah, but this time it would be both of us."

There was no doubt the car was meant to look like a flying saucer when they finished. Kade had scrounged up a large glass bowl that now sat on the roof. They'd put Everly's bicycle helmet inside it, so that it appeared to be a little spaceman peering out. Using pieces of wood wrapped in foil, he'd made the wheels look like stabilizers, as if the flying saucer had landed. All she'd planned to do was wrap the car, but this was so much better. She took some photos with her phone.

"Why did we wrap Tristan's prized possession?" Kade said when they finished and were admiring the results.

"Payback. He gave me a pastry filled with mayo."

"That's funny, but why would he do that?"

"I kind of made him think spiders were crawling on his neck."

He laughed. "That would do it. He hates spiders. How'd you get in? We keep the garage door locked."

"Picked the lock?"

"What a talented little thing you are. He probably won't discover this until the weekend. Wish I was going to be around to see his face when he does."

She wished she could be, too. The Mustang was Tristan's day-off car. The rest of the time, he drove a city-issued SUV.

"Parker and Everly will see it in the morning when he takes her to school. I'll tell them not to spill the beans. Hopefully, Everly can keep a secret."

"You know, it might be funny if she asks him why there's a spaceship in the garage."

"True. I won't say anything to her then. Just let it play out, whichever way it goes."

"If he sees it in the morning when you're around, you better let me know what he said. Guess I should go before we really do get caught."

He smiled as he opened his arms. "Give me a hug, fishing buddy."

She didn't hesitate to go to him. Kade's hugs were like hugging her brother, except her brother wasn't putting his life on the line every time he left on whatever mission the Army was sending him on. She hugged Kade tight as she sent up a prayer that he'd come home safely to his family.

The funny thing about their relationship was that they really were just friends and fishing buddies. Neither Tristan nor Parker had the patience for the sport. She thought the reason Kade did was because it was the polar opposite of his Army life and the secret missions he went on. "I couldn't care less if I catch a fish. I feel at peace on the lake," he'd once told her.

She loved to fish, and she did love to catch them. Kade had a boat he stored on Lake James, and whenever he was home and the weather was nice, he'd invite her to come fishing with him. Usually, she'd fish while he settled in for a nap.

Tristan had once invited himself along, and both she and Kade had threatened to throw him overboard if he didn't stop complaining about how bored he was. Since then, he'd been banned from their fishing trips.

"Stay safe and come home to your family," she said, then stepped away.

"I'll always come home."

He couldn't promise that, but she didn't call him out for saying it, instead praying that would always be true. She pushed on his chest. "Go get some sleep."

"Yes, ma'am."

She took one last admiring look at their handiwork, then headed home to get a few hours of sleep herself.

The next morning her phone chimed with an incoming text. A picture of Tristan appeared. He stood with his hands on his hips, staring at his Mustang. Underneath the photo was a text from Kade.

Exact quote. "Oh, she's gone and done it now."

She giggled. Jeez, when was the last time she'd giggled? Maybe when she was sixteen during a slumber party when everyone was on a sugar high. She was going to have to be vigilant because he was going to pay her back. No doubt about it.

When she got to work, she scanned the area around the building. No sign of Tristan's SUV. Safe for now. She detoured to the breakroom for a cup of coffee, then got to work.

"When you gonna announce Randal's replacement?" Mason said, walking into her office and taking a seat.

Sometimes she regretted her open-door policy. Mostly because it allowed Mason to barge in whenever he wanted. "Soon." *And it won't be you.* She was so not looking forward to dealing with him when he learned he wouldn't get the promotion.

"There's only one right choice."

She inwardly sighed. "Mason, aren't you supposed to be on jail duty in ten minutes?" *And get that scowl off your face.*

"With my experience and seniority, I shouldn't have—"

"Sorry, am I interrupting?" Tristan said, appearing in the doorway, holding two cups of coffee and a white bag.

"No. Come on in, Chief. Mason's headed out." She pointedly looked at her deputy.

Shooting her another scowl, Mason stood. "Good morning, Chief," he said, giving Tristan a smile that she never got from him.

Tristan nodded. "Mason."

From Tristan's curt greeting and non-smile, she gathered he wasn't a fan of her deputy either. Smart man. Unlike the friendly way he treated most people, Fuzz ignored Mason as he headed straight for her. Smart dog, too.

Tristan sat in the chair Mason had vacated, put one of the coffees on her desk and pushed it toward her, then pulled a pastry from the bag, along with a napkin, and set them on her desk. He removed another one and took a bite.

She sat back in her chair. Did he really think she was going to touch that pastry or the coffee? "What brings you by this morning?"

"Told Miss Mabel we'd have our recommendations to her by Friday. Thought we should get started."

"I can't this morning. I have to leave in about fifteen minutes for Probate Court." Interesting that he had nothing to say about his Mustang.

"Hmm." He seemed to be thinking something as he drummed his fingers on the arm of the chair. "Tell you what. I'm on babysitting duty tonight so Parker can paint. Why don't you come over, have dinner with me and Everly? After I get her to bed, we can do our planning committee thing."

"I don't think that's a good idea." Parker's daughter was adorable, but spending time with Tristan in his home? Not wise. She would love to see inside it, though. The brothers lived in the house they'd grown up in, and the place was big and beautiful.

"It's a great idea. I promised Everly I'd make lasagna and garlic bread for dinner. Not to brag, but I make a mean lasagna."

He didn't play fair. The night they'd met, while sitting at the bar, they'd talked about some of their favorite things to do and eat. She'd told him lasagna was her weakness.

"Say yes. You know you want to."

Wanting to and doing it were two different things. But they did need to get something in the works for Miss Mabel. The last thing she wanted was the old bat gunning for her. "Fine. What time should I be there?"

"Around six."

"What can I bring?" Somehow, he'd tricked her into agreeing.

"Just your lovely self."

"I'll bring a bottle of wine."

"Perfect." He eyed the pastry. "Aren't you going to eat that?"

"Oh, I'm not really hungry."

His eyes were alight with amusement as he picked up the pastry. "Guess I'll have to eat it." He stood and took a big bite. "These things are so good." He finished it off, then picked up the coffee she hadn't touched. "Guess I'll have to drink this, too. Sweet Tooth sure does make the best coffee." The blasted man chuckled as he walked out with her coffee and her pastry in his stomach. Hers growled.

She scowled at his back as he left. The sneaky devil had just played another joke on her.

Chapter Eleven

"I need help, Katie," Tristan said, striding up to the diner's counter, a man on a mission.

"What can I do for you, Chief?"

"Teach me how to make lasagna." What had he been thinking, telling Skye he made a mean lasagna? His mouth had gotten ahead of his brain, but he'd seen her refusal to come to dinner forming. Remembering she'd said lasagna was her favorite food, he'd thrown that out there. Now he had three hours to pull this off before Skye would be sitting at his table, expecting what he'd promised.

"Okay. When do you want to learn?"

"Now."

"Now, as in this minute?"

"Yes." Fortunately, it was the middle of the afternoon, so she wasn't busy. "Garlic bread, too." He didn't blame her for looking at him like he'd lost his marbles. "I'll owe you big."

"Why don't I make it for you, and you can pick it up in an hour or so."

"That won't work. I have to make it myself."

"I have a feeling there's a good story here. Care to share?"

"Just promised someone I'd make them lasagna for dinner. No biggie."

A slow smile spread across her face. "I see. Got a hot date, do you?"

Crap. Did that heat spreading across his cheeks mean he was blushing? Apparently so, because she laughed.

"I'll make you a deal. You tell me with who, and I'll teach you how to make the best damn lasagna you've ever had."

"You drive a hard bargain, Katie. You can't tell anyone, okay? And you especially can't ever hint to her that you know."

"Promise." She made an X over her chest.

"The sheriff."

She banged her fist on the counter. "I knew it."

Huh? "Knew what?"

"That you have the hots for Skylar. I see the way you look at her whenever she's near you."

"You're imagining things." But she wasn't. Not at all. Marsville's police chief definitely had the hots for Horace County's sheriff.

Tristan carried the pan of lasagna—made by his own hands, thank you very much—and the French bread into the kitchen. Katie had talked him out of the garlic bread, saying he didn't want garlic breath. Good thinking, that.

He glanced at the microwave clock. He had an hour before Skye arrived, enough time to shower and get things ready. After preheating the oven to the temperature Katie had instructed, he headed to his room, unbuttoning his shirt as he went. He put his gun in the lockbox he kept high on his closet shelf, then finished undressing. Shower done, he shaved, slapped aftershave on his face, then went to his closet. What to wear?

It had been a year since he'd gone on a date—her fault, that—not that tonight was a date, but it kind of felt like it was. If he got too dressy, Skye would be suspicious. Casual was the way to go. He decided on gray cargo shorts and a dark blue T-shirt. Barefoot, he returned to the kitchen.

The oven had reached the correct temperature, so he slid the lasagna in. Next, he lightly sprayed water over the French bread, then wrapped it in foil. That would go in the oven ten minutes before dinner was served.

He called Parker. Everly answered, which meant Parker was painting. "Hey, kiddo. I'm home if you want to come up to the house. Bring Fuzz with you." He'd dropped his dog off at home before going to learn how to make lasagna.

"Uncle Tris, I painted Jellybean."

He pulled the phone away from his ear. Hopefully, this shouting stage wouldn't last much longer. "Did you now?" Since Jellybean was winding around his ankles, that meant she'd thankfully painted his picture and not the cat, something she'd done before.

Between getting out of school and his arriving home, she spent her time in the studio with Parker when he was off duty. On the days Parker was at the fire station, Andrew—their housekeeper and babysitter—stayed with her until Tristan was home. She had her own paints and easel, and the kid had inherited her dad's artistic ability. She was good, and he wasn't just saying that because he was her uncle.

"Yes! You have to come see."

"How about I'll look at it after dinner, and right now

you come help me set the table?" They needed to have a little chat before Skye arrived.

"Can I have some juice and a pickle? I'm hungry."

This kid and her pickles. "Sure. Tell your dad…" He chuckled as he set his phone down. She'd hung up on him. He poured her a cup of juice, but he'd wait on the pickle until she came in. If he tried to guess what kind she was in the mood for, he'd inevitably be wrong.

She came barreling in with Fuzz on her heels and headed straight to the refrigerator.

"Whoa there, Ev, we need to get the paint off your hands and arms before you touch anything." He used his foot to slide her step stool in front of the sink. "What kind of pickle you want?" he asked while she washed her hands and arms.

"Sour," she yelled.

"One sour pickle coming up." He put a dill pickle on a saucer, then set it on the kitchen island next to her juice. He shuddered at the combination.

"Two!"

"One, or you'll ruin your dinner."

After she was scrubbed clean, he lifted her and set her on a bar stool at the island. "Remember I promised I'd make you lasagna for dinner tonight?" So, it had come to this, lying to a child. How low could he go?

Everly shook her head. "No, don't remember that. I want mac and cheese with hotdogs in it."

"Lasagna is better. It has lots and lots of gooey cheese and is even better than spaghetti." She should go for that since she loved spaghetti.

"Does it have hot dogs in it?"

"No, it has hamburger."

"I want hot dogs in it," she yelled.

"How about this? I'll cook a hot dog, and if you want to cut it up and add it to the lasagna, you can. But first you have to taste the lasagna before you put the hot dog in it."

"What the devil are you feeding my child?" Parker said, walking into the kitchen. He slid onto the stool next to Everly.

"Lousshauna," she said.

"Lasagna," Tristan enunciated.

"That frozen stuff from the store?" Parker said. "I think I'll just make a sandwich."

"Nope. Homemade." Tristan eyed his brother's paint-splattered shirt. "We're having a guest for dinner, so you might want to change your shirt. Or I can make you a plate to take back to your studio." Which was where Parker usually ate dinner, and even better. He didn't need his brother observing and commenting on his non-date night.

"We are? Who?"

"Skye."

Everly looked up at the ceiling. "The sky is coming to dinner?"

He chuckled. The kid was a trip. "No. You remember Miss Skylar?"

Everly nodded. "I like her. Does she like pickles?"

"I don't know. You can ask her."

Parker was looking at him with a smirk on his face. "So you're finally making a move?"

What was it with people thinking they knew his business? "Don't have a clue what you're talking about. Miss Mabel put us on a ridiculous planning committee, and we're having our first meeting tonight."

"Uh-huh. I think I'll stick around. Going to be fun

watching you pretend you don't want to get in her pa…"
He glanced at Everly. "In her pantry." He grinned when
Tristan snorted. "Best I could do off the top of my head."

"Does she have pickles in her pantry?" Everly said.

Parker made a choking sound, and Tristan refused
to look at his brother. If he did, they'd both burst into
laughter. He turned and got plates out of the cabinet.
When he could safely talk without laughing, he said,
"If it comes up, I made the lasagna myself."

"All right, but who really made it?"

"I did. Really." At Parker's raised brows, he sighed.
"With Katie telling me what to do."

"All that effort and you want me to believe you're
not interested in Skylar's pantry?" He smirked as he
pushed off the stool. "I'm going to change my shirt."

Tristan wanted to bang his head on the counter.
Whose bright idea was it to invite her to dinner, anyway?

Chapter Twelve

Skye parked in front of the Church brothers' house and stared at it for a few minutes. She'd driven by countless times and had always admired it. The three-story Victorian-style house was painted pale gray, the trim and front door a deep burgundy, and the windowsills white. It was a striking house, the paint colors perfect for it. She wondered if Parker had chosen them.

A wide porch stretched across the front, and dark green ferns hung between each post. A swing with a dark blue seat cushion and blue-and-burgundy pillows swayed with the evening breeze on the right side of the porch. What a perfect place to curl up with a book. Other chairs and wrought-iron tables were scattered around. If the outside of the house was this perfect, imagine what the inside had to look like.

If you'd get out of the car and go inside, you could see for yourself. She'd almost called and cancelled, probably should have, but here she was. She'd gone home early, bathed, shaved her legs, and then had spent a freaking hour deciding what to wear. You'd think this was a date or something.

Annoyed with herself and needing to remind both herself and Tristan that this wasn't a date in any way whatsoever, she'd gone with her sheriff's uniform. The hair she'd washed, blow dried, and then added some curls to with her hot iron was now in its usual bun at the back of her neck. She even had on her black, soft-leather boots.

Now that she was here, she regretted her clothing choice. Jeans and a T-shirt wouldn't have given off any vibes of the I-think-you're-hot-and-do-you-want-to-play-with-me-again kind, never mind that she did want to.

The door opened, and Tristan stepped out. He stopped, braced his legs apart, and stuffed his hands in his pockets as he stared back at her.

Well, too late to take off now. She grabbed the bottle of wine and bakery box and as she walked toward him, her hungry eyes—and boy, were they hungry for this man—roamed over him. His T-shirt wasn't a size too small like some big-muscled men wore, but it did nothing to hide his broad shoulders. She'd never seen him in shorts before, and who knew how sexy a tall, bare-foot man wearing cargo shorts was? Well, she did now.

"Thought I was going to have to bring your dinner out to your car for a minute there," he said, then belat-edly added as his gaze took in her uniform, "Sheriff."

Ignoring his dig, she stopped a few feet from him. Even a few feet weren't enough to keep his scent from washing over her. Soap and either cologne or a spicy aftershave was a potent combination. "Good evening, Chief."

His lips thinned. "How about for tonight, we're just Tristan and Skye?"

"I suppose we can do that since you're feeding me lasagna."

"Hmm." He scratched his chin. "You can be bribed with lasagna. Good to know."

"There's something about a police chief bribing a sheriff that doesn't seem right."

"I think lasagna bribery is a misdemeanor, if that even, so I'm willing to risk it." He took the bottle of wine from her, then opened the door. "After you."

All her life until coming here, she'd been Skye. It was how she thought of herself. The day she'd discovered she knew the police chief intimately—a man who'd whispered her name in her ear while his body was wrapped around hers—she'd introduced herself as Skylar so she wouldn't have to listen to him call her Skye. He called her Skye anyway.

As soon as she stepped into the foyer, she stopped, barely stifling a gasp. Ahead of her, matching curved staircases on each opposite wall led upward. A massive crystal chandelier hung between the stairs from the third story. And this was only the entry. What did the rest of the house look like?

She'd grown up middle-class, her parents able to provide the essentials and keep food on the table for their three children, but sometimes struggling if there was a surprise big-ticket expense. This was the kind of place one drove by and wondered what it was like to live in. The brothers had inherited it from their aunt, but that was all she knew about their family history.

Tristan stood by, watching her gape at the entry, and she couldn't read his expression. He probably thought she was a real bumpkin, but seriously, who lived like this?

"It is a bit ostentatious, isn't it?"

"Maybe, but it's really beautiful."

"Wait until you see the rest of the house. I'll take you on a tour after dinner."

"I'd like that."

"Uncle Tris." Parker's daughter ran into the foyer. "Did you cook my hot dog?"

He reached down and put his hands on her shoulders, stopping her in front of him. "Everly, say hello to Miss Skylar."

"Hello, Miss Skylar. Do you want a hot dog? Uncle Tris said I could put one in my lassanoa."

He chuckled. "Lasagna."

"That's what I said."

Heavens, the girl was loud for such a little thing. Skye smiled. "Hello, Everly. Can I wait and decide about the hot dog in a little while?"

"Okay. Are you hungry? Do you want a pickle?"

"Ah…"

"She thinks if you want a pickle, that will mean she can have another one," Tristan said. A large orange-and-white cat ambled in, sat, stared at them, then let loose with a mournful drawn-out meow. "It sounds like Jellybean's hungry. Did you feed him?"

Everly shook her head. "Not yet."

"Go do that now. Our dinner will be ready soon."

She danced off with the cat running after her.

"She's adorable," Skye said.

"Yes, she is. She's also very loud."

Skye laughed. "I noticed."

He reached for her hand. "Come on."

As he led her through the house, she wondered if he even realized they were holding hands. She should take her hand back, but she didn't. They walked through a formal dining room, and she tried to take it in as they passed. The table was a beautiful dark wood with ten upholstered chairs in a soft cream fabric. A large and stunning mountain sunset painting was on one wall. "Is that one of Parker's?"

He glanced at the painting. "Yes."

"It's beautiful."

"He shows promise."

Was he serious? "I think someone who's had showings in New York art galleries is a little more than just 'shows promise.'"

"Yeah, but don't tell him that. We try to keep his ego in check."

She heard the love and pride in his voice and envied the close relationship the brothers had. Her brother lived in the Netherlands with his Dutch girlfriend. She called him on his birthday, and he called her on hers, and they talked on Christmas Day. He kept inviting her to come see him, and someday, she would.

Her sister...well, Lindy was all about Lindy. She'd married an older man with more than enough money to keep her in Louboutin shoes, two-thousand-dollar Saint Laurent handbags, and designer dresses. But Lindy was happy, so who was she to judge?

Skye was the youngest, and the day after she left for college, her parents put their house up for sale, bought an RV, and didn't even bother waving goodbye. She communicated with them via Facebook now and then, and if it wasn't for social media, she probably wouldn't know where they were on any given day.

Tristan, still holding her hand, led her to the kitchen, and holy cheese balls, what a kitchen it was. It was almost as big as her one-bedroom apartment, and her head swiveled as she tried to take it all in. The most beautiful granite she'd ever seen covered the counters and a long island.

She set the bakery box down, then pulled her hand away from Tristan's and swept her palm over the cool stone. "This is gorgeous. I've never seen anything like it." The blues, grays, and whites in the granite made her think of the ocean on a stormy day. The cabinets were white and the backsplash the same blue as in the granite. The appliances were all oversize stainless steel. A large window over the sink had a view of the Blue Ridge Mountains rising in the distance.

"We remodeled when Parker got his first big paycheck. It was still the original kitchen from when the house was built and sorely needed a facelift." He set the wine down next to her bakery box.

"You and your brothers have lived here all your life?"

Something flashed in his eyes. Pain? Sadness? "No." He turned away, going to the counter behind him, and opening a drawer. "Let's open your wine."

"Miss Skylar, I painted Jellybean. Do you want to see?"

Skye smiled at the loud little girl running toward her. Parker followed his daughter into the kitchen, grinning at seeing Skye. "Use your quiet voice, Ev. You don't want to hurt Miss Skylar's ears." He walked to her and kissed her cheek. "Welcome to our home, Skylar."

"Thank you," she said as she glanced at Tristan, who was looking back at her with soft eyes. Her stomach somersaulted.

She was so in trouble with this man. Yes, she was.

Chapter Thirteen

"We'll eat in the solarium." Tristan opened the wine Skye had brought, then handed it to Parker. "Take this out to the table."

Everly hopped to Skye. "Will you sit next to me, Miss Skylar?"

She smiled at his niece. "I would love to."

"If you want Miss Skylar to sit next to you, you have to promise to use your soft voice," Parker said over his shoulder as he walked out of the kitchen.

"I can do that," she yelled.

Skye glanced at him, and Tristan grinned at her effort not to laugh. He really liked how she treated Everly. Inviting her to dinner tonight was turning out to be a brilliant idea. She was more relaxed around him than she'd been the whole of the past year. He didn't think she'd realized she'd let him hold her hand.

"Why don't you take Miss Skylar to the solarium? And remember, use your soft voice when you talk to her."

"Okay," Everly whispered.

"Can I do anything to help?" Skye said.

"Nope. Go with Everly. I'll be there in a minute."

Everly took Skye's hand. "Do you like pickles?" she whisper-shouted as they walked away.

"I do," Skye whispered back.

He narrowed his eyes at that tidy bun low on her neck. His fingers itched to pull the pins in her hair out, one by one. Her hair was glorious. Silky soft and fell halfway down her back.

Even in her sheriff's uniform, she was sexy as hell. He'd been disappointed that she came in her uniform because he knew she'd done it on purpose. A reminder that tonight was a business meeting, nothing more. Well, they'd just see about that.

Fuzz barreled through the doggie door, went straight to his dinner bowl, and chowed down.

As instructed by Katie, the lasagna had been cooling for fifteen minutes. Tristan took the French bread from the oven, sliced it, then put the pieces in a breadbasket.

Parker returned. "Need help?"

"Yeah, you can take the bread." Tristan put on oven mitts, picked up the lasagna dish, and followed Parker to the solarium.

"That looks great. Did you really make that yourself?" Skye asked when he set it in the middle of the table.

"Miss Katie helped him," Everly cheerfully offered. Parker snorted.

"Did she now?" Skye said with amusement in her eyes.

"Thank you for sharing that, Ev." Little tattletale.

"You're welcome, Uncle Tris."

The lasagna was delicious, the bread warm and soft inside, Skye's wine was good, and the conversation mostly from Everly as she peppered Skye with questions, sometimes whispering and sometimes forgetting to. Tristan was content to listen, learning more about Skye than he had in a year. She had a brother living with his girlfriend in the Netherlands, a sister who was married and didn't have any children, and her parents were traveling the country in an RV. He had the impression that it was her brother she missed the most.

"A spaceship landed in our garage, Miss Skylar," Everly said, her voice filled with wonder and her eyes wide.

"Wow. A spaceship?" Skye darted a glance at him.

"Imagine that, Miss Skylar." Tristan kept his face blank, although he wanted to laugh. It was a great prank. "How do you think something like that could happen?"

She shrugged. "How would I know?"

Oh, you know, sweetheart.

"I wanted to see it fly, but it was gone when I got home from school," Everly said. "Have you ever seen a spaceship, Miss Skylar?"

"Stop talking for a few minutes and eat your dinner," Parker told his daughter.

"I love lashana," she said after taking a bite.

"Lasagna," he and Parker said together.

She dramatically rolled her eyes as only a five-year-old could. "That's what I said."

"I love it, too." Skye took the last bite of hers, then grinned at Everly. "Yum."

"Yum," Everly echoed.

"If you're finished, why don't you take Miss Skylar to the studio and show her your painting while I clean up?"

"Uncle Tris, you forgot my hot dog."

He hadn't, but he was hoping she would. "Looks to me like you didn't need it. Miss Skylar brought..." He glanced at her.

"Cupcakes."

"Show her your painting, and then you can come back in and have one."

"Cupcakes! Oh, boy." Everly jumped up. "Come on, Miss Skylar. I painted Jellybean."

"I should help you clean up," Skye said.

"Thanks, but I got it. Go with Parker and Everly, and I'll come down shortly."

"Okay. Dinner was really good."

"Thanks."

After loading the dishwasher and putting the remainder of the lasagna away, he headed to Parker's studio. When he got there, Skye was standing behind Everly, watching her paint.

Everly was putting the finishing touches on her portrait of Jellybean, and every time he saw one of her pieces, he was struck by how talented his niece was, especially for her age. If she kept at it, he thought she would surpass Parker in her abilities.

"That's amazing, Everly," Skye said. "It looks just like Jellybean. I love how you have him sleeping in that spot of sun on the floor."

"I trip over the da...darn cat every day because he's right in the middle of the floor," Tristan said. "He needs to find a new place to sleep."

Everly gave him her patented eye roll. "You can't tell a cat what to do, Uncle Tris. They do what they want to." She seemed to consider that. "I wish I was a cat."

"I know the feeling," Skye said.

He loved that Skye and his niece were bonding, but

it was his turn to have time with the sheriff. Parker was already lost in whatever he was painting now, and this was the time of the evening when Tristan would distract Everly, his gift to his artistic brother, who wasn't happy if he wasn't painting. But not tonight. Parker would just have to deal.

That wasn't really fair, though. Parker spent time with his daughter until she fell asleep, but then he'd leave Tristan to keep watch over her while he spent hours on whatever masterpiece he was creating.

Tristan's paycheck covered his personal expenses, groceries, and Andrew's wages. Since Andrew kept their house clean and the refrigerator stocked, that was money well spent. Parker paid for everything else— such as the much needed and expensive remodeling. Tristan and Parker both refused to take any money from Kade. He was serving his country and risking his life in doing so. He could blow all his money on whatever he wanted for all they cared.

Tristan walked to the other side of the room and stopped next to Parker. "I'm taking Skye up to my floor, so Everly's all yours. She's going to want a cupcake when she finishes her painting. They're on the kitchen counter."

"'Kay."

Parker might or might not have heard him. When he was in his zone, you could set off a firecracker under his feet and he wouldn't notice. The only two things that could penetrate his concentration was Everly or a call on his firehouse radio.

He walked back to Skye and Everly and put his hand on his niece's shoulder. "Tell Miss Skylar good night."

"Night."

Like her father, Everly was lost in her art. Fuzz was spread out on the floor, and Jellybean was busy boxing his nose. He left them to it and took Skye's hand. "I promised you a tour." And again, she let him hold her hand while they walked back to the house.

Chapter Fourteen

He was holding her hand again. Skye wished she didn't like it. She was a competent, strong woman. She had to be, considering she was surrounded by an abundance of testosterone. She was perfectly capable of protecting herself, thank you very much. Yet Tristan's large hand wrapped around hers made her feel protected, cherished even. It was an odd feeling.

Holding hands with a man wasn't something she'd particularly liked in the past. Her only serious relationship had been with Danny, and when he'd held her hand, it was a show of ownership, not for the intimacy of it. She hadn't appreciated the control he'd tried to exert over her. But holding hands with Tristan was... different. It was intimate in a way holding hands with Danny had never been.

Then, as they neared the back door of the house, he began to caress his thumb over the top of her hand. Weird tingles traveled up her arm. She wanted to snatch her hand away because she didn't need tingles in her life. Not from a cop. He dropped her hand to open the door, and she was both relieved and missed that hand he'd had wrapped around hers.

"We have some wine left from dinner, but you have to drive home, so maybe something else?"

"Yeah, wouldn't be good for the sheriff to get pulled over for a DUI."

He smiled. "No, but I'd bail you out of the pokey."

Not only did he need to stop holding her hand, but he should stop smiling at her like that. "Good to know. I'd love a cup of coffee."

"Perfect." He opened a cabinet, took out a plate, and handed it to her. "Put a couple of those cupcakes on this while I make us coffee."

She put three cupcakes on the plate, two for him and one for her. "I'm amazed at how talented Everly is. I guess she inherited that from Parker."

"Him and maybe her mother."

"Do you mind me asking about her mother? Does Everly spend any time with her?"

"Nope." He leaned back against the counter. "I've never met her. Parker met her when he was studying art in France. He doesn't talk about her, but from the few things he's said, she didn't want anything to do with a baby."

"Wow. How could a mother not want her child?"

"Beats me. He'd been gone for three years, then without a heads-up, he came home with a two-week-old baby. You ever see the movie *Three Men and a Baby*? It's an oldie."

"I don't think so."

"Stream it sometime and you'll see exactly what it was like for us with a newborn baby in the house. We were clueless."

"From the little time I've been around her, she

doesn't seem any worse for the wear having three men raise her."

"She's an awesome kid. Just don't get between her and her pickles, though. She'll get vicious." The first coffee pod finished brewing, and he popped in another one. "Cream and two sugars, right?"

"How do you know that?"

"I'm a cop. It's my job to be observant." He winked, then added the cream and sugar to her cup.

He needed to stop doing things like knowing how she preferred her coffee and winking at her. And going barefoot? Why she found that sexy was puzzling.

After his cup filled up, he gave her one of his panty-melting smiles—another thing he needed to stop doing. "Grab your coffee. We're going up to my quarters on the second floor." He picked up his cup and the plate with the cupcakes.

He was taking her to his bedroom? "Um, can't we stay down here?"

"I thought you wanted a tour." He walked out of the kitchen, and after a few seconds of internal debate, she followed him. Odd that she trusted him, considering she didn't really know him. Or maybe she did, more than she'd realized. Otherwise she wouldn't be trailing after him.

"Parker and Everly have their rooms down here," he said when they reached the first of the twin stairs leading up. He lifted the hand holding his cup toward a hallway. "Down that hall. Our quarters are off-limits to each other, so I can't take you on a tour of their rooms." He leaned his mouth near her ear, as if he was about to tell her a secret. "I'm not against sneaking you in, though, if you want. You just can't rat me out if I do."

"Let's save our sneak invasion on Parker and Everly's rooms for another time. Just so you know, if you're taking me to your bedroom, I'll go back to the kitchen to drink my coffee and eat my cupcake."

"Well, there goes my wicked intentions." He comically waggled his eyebrows. "But I have other rooms for you to choose from. Put your coffee on the stairs a minute." He set the plate and his coffee down. "There are two rooms down here you'll want to see before we go up."

She set her cup next to his, then followed him across the foyer. "This is a beautiful library, or is it a living room?"

"A combination of both."

The floors were a dark wood and the walls a sage green. Thin streaks of pale green snaked through the white marble fireplace. The furniture pieces were upholstered in a green, yellow, and white print. An entire back wall was custom-built bookcases filled with books.

"Who's the reader in the family?" She walked over and scanned the titles. They were an eclectic mix of fiction and nonfiction.

"My aunt was."

The edge in his voice caught her attention. "She seems to have had a wide-ranging taste in books."

"She was a voracious reader." He walked to one of the shelves and put his hand on an empty spot. "We weren't allowed to touch her books. After she passed, Kade and I decided we'd read every damn off-limit book, whether it interested us or not. I've gotten this far. The books that go here are upstairs." He pointed to another empty space. "Kade has the ones that go there on base with him."

"Why would a book lover ban children from learning to love books?"

"Because she resented our being dumped on her."

"Dumped? Your parents—"

"Mother. She liked to party, and three boys were apparently too much of a burden for a party girl. I was nine when she brought us to her sister's house. Said she'd be back in a few days. That was the last anyone saw of her."

"What about your father?"

"He split before Parker was born." He took her hand. "Come. I have one more downstairs room to show you."

Well, that was a heartbreaking story. She wanted to know more, but he was obviously done talking about it. That was for the best, though. Her heart hurt for the little boys no one wanted, and she didn't need it softening toward him. And this thing he had about holding her hand, she liked that entirely too much.

"The media room," he said.

"Wow! It's like stepping into one of those old movie houses." She pulled her hand away from his and moved to the middle of the room. Turning in a circle, she took everything in. The walls were painted dark gold, and panels of red velvet drapes hung from the ceiling about every ten feet. Also hanging from the ceiling were four ornate crystal chandeliers. Instead of rows of typical theater seats, there were three rows of plush black leather recliners.

"Was it always like this?"

"No. It was our aunt's sick room the last year of her life. Before that, it was just an empty room the entire time I lived here. It was Parker's idea to make it a media room. He designed it."

"Well, it's amazing. Oh, a popcorn machine." She walked over to it. "This is so cool."

"Come over some night to watch a movie, and I'll make you popcorn."

"Maybe." She wouldn't. This man was just too tempting. "Aren't we supposed to be discussing our committee crap?"

He laughed. "That's a good word for it. Yeah, I guess we should get to it."

They retrieved their coffee and the cupcakes. At the top of the stairs was an open space, with a wide hallway in the middle. One of the twin stairs continued up.

"Those lead to Kade's quarters." He headed for the hallway.

Her assumption that he was taking her to his bedroom had been wrong. He led her to a room that was a total man cave—a cushy brown leather sofa and matching recliner, a slate fireplace, and one of the largest TV screens she'd ever seen. More of what she was sure was Parker's art was scattered about on the walls. It was a room she could happily hang out in to watch a baseball game.

"I guess we better get down to business." Before she decided it would be a good idea to snuggle up with him on that cushy couch.

Chapter Fifteen

Tristan set his coffee and the plate of cupcakes on the coffee table. He'd rather get naked with her on his over-size sofa...well, start there, then move to his king bed. But down to business it was.

She settled on one end of his sofa, and he liked seeing her there. Really liked it. He could imagine her here, watching a football game with him...actually, watching anything with him. Even sentimental romance movies if that was her thing.

"Your home is beautiful. I've driven by it a lot and always wondered what the inside was like."

"Thanks. We've done a lot to fix it up since our aunt died. All the downstairs renovations are done. We're in the process of adding a mini kitchen in my quarters so I don't have to go down for a drink or snack. That's the last thing to finish on this floor, then we'll start on Kade's rooms."

"I have to say that I'm impressed with how neat and clean everything is considering three men, one child, a dog, and a cat live here." She brushed her hand over the leather cushion, then held her palm out. "Not even any animal hair."

"We have Andrew to thank for that."

"I don't think I know an Andrew."

"Andrew Shaughnessy. The sweetest young man you'll ever meet. He's been a godsend. Not only does he keep our house clean, and loves doing it, but he does our grocery shopping and cooks a lot of our meals. If Parker's on duty at the fire station and I'm held up, he watches Everly until one of us gets home."

"You're lucky to have someone like that."

"Believe me, we know." He picked up the plate and held it out to her. "Let's finish our coffee and cupcakes, then we'll get to work." There wasn't much to discuss, probably not even thirty minutes' worth. As soon as they finished, she'd bail. Thus, he was trying to delay her departure.

It had taken a year to get her in his house, and he wanted to keep her here for a while. He wanted to talk about something besides Miss Mabel's ridiculous plan to reopen the museum. The problem was, although he'd known her intimately, he knew so little about her and wasn't sure what to talk about.

She moaned after taking a bite of the cupcake. "These are so good."

Her moan went straight to his groin, and he almost asked her to do that again. His brain jumped in before he got stupid. One wrong move like that, and she'd be gone girl before he could blink his eyes.

"Sweet Tooth is the best." He finished his cupcake, then picked up his coffee. "What made you decide to leave Florida to come up here?" He'd always wondered about that. She'd been the chief deputy sheriff, the second highest rank in a sheriff's department three times the size of Horace County's. Why had she left?

"Just ready for a change."

Her gaze had fallen to the floor when he'd asked his question, and his gut said there was more to it than that. "Things are a lot quieter here than what you had to be used to."

"Believe me, I appreciate that more than you can know."

There was a story there, and he wanted to know what it was. Was it the answer to the puzzle that was Skylar Morgan? The reason she'd erected thick walls around herself…at least where he was concerned?

Over the past year, she'd proven to be intelligent, capable, and better in the role than the previous sheriff. Her deputies liked and respected her. Well, except for Mason, but the man was an ass, so he didn't count.

"What happened, Skye? What made you—" His phone buzzed. Relief flashed in her eyes at the interruption. He wanted to ignore the call, and a glance at the screen had him wishing he could ignore it when one of his officer's names appeared. Kyle Jenkins wouldn't be bothering him at home if there wasn't trouble.

"Tell me you're just calling to say you'll pick up the doughnuts in the morning."

Kyle laughed. "You're funny, Chief, but no."

"Aren't you off tonight?" Was he going to have to bail one of his cops out of jail?

"Yeah. I don't know if this means anything or not, but I'm at Beam Me Up. Stopped by for a beer and to play some pool. There's a dude here I've never seen before asking a lot of questions about the sheriff."

Tristan sat straight up. "What kind of questions?"

"Personal ones. Is she seeing anyone, where does she hang out, where does she live, things like that."

"Answer those questions as vaguely as you can, buy

him a beer, just keep him there however you can. I'm on the way."

"Trouble?" Skye said when he disconnected.

"Not sure, but you need to come with me."

"What's going on?"

"I'll explain in the car. Give me two minutes to put on pants and shoes." That done, he collected his wallet, keys, badge, and gun. Like him, his officers knew the residents of Marsville, and it was concerning that a stranger was asking about Skye.

When he returned to his sitting room, Skye was standing at the top of the stairs. "Let's go." He called Parker as they walked down. "I've got to go out on a call. Send Fuzz to the house." When they reached the foyer, Fuzz raced to him. All Parker would have had to say was "Work" for Fuzz to know duty called.

"Why don't I follow you?" Skye said when they were outside.

And then she could go home after they checked out the stranger asking questions about her? Didn't work for him. "No, I need to tell you what's going on. Besides, we still have to talk about traffic lights and parking meters."

She shot him a disgruntled look. "Fine, but I need to get my gun out of my car."

He quietly chuckled as he headed for his police SUV. Hopefully, she wouldn't use it to shoot him. He opened the back door, and Fuzz jumped in. Although Tristan kept a leash in the car, he didn't use it. Fuzz never left his side when they were working unless Tristan parked him somewhere and told him to stay. For sure, he would attack if given the command, but he'd never made that decision on his own as long as his people—

Tristan, Everly, Parker, Kade, and even Jellybean—weren't being hurt.

Tristan opened the passenger door for Skye. Once they were underway, he said, "Know anyone who might be asking questions about you?"

Her gaze jerked to his. "What are you talking about?"

"That was Kyle Jenkins on the phone. He's at Beam Me Up. There's a man he's never seen before asking around about you. Where you live, who you're seeing, stuff like that. You got any idea who that might be?"

Chapter Sixteen

"I don't." Skye didn't like the idea of someone asking questions about her. Most anyone living in Horace County wouldn't be a stranger to Kyle, especially if it was someone she or one of her deputies had arrested.

"We'll find out his name when we get there."

"You bet your ass we will."

He laughed. "Do me a favor. Anytime you go betting my ass, make sure you're the winner."

Why did he have to go and make her think of his very fine tush?

Nothing was far away in Marsville, and ten minutes after leaving Tristan's house, they arrived at Beam Me Up. She was out of the car as soon as it stopped.

"Slow down, Sheriff." Catching up to her, Tristan put a hand on her shoulder. "Let's ease in and see if you recognize our mystery man before he sees you."

He was right. As much as she wanted to storm in and confront whoever it was asking questions about her, she stopped outside the door. "Call Kyle and see where the man is right now."

"I'll text him." A few moments later, he stuck his phone back in his pocket. "They're playing pool."

"Great. He won't see us come in."

Tristan opened the door, and then he and Fuzz followed her in. She headed for the end of the bar, where she would be able to see the pool tables. He stopped next to her, close enough to feel his body heat and smell his spicy scent. He was distracting. She huffed an annoyed breath as she took a few steps away.

"Kyle's at the second table," Tristan said as he closed the distance she'd put between them. "Recognize the man with him?"

She sure did. What the hell was he doing here? She strode to the man she'd hoped to never see again. He was leaning over the table, cue stick in hand. "Why are you here, Danny?"

The man who'd tried to ruin her life lifted his gaze to her and had the nerve to smile. "Skye." He dropped the cue stick, then came around the table, arms out as if he meant to hug her.

Not if he was the last man on earth. She held her hand up, palm out. "You touch me, and I'll hurt you."

"Aw, baby. You don't mean that." His eyes shifted to Tristan, who'd moved so close to her that their arms were touching. "Who's he?"

"Tristan Church, Marsville's police chief. And you are?" Tristan said.

"He's nobody," she said. "And he's leaving. Go home, Danny, and don't come here again."

"I'm her fiancé," her ex had the gall to say.

Tristan glanced at her. "I don't think she agrees with you. Do you, Skylar?"

"Why don't you butt out, man, since this is none of your business?" Danny puffed out his chest and moved into her space.

She should have left her gun in the car, then she

wouldn't be tempted to shoot him. When he put his hand on her arm, both Tristan and Fuzz growled. She rolled her eyes. Next, all three of them would be peeing on her to claim their territory.

When Kyle moved to the other side of her so that she was sandwiched between him and Tristan, she sighed. *Men!* She was the sheriff. She carried a gun. She could take care of herself, thank you.

"You!" She pointed at Danny. "Outside." She narrowed her eyes at Tristan. "Wait here while I send that one back under the rock he crawled out from."

He snorted. "Yes, ma'am."

As she followed Danny out of the bar, she glanced over her shoulder. Tristan had turned to watch her, but he was staying put. If the roles had been reversed between him and Danny, Danny wouldn't have trusted her to be alone with another man.

Not that she and Tristan were a couple, but chemistry sizzled between them whenever they were in the same room. If not for the jerk walking ahead of her and the games he'd played, she wouldn't have been so skittish when it came to having some playtime with a certain hot police chief. But what if they gave into this thing brewing between them?

What if it turned sour and his true colors showed? *You're seeing his true colors. Don't judge him by the way Danny treated you.* Was she seeing the real Tristan, though? She'd never thought Danny could turn on her the way he had.

Danny stopped and held open the door for her. As she walked past him, Fuzz appeared at her side. She almost laughed. Tristan was respecting her wishes by staying put, but she hadn't included his dog in her instructions. Fuzz wouldn't leave his side without being commanded to do so, which meant Tristan had sent him to guard her.

"I've missed you, babe," Danny said as soon as the door closed behind him.

"I'm not your babe." She'd told him early on that she didn't like being called babe, especially in front of her fellow cops, but he'd ignored her. She should have recognized that for the red flag it was.

When he reached a hand toward her, she stepped back and crossed her arms over her chest. "The faster you tell me why you're here, the faster you can go back home."

"Don't be like that, Skye. I know I messed up, but we love each other. Come home with me. I promise, things will be different this time."

"No. You don't have it in you to be different."

He'd cheated on her, and that was something she couldn't get over. He'd do it again, given half a chance. When she'd caught him, he'd blamed her. "You've gone cold on me, babe," he'd said. "She didn't mean anything, but a man has needs, you know?"

Whatever. She'd been gone a year. Why was he showing up now? He didn't do anything without a reason.

"Why are you really here, Danny?"

"For you, babe."

Yeah, right. "I don't trust you. I don't like you. I don't want you here. Go home, and don't come back."

Anger flared in his eyes, then he blinked it away. He smiled. She didn't trust that smile one bit. It was the one he'd give her when he was determined to get his way. Danny was a gorgeous man...almost too pretty. Black hair, smoldering black eyes that could melt a girl's panties off, high cheekbones, and pouty lips.

When he'd turned his attention to her, she'd felt breathless. He'd relentlessly pursued her, and she'd learned the hard way that his beauty was only skin-deep. Underneath the façade was a vain, selfish, immature man-child.

Tristan wasn't gorgeous like Danny, but he was definitely easy on the eyes. Real easy. There was also a ruggedness about him missing in Danny. He wasn't afraid to get his hands dirty, and she liked that about him. Another difference, Tristan had kind eyes, and he cared about people. Take Melissa. Danny would never inconvenience himself with taking the time to help a teenager get on the right track. How had she ever thought Tristan would, for any reason, try to ruin her the way Danny had?

A group of laughing people came out. She recognized them and shook a finger at them. "I hope one of you is a designated driver." She already knew this group of friends took turns being responsible when out partying, but she was tired of talking to Danny.

Jeff Blair pointed at his chest. "That's me tonight, Sheriff. Only had one beer."

She gave him a thumbs-up. The two girls eyed Danny, and appreciation lit their eyes as their gazes slid over him. "Enjoy the rest of your evening," she said to encourage them on their way.

As they walked away, Danny put his hand under her elbow. "Let's go back to your place, babe, where we can talk in private."

"Nothing to talk about."

"Babe," he said in that sultry voice that used to make

her feel gooey inside. He stepped in front of her and pulled her to him. He crashed his mouth to hers as she pushed against his chest.

Furious, she bit his bottom lip. When he let go of her, she fisted her hand and punched his chest. "Don't ever touch me again."

The anger that had flashed in his eyes earlier returned and stayed. He rubbed his bottom lip. "Why do you have to be such a bitch?"

Fuzz growled, and she rested her hand on top of his head. "You need to leave before I tell the dog he can bite your ass. And don't come back." With Fuzz at her side, she walked back inside.

It still puzzled her as to why he'd shown up after all this time, but one positive thing came from his visit. Tristan wasn't like Danny. Maybe it was time to let herself have some fun with a sexy police chief. But only if he would agree to her conditions.

Chapter Seventeen

It had been damn near impossible to stay behind and let Skye walk outside with that man. Tristan was good at reading people, and the man claiming to be her fiancé wore an air of entitlement and ownership. Tristan knew there were men who thought they had the right to own a woman, but that was bullshit. The problem was, men with that attitude could get mean.

He'd wanted to walk out with her, but he understood it was something she needed to deal with on her own. In her place, if an ex—there was no way the man was her fiancé—showed up, he'd want to deal with the situation on his own. He didn't trust the man, though. It hadn't occurred to her to include Fuzz in her command, so he'd sent his dog to watch over her.

While he waited, he went to the bar, choosing a stool where he could see the door. As much as he believed Skye hadn't been happy to see the man, what if she wanted him back? He had to admit the guy could have stepped off a calendar of hot dudes.

"If you ever looked at me the way you do her, we'd have about ten kids by now," Jessie said as she set a beer in front of him.

He laughed. They'd lost their virginity together on

senior prom night. Jessie was an awesome girl…woman now, but they both knew they hadn't been meant for each other. Her taste ran to men like her husband; inked from neck to ankles and who Tristan would go to if he ever decided to get a tattoo. The man treated her like a princess, and Tristan loved knowing she was happy.

"You probably shouldn't tell Ben you said that."

She grinned. "Ben knows he's my forever man, but I use you to get him hot and bothered."

"Huh?"

"Yeah." She winked. "He knows you took my cherry, and all I have to do is remind him how hard I once crushed on you for him to prove he's all the man I need. So, thank you, cherry stealer."

Tristan was seldom at a loss for words, and also… TMI. He could have gone forever without that bit of information. As he struggled for something to say, something over his shoulder caught her attention.

"Here comes your girl and dog," Jessie said. "Let me know if she wants my special send-the-bastard-on-his-way drink."

"You've gotten weird, since you were that nice, quiet girl I took to the prom in high school."

"Weird can be good," she tossed over her shoulder as she walked to the other side of the bar.

He swiveled on the bar stool when Skye and Fuzz walked in. She marched straight to him, and he thought… *She's magnificent.* As much as he wanted to go to her and demand what dragon she wanted slayed, he stayed still.

Skye could slay her own dragons, and that made her the hottest woman he'd ever had the honor of knowing. As she walked to him, her eyes capturing his, something was different. The woman who'd shied away from him since the moment she'd realized she'd spent an amazing night with Marsville's police chief was coming at him, clearly on a mission. Whatever that mission was, he was onboard.

She stopped in front of him, leaving only inches between them. "You ready to get out of here?"

"Your fiancé gone?" There had never been a hint she'd once been engaged. Did that not-so-little fact have anything to do with those thick walls she'd erected around herself?

"He's not my fiancé." She took a few steps away, then glanced over her shoulder. "You coming?"

There was something different about her, and whatever it was, he liked it. "Lead the way, Sheriff." He'd let his voice drop on *sheriff*, and she'd looked back at him again, and ah…that glint in her eyes! As if she knew a secret, one he'd very much like.

As he slid off the bar stool to follow her out, he noticed a man leaning against the bar and staring hard at her, a stranger with mean eyes. He was a big guy, muscled, with tats covering his neck and both arms. A teardrop was under one eye, a sign that he'd served prison time. Sometimes that particular tattoo meant the wearer had committed murder.

Tristan stepped in front of the man, blocking his view of Skye. "You just passing through town?"

The man's gaze dropped to the badge on Tristan's belt, then slid over to the gun on his hip, then down at the growling dog next to Tristan's leg. "Yeah, just stopped for a beer before moving on, Officer."

"Chief, as in police chief. Don't take too long to move on."

The man lifted his beer bottle, giving Tristan a mocking salute.

Tristan detoured to the end of the bar where Jessie was. "Keep an eye on that man. If he sticks around, let me know."

She glanced at the man. "I will. He's scary."

Jessie had bartended long enough to have a good sense of people, and if she thought he was scary, then he was. Fuzz was no fool either. He rarely growled at anyone, even strangers, but he'd let his feelings be known to Skye's ex and this man.

"What was that all about?" Skye asked when he caught up with her.

"Just trying to keep trouble from happening before it happens."

When they got to his SUV, she held out her hand. "I'm driving."

"Bossy woman," he muttered, hiding his grin when she laughed. Whatever this new mood of hers was, he liked it. He tossed her the keys, opened the back door for Fuzz, then buckled himself into the passenger seat.

He waited for her to explain the part about having an ex-fiancé, but they were halfway back to his house, and she hadn't said a word. She did, however, keep glancing at him, and he could almost see the smoke coming out of her ears. "What?"

"If I'd told Danny I was driving, he would've gotten all pissy."

"Sounds like Pretty Boy is an ass."

"That he is."

He was damn glad she thought so. "Want to tell me what that was all about?"

"When we get back to your place. Then after I finish off that bottle of wine, you can let me crash on your couch or drive me home. Your choice."

"My couch is very comfortable." His bed even more so.

"I'm not happy talking about this," Skye said from the corner of his couch.

"Then don't." He wanted her to, though. He wanted to know who Pretty Boy was and why he'd shown up. What had they talked about when they'd gone outside? She'd removed her shoes and socks, and had curled her legs under her, but not before he'd caught a glimpse of her blue toenails. So, the uptight sheriff had a wild streak. He liked it.

"The only way for you to understand why I freaked out when I learned who you were is to tell you about Danny." She took a healthy drink of wine, then stared down into the contents of the glass. "You saw him. He's gorgeous. When he started paying attention to me, I was flattered. He could have any woman he wanted."

"Have you looked in a mirror, Skye?" Did she not see that she was beautiful? Any man would be interested in her.

She shrugged. "I know men think I'm attractive. It's just he literally had women throwing themselves at him." She lifted her gaze to his. "The thing about Danny is that he's not so pretty on the inside."

"He called you his fiancée."

"Ex. We dated for eight months, and I thought he was the one. When he asked me to marry him, I didn't hesitate to say yes. The very day he put a ring on my finger, things changed. Danny's a cop. I was the chief deputy sheriff. I thought that gave us a lot in common. We understood the demands of each other's jobs.

Turned out he was jealous that I had a higher rank than him, something he'd hidden until he considered me his. When he failed his sergeant's exam because he didn't study, it got worse.

"Then the jealousy started. I have two best friends in Florida. He resented any time I spent with DeAnna and Kerry, and that was basically once a week at our standing Sunday brunch. Apparently, that meant he wasn't the most important thing in my life. Then he started accusing me of flirting with any man I talked to, including my coworkers."

"None of that sounds like something you would have put up with." Not the sheriff he knew, anyway.

"I put up with it longer than I should have. He showed up tonight to ask me to come home."

"You're not considering that, are you?" He really should have thrown Pretty Boy's ass in jail.

"Not a chance in hell."

His heart started beating again. "But why show up a year later? Something doesn't sit right about that."

"I know. Danny never does anything without a reason, and it's always about him. But it's not going to happen, so who cares? Not me." She finished off the wine, then poured some more. She frowned at the glass. "I never have more than one."

"Tonight seems like a good reason to make an exception." He was drinking coffee in case she decided she wanted him to drive her home, but he hoped to talk her into staying the night. Preferably in his bed, even if all he did was hold her.

"You can say that again."

"Tonight seems like a good—" He grinned when

she slid her foot out from under her and poked his leg with her toes.

"That was a figure of speech, silly."

He grabbed her foot before she could take it away and put it on his leg.

"What are you doing?"

"Giving you a foot massage."

She groaned when he pressed his thumbs into her arch, and the sound went straight to his groin. The affect she was having on him was growing obvious.

He grabbed a pillow and put it on his lap, then rested her foot on it. "I assume you were the one to break it off?"

"Yeah." She leaned her head back and closed her eyes. "That feels so good. Anyway, he decided I should quit my job, said he worried about me putting myself in danger. That was total bull. He didn't like that I was the chief deputy sheriff. He thought that made him look bad, that I was more important than him."

"At least all that came out before you married him, not after." And before there were any children caught in the middle. From what he'd observed over the past year, Skye had her act together, and she wasn't a selfish person. He couldn't see her dumping her children on an aunt who didn't want them, promising it was only for a few days. What a joke that was.

"Believe me, I will be forever thankful for that. But it got worse before it got better. After I broke up with him, he started rumors about me. Claimed he'd ended it with me because he'd caught me cheating on him. As if that wasn't bad enough, he claimed that I had pocketed some money and drugs on a combined police department-sheriff's department operation. The sheriff was forced to open an investigation."

"The sheriff believed him?" It was probably a good thing he hadn't known all that when they'd been at Beam Me Up. He would have found a reason to slap handcuffs on her ex and haul him off to jail. Then he would have lost the key to the cell.

"No, not at all, but he had to investigate. I didn't like it, but I understood." She finished her second glass of wine, then eyed the bottle.

"Go for it. I've got you tonight." It was hard to hide his rage, but he somehow managed it. What he wanted to do was hunt the asshole down and beat the ever-loving shit out of him.

She waved a hand at him. "You're a good man, Chief."

He snorted. "That must be the wine talking. I should have recorded you saying that so when you deny it, I could play it back for you."

"Not admish...admissible—" she beamed at getting the word right "—in court."

She was cute when she was tipsy. "Is all that why you left Florida?"

"Yeppie. Decided to put turd face in my rearview mirror. Start over somewhere no one knew me and wondered how much of his BS was true."

"Well, I'm glad you did." The pieces fell together in his mind. "What he put you through is the reason you didn't want anything to do with me once you found out I was a cop." It wasn't a question. A part of him understood why she'd reacted the way she had, but another part of him resented that she'd lumped him in with her ex. "I'm not him, Skye."

Those blue eyes that had been nothing but ice for the past year when looking at him turned warm. "I know."

She'd whispered the words, almost as if she didn't want him to hear her admission, but he had. There was no going back to the tension-filled relationship of the past year. He wouldn't allow it.

"Give me your other foot." And that was only the beginning of what he wanted from her.

Chapter Eighteen

There had been times since leaving Florida that Skye thought she should have stayed and stood up to Danny. That she shouldn't have let a man ruin her reputation because of his ego and run her off a job she loved, but she'd grown tired of fighting his lies. She'd also been disappointed in the men who knew her, knew Danny's lies for what they were, but hadn't stood up for her. Maybe it was her sloshed mind talking, but Tristan would have stood by her.

She peered at him through blurry eyes. More than one glass of wine always did that to her, make her vision go fuzzy. One reason she limited herself. But tonight, the limits were gone. Like magic. Poof. Now you see them, now you don't.

It was Tristan's fault for making her feel safe to let down her hair, so to speak. Speaking of hair…the bun riding low on her neck was uncomfortable. She straightened her leg, letting him have her other foot, then leaned over and handed him her empty glass. With an amused smile on his face, he took it from her, then set it on his coffee table.

She frowned. "I coulda done that."

The amusement lighting up his eyes grew brighter. "Why, when you have me to do it for you?"

"Good answer." It really was. She was about to do something. What was it? Oh, right. Get rid of the stupid bun that was crinking her neck as she tried to get her head comfortable on his marshmallowy soft couch. Maybe he'd let her borrow his couch whenever she wanted to take a nap. And maybe he'd be on hand to give amazing foot massages. She sighed her pleasure as she pulled out the first bobby pin, then a second one.

"You keep making those sounds, Sheriff, and I'm not going to be responsible for what happens next." Heat simmered in his dark brown eyes.

"Yeah?" She hadn't wanted a man this much since... well, the last time she'd spent the night with him.

"Oh, yeah," he said.

She pulled the rest of the pins out of her hair, then combed her fingers through it, letting it fall over her shoulders. She knew from their night together that he loved her hair, and from the way his eyes followed her movements, that hadn't changed.

"I have conditions." Had she blurted that out? By the puzzled look on his face, apparently so. She blamed that smolder in his eyes and the wine. Well, she'd opened the door, so she might as well walk through it. She waved a hand between them. "You and me. For...you know."

The hands that had been massaging her feet stilled. "No, I don't know. Why don't you spell it out for me?"

"We could see each other. If you want to."

"You mean date?"

"No!" She pulled her feet back and sat up. "Not date, just spend time together. Privately."

"Are we talking about sex?"

She nodded. "No one needs to know." He was a man. He didn't have to worry about being gossiped about. People found out he was having an affair, no biggie. She was a woman. Eyebrows would be raised; the whispers would start. She knew what it was like to be talked about, had lived through it once, never planned to allow herself to be put in that position again.

"I see." Something like disappointment flashed in his eyes. "So that's your condition?"

"One of them. We don't see each other more than twice a week. More than that increases the risk of someone finding out. And no feelings for each other. Just sex."

"Just wham, bam, thank you, ma'am?"

She frowned. "Why would you have a problem with that? Isn't that every man's dream? Free sex with no strings?"

"Conditions accepted." He stood. "Time for bed."

"Uh…now?"

"Yes, now."

"But we haven't talked about museum stuff." She thought they'd discuss how their affair would work and decide on a schedule. She would have time to mentally prepare.

"We'll do that tomorrow. I'll come to your office." He held out his hand. "Come with me."

She stared at his hand. If she asked him to drive her home, she knew he would. But if she did, he might change his mind. She wanted this, so she put her hand in his. He led her past an alcove that was under construction.

"That's going to be my new mini kitchen," he said as they passed it.

"Oh, cool." When they entered his bedroom, her gaze went straight to his bed. In a few minutes, they would be in that bed together. That both excited her and freaked her out a little. Was she really ready for this, for him?

He moved in front of her and put a finger under her chin, lifting her face. He lowered his mouth and brushed his lips over hers. It was the gentlest of kisses, unlike the ones he'd given her during their night together, where it seemed as if he wanted to devour her.

For some reason, his tenderness made her want to cry. After Danny, she'd built thick walls around herself, not letting anyone in. She'd done it to protect herself, but she'd been lonely. His soft kiss told her he cared, and she wasn't ready for that. All she wanted from him was sex, not feelings.

"You have the softest lips," he murmured against her mouth. He lifted his head, then stepped back. "Stand by a minute." He went to a chest of drawers and returned a moment later with a soft gray T-shirt and handed it to her. "I assume you don't want to sleep in your uniform?"

"Sleep?"

"You know, that thing you do when you close your eyes."

"I thought…" That they were going to have sex, but obviously he wasn't interested. She'd practically thrown herself at him, and now she was embarrassed.

"I know what you thought, but as much as I want you, not tonight." He trailed the back of his hand down her cheek. "I don't know if your offer was the wine talking, and I won't take advantage of you. I won't be your regret. When you're thinking with a clear head, then you can tell me if the offer still stands. If it is, I'm all in."

Tears burned her eyes, and she blinked them away.

She'd never felt this protected and cared for. Not that she couldn't protect herself, but her heart knew she could trust him to be there for her whenever she needed a helping hand, someone to stand at her side.

"Bathroom's in there." He waved to an open door. "There's a new toothbrush in the drawer to the left of the sink."

"Okay." In the bathroom, she turned on the cold water and splashed her face. Her friends with benefits offer wasn't a product of her wine-soaked brain, but she loved that he wanted to make sure. All they had to do was keep their affair secret and simple, and no one would get hurt.

Famous last words, a mocking voice said in her head.

Chapter Nineteen

When Skye walked out wearing nothing but his T-shirt—and maybe her panties, but he wasn't sure about that—Tristan called himself three times a fool for telling her all they were going to do tonight was sleep.

At seeing him, she stopped and they stared at each other, the air between them hot and heavy. His T-shirt covered her to midthigh, leaving her legs bare, and her long hair fell down her back and over her shoulders. He groaned. He'd had one glass of wine hours ago at dinner, but he was drunk with desire and something else.

The something else was elusive. He didn't have a name for it, but he wanted to explore it. He'd felt more than simple lust for her from the beginning, and he suspected they could be good together if she'd only open her mind to it.

Now he understood the reason for her walls. Her ex had done a number on her, but he wasn't that man. The only thing he had in common with her ex was that they were both police officers. He just had to prove he would never hurt her, no matter what happened between them.

Before he forgot that sex was off the agenda—for tonight anyway—he glanced away, breaking their connection. He walked to the bed, then pulled back the covers. "In with you, my lady."

She giggled, and it was a sound so foreign to the always-serious Skye he knew that he could only stare at her.

"What?"

"Nothing. Come on." He vowed then and there to bring laughter into her life. And he would tear down those walls, one damn brick at a time. He thought, hoped, he'd obliterated a few tonight.

Once she was in his bed, he pulled the covers up to her chin. "I'll be back."

"Mmm."

He chuckled. She was already drifting off. After a quick shower and wearing a pair of plaid pajama bottoms and no shirt, he slipped into bed behind her. Her knees were curled up to her chest, her hands tucked under her chin, as if even in sleep, she kept that wall of protection around her.

She'd been hurt by a man who'd supposedly loved her, a man who'd betrayed her, and Tristan had never wanted to physically hurt someone before, but he'd like ten minutes in a room with Pretty Boy. He'd also never in his life felt so protective of a woman as he was her. He wrapped his body around hers. She sighed, as if even in sleep, she recognized he was keeping her safe.

Until her, he'd never met a woman he wanted to hand over his heart to, and funny thing…he'd been looking. Even though they'd been clueless when Parker brought Everly home, he'd loved having a baby in the house. They all had, and he wanted more kids running around this big house. He wanted to go to sleep holding the woman he loved, and he wanted to wake up with her in his arms.

Now here was a woman who resisted having any kind of personal relationship with him, and before her, he would have shrugged and moved on. Why her, he hadn't a clue, but he wasn't moving on, not from Skylar Morgan. He wanted her in his life with a longing he didn't know what to do with.

Her hair tickled his nose, and he closed his eyes as he inhaled her scent. Why had he agreed to her absurd conditions? He did not want to be her dirty secret. He fell asleep devising ways to breach Skye's defenses, starting first thing in the morning.

"Wake up, sleepyhead." Tristan chuckled when Skye pulled the pillow over her head. "What was that?" he said when she muttered something.

"Muffermmph."

"If you say so." He picked up a piece of bacon, lifted her pillow, and waved the bacon under her nose. Her nose twitched, reminding him of a rabbit. She opened her mouth, and he let her take a bite, then took the rest away.

"Tristan?"

"Yeah?"

She pushed the pillow away, then frowned at him. "What are you doing in my bed?"

"Look around you, Goldilocks. You're in the big bad wolf's bed." And the big bad wolf would very much like to crawl in there with her and remind her what she'd been missing the past year.

She slapped her head. "Right. The wine." She lifted

the cover and peeked down at herself. "Did you change my clothes?"

"No, you did that all by yourself in the privacy of my bathroom. Full disclosure, though. I slept with my body wrapped around yours. Before you slap me because that pisses you off, you snuggled into me and sighed when you felt my touch."

To keep her from thinking too hard about that, he quickly said, "I've got your favorite breakfast." He put his palm on her cheek and turned her face toward the small table he'd set up next to the window. "Except for the buttery biscuits you love so much. I tried. Even watched a YouTube video, but my biscuits could have been used as weapons."

"How do you know my favorite breakfast?"

"Because I pay attention. Parker's at the firehouse this morning, so I have to get Everly up and ready for school. Your clothes are on the end of the bed. Enjoy your omelet."

The omelet wouldn't be as good as the Kitchen's, but he thought he'd done pretty well with it. He'd watched that on YouTube, too. He resisted the urge to stick around and see her reaction when she took her first bite.

Subtly romance her, he reminded himself as he walked away.

Chapter Twenty

"Sheriff?"

"Hmm?"

"I asked if you want me to cover for Mason until he shows up."

"Sorry. I have some things on my mind." Like Tristan. What was he up to? She'd made a friends-with-benefits offer, and all he'd done was sleep next to her... well, he'd said he'd held her all night. Too bad she'd slept through that.

This morning he'd made her an omelet almost as good as the Kitchen's but hadn't stayed to eat breakfast with her. He'd even set up a little table next to the window with a view of the mountains. It had been a romantic breakfast for one. After she ate, she'd dressed and gone looking for him. He'd been busy with Everly, so she'd told him she was leaving. All he'd said was that he would call her later. She glared at her phone, annoyed that she'd been waiting for it to ring all morning.

"Sheriff."

"What?" She sighed. "Sorry, Johnny. What's Mason's excuse this time?" This wasn't the first time he'd been late for jail duty. He could resent the assignment all he wanted.

"A flat tire."

"Hasn't he used that one before?" He'd been pushing his luck for months now, and she was done with him.

"Yes, ma'am."

She glanced at her watch. "He's over an hour late." It didn't take that long to change a tire. "I'll go over and cover for him until he arrives." She wanted to be there when he did. "I'm going to suspend him for a week, so stick around. After he's gone, I'll call you. You can come over and take his place for today. I'll rework the schedule this afternoon." If she was lucky, Mason would go ballistic, giving her grounds to fire him on the spot.

"He's not going to react well to that."

One hoped. "I want to talk to you about something. Stop by in the morning before you go out on patrol."

"Will do. Good luck with Mason."

As she pulled into a parking space at the county jail, her phone buzzed, Tristan's name coming up on the SUV's screen. "What can I do for you, Chief?" Her tone was sharper than she'd intended, but she wasn't having a good morning.

He chuckled. "So many things, but we'll save that conversation for some other time, Sheriff. Are you in your office?"

"Nope. I'm at the jail. I have to deal with Mason. Talk to you later." She disconnected. As soon as she did, she regretted it, that and her irritation with him. He hadn't done a thing wrong. She'd had too much to drink, and he could have taken advantage. Instead, he'd held her all night and then had made her breakfast. She'd call him later and apologize. Plus, she wanted to know what all the "so many things" were.

The first thing she heard when she walked inside

was Earl singing. If Earl was here, so was Billy. The amusing part, when Earl went to jail, so did Billy. The story went that the first few times Earl was arrested drunk driving his lawnmower home from Beam Me Up, not only did Earl cry all night, asking for Billy, but that Billy somehow figured out where Earl was and showed up at the jail, butting anyone who got in his way of getting inside.

The previous sheriff had given up trying to keep Billy out, and now, when Earl was arrested for lawnmower drunk driving, Billy was hauled off to jail with him. She gave Earl credit for knowing he was going to get drunk and riding his lawnmower to Beam Me Up instead of his truck. More amusement, Billy and Fuzz were the only animals allowed in the bar. Fuzz she got, but a goat in a bar? Only in Marsville.

She smiled as she headed for Earl's cell. She liked the old man a lot, and… She stopped when Mason strolled in as if he didn't have a care in the world. After quickly activating the recorder on her phone, she crossed her arms and waited for him to notice her.

At seeing her, his eyes widened, then he smirked. "Checking up on me, boss lady?"

"Just how long does it take to change a tire?" She tapped her finger on her watch. "You're almost two hours late."

"Well, I'm here now."

"This is the third time you've been late when on jail duty, and you've already used the flat tire excuse before. You seem to think—" She paused when Tristan and Fuzz walked in. She would swear the dog and man gave Mason the stink eye.

"Morning, Sheriff, Mason."

Skye nodded. "Good morning, Chief." Mason seemed to think the interruption meant he could walk away. She grabbed his elbow. "Let's step outside."

He tried to pull his arm away. "I don't need a damn lecture."

She tightened her grip. "Outside. Now."

With a grunt to let her know he wasn't happy, he headed for the door. She glanced back at Tristan and shook her head, telling him not to get involved.

As soon as the door closed behind them, Mason turned on her. "You get off on embarrassing me in front of the chief? I don't appreciate your lack of respect."

"Respect has to be earned, Mason, and you haven't earned it. You've had a poor attitude since the day I was appointed sheriff, you don't show respect to your fellow deputies, and you resent the responsibilities of your job."

His eyes turned mean. "You think you're hot shit, but when you showed up, getting the job that should have been mine, I wondered what made you leave a cushy chief deputy sheriff's job to come to a Podunk town." He stepped into her personal space, his expression pure menace. "So I made a little trip on my days off to your old stomping grounds. Had a few beers with some of your buddies from the sheriff's department. Thought it was a wasted trip until I found one that had some interesting things to say about you. Want to know what Gary Jerrican had to say?"

Oh, she knew exactly what Gary would say. He was Danny's best friend, one of the few deputies who believed Danny's lies. Even though she was furious with Danny for the lies, Gary for gossiping about her, and Mason for going out of his way to dig up dirt on her, she crushed the urge to defend herself. She couldn't show him any weakness.

She also crushed the urge to step back or better yet, push him away. "You need to worry about yourself and the responsibilities of your job, Mason. You're suspended without pay for a week. Take the time to think about how much you want to keep your job, because you need to be a changed man when you come back or there won't be a job waiting for you."

His face turned red, and he bumped his chest against hers. "You don't want to mess with me, lady, unless you're ready for everyone to know what a conniving bitch you are."

"Back off right now before I fire you on the spot." She didn't bother telling him that the mayor and town council were aware of what had gone down in Florida. She'd been upfront about everything during her interview, and a few days later her former boss had backed up her story on a Zoom call with them.

"You do, and I'll file a sexual harassment complaint that you came on to me. It'll be my word against yours, and with your history—"

A low growl sounded, and she glanced down to see Fuzz staring up at Mason. The dog's ears were pinned back, and his lips lifted, showing his teeth. Mason finally removed himself from her space. For that alone, Fuzz was her new hero.

"Tell you what, Mason. You're fired. I'll follow you to the station so you can turn in your badge, gun, and car."

"You're going to be fucking sorry, bitch."

Chapter Twenty-One

The tension between Skye and Mason was escalating. Tristan pressed his feet to the floor to keep from storming out the door and...what? Playing hero? Well, yeah. He'd love to be her hero, but this was her battle. If he interfered, she'd probably shoot him.

When Mason bumped against her, he growled. Fuzz had his nose stuck against the glass door, and he growled right along with Tristan. He got the warning look to stay out of it that she'd sent him before walking out with Mason, and he understood that if he went out there it would undermine her authority, so he kept his feet glued to the floor. He deserved a medal.

Fuzz growled again, and Tristan eyed his dog. "Go protect our girl," he told Fuzz as he opened the door.

Fuzz shot out the door, a dog on a mission. "Feel free to bite him," he said after the door closed behind Fuzz. A few minutes after Fuzz joined them, Mason stormed toward the parking lot. A pity Fuzz didn't get a good bite in.

Tristan opened the door for her and Fuzz. "You okay?"

She glanced back when Mason's tires squealed as he tore out of the parking lot. "Yeah, I just fired him.

Would you do me a favor? Mason was on jail duty today. Can you hang out until Johnny gets here?"

"You bet. I came over to see if Earl was sober enough for me to sign him out and take him and Billy home."

"Is that really the reason you showed up?"

Busted. "No. I don't trust Mason and wanted to make sure he didn't pull a stupid stunt."

"Who knows what he might have done if you hadn't been here." She studied the floor. "Thanks."

"Sorry, I didn't hear you. Could you say that a little louder?"

"Nope." She smirked, then pivoted and walked out.

"She's something else," he said to Fuzz. "Come, let's go see your favorite goat."

Fuzz knew the word *goat*, and knowing Billy was here and where, he headed for the cells.

"You here to get Earl?" Jill asked at seeing them. She was the detention officer, the only permanent employee at the jail.

"I am. By the way, Mason won't be on duty today. The sheriff is sending Johnny to cover for him. I'll hang around until he gets here."

"Not like Mason does anything when he's here."

Not like that was a surprise. Goat bleats and happy dog yips filled the air. He glanced at Jill and rolled his eyes. "Star-crossed lovers."

She laughed. "Those two are a riot."

They were a real comedy team all right. The door was never closed when Earl was in the cell. Billy didn't like being locked up, so he was allowed to hang out wherever he wanted when Earl was here. There wasn't any need to lock Earl in anyway. He never left the cell until Tristan or one of his officers or one of Skye's deputies came to drive him back to Beam Me Up to get his riding mower.

It was Earl who insisted on going to jail. He was never arrested or charged with anything, but from the beginning, he'd refused to let anyone take him home. He'd once told Tristan his regrets when they came were too big a burden to carry home with him.

Tristan entered the cell, taking a seat next to Earl on the bunk. They both watched Fuzz try to get Billy to play tug of war with Fuzz's KONG toy. Thankfully the rubber was too hard to eat, because Billy was giving it his best effort. The dog and goat really were entertaining.

"You about ready to go home?"

Earl grunted.

That meant yes, he was. Last night's drunk was because it was the anniversary of his wife's death, which was common knowledge. The other two nights a year he tied one on were a mystery, and people had speculated all kinds of reasons. Earl refused to talk about it, but he had been in the military during Desert Storm, and Kade thought Earl's drunk nights had something to do with that. It was as good a guess as any.

Johnny walked in, coming to a stop at the open cell door. "I see Billy got in trouble again last night."

Earl frowned. "Billy didn't do nuthin'."

"Just pulling your chain, buddy."

Earl grunted. He didn't like anyone dissing his goat. Tristan stood and put his hand on Earl's shoulder. "Let's get you and Billy out of here."

Earl, his goat, and Fuzz followed him out. Because Earl refused to ride in the front seat of a police car, Tristan opened the back door. The three of them piled in. He shook his head, chuckling as Billy and Fuzz bounced around Earl.

Five minutes later, he pulled up next to Earl's lawn-mower at Beam Me Up. A few minutes after that, Earl rode away with Billy standing like a hood ornament on the engine cover. "Gotta love this town," he muttered.

Fuzz whined, already missing his friend.

"Suck it up, buttercup. Billy didn't even glance back at you."

Kind of like how Skye ignored him. Since he wasn't so keen to suck that up, he turned toward the sheriff's department, making a stop on the way.

"You're out of your mind if you think I'm going to eat that," Skye said when he set a cream-filled pastry on her desk, along with a cup of coffee.

"No funny business. Promise." He picked up the pastry and took a bite. "See." He perched on the edge of her desk.

She sat back in her chair and narrowed her eyes. "Uh-huh. What's the catch?"

"You wound me, Sheriff. I come bearing gifts, and you're questioning my thoughtfulness."

Her brows furrowed as she eyed the pastry. "You swear there's nothing in there but cream?"

"Pinky swear." He held out his pinky finger.

"What are you? A twelve-year-old girl?"

"Sweetheart, you know for a fact how far from the truth that is." He wiggled his finger.

She rolled her eyes as she wrapped her little finger around his. "You're ridiculous."

"*Au contraire.* I'm a handsome devil, is what I am." He winked, grinning when he caught her trying to hide her smile. Time to get serious for a minute, though. "Mason give you any trouble when he turned in his gun and badge?"

"Other than telling me he'd make me sorry? No."

"That's a threat, Skye. You need to watch your back." He'd sure as hell be watching it, even if she said—and she would—that she was perfectly capable of protecting herself.

She picked up her phone and wiggled it. "Got it recorded."

"Good thinking. I wish I didn't think the day would come when you'd need it, but I can't." He pushed off her desk. "We still need to have a committee meeting. The rest of my day is full, so dinner tonight." When she opened her mouth, to no doubt object to spending the evening with him, he said, "It's a business dinner, nothing more." Unless he could talk her into more.

"Fine. Where should I meet you?"

Nice try, sweetheart. "We have reservations at seven, so I'll pick you up at six thirty." He left before she could argue. He'd come close to telling her to wear something besides her damn uniform but had managed to keep his mouth shut. That they had reservations somewhere was hopefully enough of a hint that they weren't eating at the Kitchen.

What would she wear? He couldn't wait to find out.

Chapter Twenty-Two

Enough was enough. She'd changed clothes three times already. Skye glared at her reflection in the mirror. How long had it been since she'd worn a dress? The last time had been a dinner out with Danny, so over a year ago. Wearing this dress, in fact.

She reached behind her to unzip the back, then paused. She liked this dress, but it needed new memories. The sleeveless dusty rose dress didn't show any cleavage and the hem of the flared skirt stopped just above her knees. The high-neckline bodice was fitted, and a thin silver belt drew the eye to her waist. It was a classic, yet sexy, and she was going to wear it.

She was hopeless when it came to makeup, so mascara, a hint of blush, and some lip gloss and she was done. The first thing she'd done after getting out of the shower was put on the strappy heel sandals to try and get used to walking in them. She hated heels, hadn't worn any since leaving Florida, but she'd look pretty silly wearing flip-flops or her work shoes. Hopefully, she wouldn't fall on her face.

All right. She was ready, and what was she supposed to do with herself until Tristan would get here? And why was she nervous? This was just a business dinner, not a date. Maybe she should change. Wear something more businesslike.

Her doorbell chimed. Okay, it was too late to change. Problem solved. And she was kind of glad. She wanted to see appreciation in Tristan's eyes. Wearing the sandal heels for an hour to get used to them had been a great idea, as she didn't trip over her feet when she opened the door and was treated with the vision of Tristan in a suit.

"Hi," she gushed. No. Nope. Nada. She did not gush over men. Well, she never had before, but if any man was gush-worthy, it was the one standing in front of her. His gaze roamed over her, and his eyes deepened to the color of rich, dark chocolate.

"Hey, beautiful." He gave her a shy smile. "Is it okay to say that?"

"What girl doesn't like hearing a man say that to her?" He was flirting with her, and she liked it.

"Good to know." He stepped to her and brushed his lips over hers, nothing more than a soft touch, but her heart hammered in her chest. "Is that okay?"

"For a business dinner, probably not." But he was welcomed to do it again.

"We might discuss a little business, but this is not a business dinner, Skye."

"No? What is it then?"

"A date."

"That's not—"

He touched his finger to her lips. "Don't overthink it, Sheriff."

"Okay." She'd try not to, at least for tonight. "Let me grab my purse." Her one-bedroom apartment was small, and it was only a few steps to the kitchen counter where she'd put her clutch. The only things in it were her cell phone, lipstick, a credit card to hire an Uber to get home if needed, and her gun.

After locking up, he put his hand on her lower back as they walked to his car. For a year, she'd convinced herself that she didn't miss a man's touch. It only took a moment of Tristan's palm resting low on her spine to remember how much she did like it. Or maybe it was just because it was him, only his hand she wanted touching her.

"Oh cool," she said when she saw his car. "I get to ride in the Mustang."

He opened the passenger door. When she was seated, he leaned down. "Only special people get to ride in my spaceship." He chuckled as he closed the door.

Oops. She shouldn't have reminded him that he owed her a prank. He walked around the front of the car, and she sighed. The man was dead-on sexy. Why did she have to be attracted to a cop? Why couldn't he have been anything but a police officer? But he was, and this was his town. If they made their relationship public and it ended badly, fair or not, she'd be the one to suffer for it. She wasn't going to lose another job because of a man, even one who made her feel things no man before him ever had.

He slid into the car, then reached over and curled a lock of hair around his finger. "Have I ever told you how much I love your hair?"

"Not that I remember."

But he had. The night they'd spent together, he'd told her that several times. He'd been fascinated with her hair, had played with it, and had wrapped it around his fist when she'd pleasured him. Warmth spread through her just thinking about that night, about his hands on her, the places on her body his mouth had kissed.

He let go of her hair. "I've dreamed about it, you know. How it felt sliding over my skin, like a teasing feather, how it turned you on when I wrapped my fist around it, taking control. You liked when I took control. Why is that?"

Dear God, he needed to shut up before she combusted.

"Know what I think?" He turned the key in the ignition, then backed out of the parking space.

She waited for him to answer his question, but he stayed silent as they drove away from her complex. Fine, she didn't care what he thought. She stared out the window. Where were they going? Marsville was the other way. He'd said they had reservations, so the Kitchen was out. There was a steakhouse in town, and she'd assumed they would go there. Since she wasn't a big fan of steak, she was okay with that not being their destination.

When he chuckled, she kept her attention on the passing scenery. He wanted her to ask what he thought, and even though she was dying to know, she wouldn't give him the satisfaction of asking. Besides, he was entirely too amused.

"Since you're dying to know, I'll tell you."

What, he was reading her mind now?

"This is my theory. You need to be in control in your personal life and on the job." His gaze darted to her, probably to see if she was listening. She was. "That's cool. Everyone should have the confidence to take control of the things important to them. Especially if they're a woman. But in bed—" his gaze locked on hers

"—you like it when a man takes control." He smirked. "If that man is me, anyway."

"Arrogant much, Chief?"

He was right; she had loved the way he'd taken control the night she'd spent with him. And that was weird now that she thought about it. She had never allowed another man to dominate her in bed. With Tristan, though, it was different.

"No, I just have you figured out, Sheriff."

"You think so, huh?" He said *Sheriff* the way he'd once whispered her name in her ear, and goose bumps dotted her skin.

He gave her a wicked grin. "I know so. And, Skye, you ever want to dominate me, just say the word."

Yes, please. She needed to change the subject before she embarrassed herself by panting. "How's it going with Melissa and Miss Bauman?"

Chapter Twenty-Three

"Sure, we can change the subject," Tristan said. "Or we can talk some more about how much I love—"

"Melissa. Talk about Melissa!" She pulled at the top of her dress. "Does this car have A/C?"

"Getting hot and bothered, yeah?" He laughed when she shot him a glare. "Fine, Melissa it is. Surprisingly, that situation seems to be working out. I think Melissa likes earning her own money and Miss Bauman likes having someone to boss around. As soon as Miss Bauman paid her, Mary Beth took Melissa to the pharmacy and Melissa admitted to stealing the earrings, paid for them, and promised to never do it again."

"That's great. Your idea to put the two of them together was clever."

"I'm a clever guy."

She punched his arm. "And humble, I see."

"That's me. Humble and clever." He turned on the road leading to the lake, frowning when the car behind them that he'd been watching turned, too. It was probably someone also going to the resort, but he didn't like that the car had been keeping the exact distance between them. No one drove like that unless it was on purpose.

"Are we going to the resort?"

"We are. Have you ever been?" He'd taken dates to the resort's restaurant a few times. It was pricey but the food was excellent, a place to impress a girl. Well, most girls. Skye would probably be just as happy with a burger at the Kitchen. He liked that about her, but he wanted to make tonight special.

"No, I haven't. Is it good?"

"Skye." He tsked. "Would I take you someplace that had crappy food?"

"Okay, silly question."

He stopped at the valet stand, one of the valets opened her door and the other came around to his side. He handed the kid his key.

"Cool car, man."

"It is. No drag racing."

The kid laughed. "You're no fun."

"True, but I am clever and humble, or so my date says." He grinned when Skye rolled her eyes.

The car that had been behind them had turned into the public parking lot, and since he couldn't think of a reason anyone would be following them, he decided it wasn't anything to worry about.

He rounded his car, stepped next to Skye, and put his hand on her lower back. When she didn't slap him silly for touching her, he considered it a win. "How much you want to bet he won't be able to resist taking Marilyn for a spin?"

"Marilyn?" She lifted her gaze to his. "You named your car Marilyn?"

"Well, she does have sexy curves like Miss Monroe." He hadn't named his car, but he liked getting those eye rolls that said he was ridiculous. Until recently, she'd always been so serious, especially around him. He thought he was finally seeing glimpses of the real Skylar Morgan. That there were cracks in those thick walls she'd built around herself. She wasn't ready to admit it yet, but she needed his silliness and his practical jokes.

"Beautiful view," she said after the hostess seated them.

"Sure is." Although he was looking at her when he said that. He'd requested a table by the window when he'd made the reservation, and the setting sun had turned the sky pink. The lake water was calm, and the sun's reflection danced like glittering diamonds on the surface.

"I'd love to come spend a day or two here and just vegetate. I probably wouldn't leave the room's balcony except to eat."

"We should do that."

Her eyes widened. "We?"

"Someday." When he could convince her they didn't have to hide their relationship. "What do you do for fun?"

"Um…"

He raised his brows at the blank look on her face. "Okay, let me rephrase that. What do you do when you're not working?"

"Sleep?"

"Skye, Skye, Skye. You are in serious need of an intervention." He grinned. "And I'm just the man to do it." He knew she had fun in her. She'd spaceshipped his car and that had been hilarious.

"I go fishing." She beamed as if she'd aced a test.

"Boring. When's your next day off?"

"Why?"

"Because I'm going to give you a fun day."

"I don't—"

Their waiter appeared. "Good evening. I'm Stan. What can I get you to drink?"

"I'd like a glass of Pinot Grigio," Skye said.

"Same for me." He'd prefer a beer, but this was a fancy place, so he'd try to be fancy.

"Our chef is offering two specials tonight. A roasted duck with a tangy chili and orange marmalade glaze, and a prime rib roasted and then blackened on a cast iron skillet. Both are superb. I'll get your drinks while you peruse the menu."

Skye pushed her menu to the edge of the table. "You've sold me on the duck."

"And I'll have the prime rib, medium rare." He handed the waiter his menu. "I…" His gaze caught on the man sitting at the bar. What the hell was he doing here?

"You what?"

"I've never tried duck. You'll have to give me a bite of yours."

The waiter returned with their drinks, and while Skye's attention was diverted, Tristan subtly eyed Mason. As far as Tristan could tell, he was alone. Was it a coincidence that Mason was here, or had he followed them?

Mason wasn't looking at them, so did he know they were here? Even if it was a coincidence, Tristan wasn't happy to see the man here. If Skye saw him, it would ruin their night. She was already edgy about anyone seeing them out together.

Thanks for that, Pretty Boy. He wanted to hunt the shithead down and stuff his balls down his throat for hurting her. Because of what her ex had put her through,

Tristan didn't blame her for being cautious, but he wasn't her ex. He got that she had no way of knowing that, the reason he'd agreed to her ridiculous conditions.

He glanced at the bar again. Mason still hadn't looked their way. What was his game, if he was actually playing one? One reason Tristan had decided on the lake resort for dinner was because it was unlikely anyone from Marsville would be here. He held a mini debate with himself. Tell her Mason was here? Don't tell her? He didn't want their night ruined, so he decided to let it play out. Hopefully, Mason was only here to have a drink and would leave soon without Skye seeing him.

Was this where he'd come for a drink, though? The answer was no. Since he was single, he could be meeting a date. But Tristan had to consider that Mason had indeed followed them, and if so, that was concerning. He would be keeping an eye on the ex-deputy. A real close eye.

Chapter Twenty-Four

"Dinner was amazing," Skye said as they drove back to Marsville.

"Then we'll go back soon."

He spoke as if they had more dates in their future. She let his comment go for now. They were a few blocks from her apartment when Tristan's phone chimed. His cell was in the cup holder, and Skye saw Parker's name on the screen.

"Answer that for me," he said. "Tell Parker I'm driving."

"I'll put it on speaker." That done, she said, "Hi, Parker. Tristan's driving, but I have you on speaker."

"Hi, Skylar. I was actually calling about you. I'm sorry to say I have some bad news. There's a fire at your apartment."

"What?" They turned the corner to her street, and she gasped at seeing two fire trucks and several police cars, their blue lights lit.

"We're pulling up now," Tristan told his brother.

"Okay, I'll come talk to you."

"My apartment," she breathed as Tristan came to a stop. Fire hoses snaked across the lawn and all the windows she could see were busted. The complex wasn't

big, only eight single story apartments. It looked like
the fire was contained to her place, thank God.

Tristan reached for her hand. "I'm sorry, Skye. Not
the way I wanted your night to end."

"Maybe it was just a minor fire." Had she left something on, her curling iron, the stove?

"Here comes Parker. Let's hear what he has to say."

She was shell-shocked, and when he got out of the
car, she stayed frozen in her seat. The passenger door
opened, and he leaned in and held out his hand. "Let's
go to work, Sheriff."

It was the perfect thing for him to say, a reminder
that she was the sheriff and that she did have a job to
do. She put her hand in his and stepped out of the car.
They met Parker at the front of Tristan's car.

"How bad is it? What about my neighbors? Are they
all okay?" *Please say it was just a minor fire.*

"I'm sorry, Skylar. Your apartment is a total loss."

She sank back against the car hood. "Everything?"

Parker's eyes were filled with compassion. "Yeah.
The good news is we were able to contain it to your
apartment. Your neighbors are fine."

Tristan leaned next to her, and she realized he was
both holding her up and lending her strength. She gave
him a grateful smile.

"It's not just the fire," Parker said. "We got that out
pretty fast thanks to your neighbor. Clarissa was bringing in groceries and saw the flames through your window before the fire spread and called it in. The fire was
deliberately set."

"Arson? Who would want to burn down my apartment?"

"Whoever it was also searched your apartment and

cut up your furniture. My guess, they were looking for something."

She frowned. "Like what?" She didn't have anything anyone would want.

Tristan rubbed the back of his neck as he glanced at her. "Do you think Mason is capable of doing something like this?"

Parker's gaze darted to his brother's. "Mason Culpepper? Why would you think he'd set a fire in Skylar's apartment?"

She sure didn't want to believe Mason would be that vindictive. "I'd rather think it was some kids messing around or looking for drugs." If so, they sure didn't know this was the sheriff's apartment. "This seems an extreme reaction to being fired. If Mason did it and we can prove it, he'll go to prison. Would he really risk that happening?"

"You fired Mason?" Parker asked.

"Yes."

"He threatened her, told her she was going to be sorry for firing him." Tristan stared at the fire trucks parked in front of the building. "He was at the restaurant tonight." He glanced at Parker. "We were at the lake resort."

That was news to her. "You saw him there?" When he nodded, she said, "Why didn't you tell me?"

"I didn't want to ruin your evening. He was at the bar for a while. Left around the time our dinners were served. He never looked our way that I saw, so I assumed...hoped that it was a coincidence."

"I don't like this," Parker said. "The resort isn't someplace Mason would hang out, so why was he there the same night you were? And if he left, what thirty or forty minutes before you two did, he had plenty of time to get here and do this."

She couldn't wrap her mind around Mason risking lives just to get revenge on her. "I'll talk to him as soon as we finish up here."

Tristan shook his head. "No, you're personally involved. This is a police department investigation, and I'll interview Mason. Forward me the recording with his threats. It needs to be documented and entered as evidence."

She didn't like it, but she couldn't argue. "Do you know how the fire was started?"

"An accelerant, but I haven't identified what yet. There were two hot spots, one in your bedroom and one in the living room."

"And no one saw anyone suspicious?" Why would someone do this?

"No. Johnny talked to the ones at home. Nothing so far. We're also hoping someone has a security camera that caught our firebug. I'm just thankful your neighbor saw the flames when she did." Parker glanced over to where Clarissa stood with some other neighbors as they watched his men roll up the hoses. "It could have been much worse."

"I'll make sure to thank her. Can I get into my apartment?" These heels were killing her feet. She really hoped she could salvage some shoes and clothes.

"Sorry, no. It's a crime scene until I finish my investigation," Parker said. "You can get in first thing in the morning. Why don't you let Tristan take you to our house for tonight?"

Tristan put his hand on her shoulder. "You good with that?"

"If it's not too much trouble for you." She could go to one of the motels, but she didn't want to be alone tonight.

"Silly girl."

If anyone else had said that to her, she would have punched their nose. Weirdly, hearing it from Tristan made her belly warm.

Parker pulled his fire helmet from his head, swiped his damp hair back with his palm, then stuck his helmet back on. "You going to try to talk to Mason tonight?" he asked his brother.

"Yeah, if I can run him down."

"Why don't the three of us meet up for breakfast after I get Everly off to kindergarten?"

"That works." Tristan bumped fists with his brother, then pulled her next to him. "Let's get you out of here."

She looked back as they walked to his car. Her poor apartment. She didn't have much since she'd walked away from everything she owned with Danny. What little she did have, mostly clothes and shoes, was probably ruined, both from the fire and water. The good news, three of her uniforms were at the cleaners. The biggest loss would be her laptop, but thankfully she stored all her files in the cloud. Such a pain. At least she had her gun and her only credit card in her purse.

"I wish there was an all-night Walmart nearby. I need a pair of shoes." Along with underwear, a few T-shirts, jeans, and toiletries for a start.

"Hmm" was all he said.

He closed the door after she got in the car. As he walked around the front, he pulled out his phone. Who was he calling? He stopped, talked to someone for a minute, then stuck his phone back in his pocket.

"You okay?" he said when he was seated. "Never mind. That was a ridiculous question."

"I'm okay." Truthfully, she was numb. And her feet hurt. She slipped the heels off and sighed. There was no way she was putting them back on. She'd go barefoot until she could get new shoes that were comfortable.

"You're not okay. Who would be? You know, you can lean on someone else occasionally."

"You got someone to recommend, Chief?"

"I sure do, Sheriff." He glanced at her and winked.

She laughed, and dear God, that felt good. It was also a surprise. This was not a night she thought she'd find something to laugh about. Not after losing everything but the clothes on her back. Had Mason torched her apartment? She just didn't see it, but who else had she pissed off lately?

When Tristan drove past the turn that would take them to his house, she glanced behind her. "Um, that was your turn. Did you forget where you live?"

"Nope."

"Are we going to talk to Mason?"

"Nope."

"You're a real PITA, you know that?"

He laughed, and crazy thing…making him laugh did that funny warm thing to her stomach again.

"Where are we going?"

"Say *please*."

"Please. Happy?" What was he up to? That was another thing about him. He kept surprising her. Like telling her to say *please* just to mess with her. She'd never liked being messed with until him. She might be losing her mind.

"Since you were so sincere with your little please—"

he dramatically rolled his eyes, which made her laugh. Again! "—Fanny is meeting us at her shop. You need stuff. She has stuff."

This man!

"That was really nice of Fanny to open her shop just for me," Skye said as they both dropped shopping bags on his bed. She even had new shoes, black high-tops for work, pink sneakers, and a pair of sparkly flip-flops. She still couldn't believe she'd let Tristan and Fanny coerce her into getting pink shoes and flip-flops with crystals on the straps.

"You've lived here long enough to know that we take care of our own."

She had seen many examples of that since she'd moved here, but she'd never felt like that applied to her. Even after a year, she still thought of herself as an outsider. But was that the town's fault? Other than to do her job and stopping in at the Kitchen on Monday mornings, she'd kept to herself. Maybe it was time to make some changes in her life.

Chapter Twenty-Five

It bothered Tristan that Skye seemed surprised that he would ask Fanny to open her shop and that Fanny would agree without hesitation. She didn't expect to be taken care of, nor would she ask for help.

The little she'd said about her family gave him the impression they weren't close, so maybe they weren't the kind of people who leaned on each other. Then there was Pretty Boy and what he'd done to her. He guessed she had learned the hard way she could only depend on herself. But she had him now.

He glanced down at her new flip-flops and smiled. Refusing to put those sexy shoes back on, she'd walked barefoot into Fanny's shop. She hadn't wanted pink sneakers or sparkly flip-flops, but Fanny didn't believe in plain anything. When Skye had asked for white sneakers, Fanny stated she wouldn't put boring shoes on anyone. The black high tops that happened to be Skye's size had been a special order for someone else. Fanny had grudgingly let Skye have them.

"I'm going to head out. Andrew's here, so you don't have to worry about Everly. You won't even see him. He sleeps in the room next to Everly when he's here overnight."

"Okay."

"I'm sorry our night didn't end the way I planned."

Exhaustion lined her face but she managed a smile. "Me, too. We still haven't talked about museum stuff."

"That can wait." He stepped to her and wrapped his arms around her. "I don't know how long it will take me to track down Mason. Make yourself at home, and we'll sort everything out tomorrow."

"You don't mind if I use your shower?"

"Use anything of mine that you want. When I get back, I want to find you in my bed asleep."

"Yes, sir." She rested her head on his chest.

He kissed the top of her head, then reluctantly stepped away. "Hopefully, I won't be long."

"Tristan?"

He stopped at the door. "Yeah?"

"Thank you. For arranging a shopping trip. That was really a nice thing to do."

"You're welcome." There were a lot of things he'd like to do for her if she'd give him half a chance.

Fuzz followed him to the stairs. "No, buddy, you need to stay here on this one. Keep an eye on our girl." His dog liked her, and maybe he could be a comfort to her.

The lights were off at Mason's, but his car was in the driveway. After exiting his SUV, Tristan slipped off his suit coat and left it on the seat. He wanted to think that Mason hadn't set fire to Skye's apartment, but he wasn't ruling it out, so he approached the door with caution. He rang the doorbell, then stepped to the side. A minute passed with no sign of life, so he rang it again. A light came on inside, and moments later, the door opened.

Mason's brows furrowed. "Chief?"

Seeing that he only wore pajama bottoms, no weapon in sight, Tristan stepped in front of him. "We need to talk."

"Sure. Come in."

Inside, Tristan glanced around. The place looked like a bachelor's pad, chrome and black leather. Mason considered himself a player, but from Tristan's observations over the years, he struck out more than he scored.

"I'll get right to the point," Tristan said. "Where were you tonight?" He knew where Mason had been earlier in the evening, but he'd pretended not to see the former deputy. He was curious if Mason would admit he'd been at the resort.

Mason blinked. "That's a cop question. Do I need a lawyer?"

"I don't know. Do you?"

The surprise on Mason's face at the question seemed genuine, but if he had set Skye's apartment on fire, he would expect after getting fired that the suspicion would fall on him and would be prepared. "Why don't you tell me why you're standing in my living room at midnight interrogating me like a suspect. What have I supposedly done?"

"I'll answer that after you tell me where you were tonight."

Mason scratched his belly, looking as if he didn't have a care in the world. "I had two beers at the resort bar as you well know since you saw me."

"Why were you there?"

"Because I wanted a beer. Is that a crime now?"

"Long way to go for a beer." He didn't bother asking if Mason had followed them there. He'd deny it, and Tristan wasn't even sure it had been Mason in the car behind them.

"So what? I felt like taking a ride and that's where I ended up."

On the same night Skye was there? It was too much of a coincidence to believe. "Where'd you go after that?"

"I came home, ate a ham sandwich while I watched a baseball game, then went to bed."

"Did you talk to anyone after you got home? A neighbor, someone on the phone? Anyone who can verify you were here?"

"No and no. This is getting annoying, Chief. Why the questions?"

"Were you anywhere near Sheriff Morgan's apartment tonight?"

"No, I was not. What's the bitch accusing me of?"

"Careful, Mason." The man was either innocent or a skilled liar. "Someone broke into her apartment tonight and set it on fire."

Mason's eyes slitted. "And she's accusing me?"

"Actually, she doesn't want to believe you'd do something like that. The thing is, you're the only person who's made threats against her."

"I think it's time for you to go, Chief." Mason walked to the door and opened it. "You want to talk to me again, it will be through my lawyer."

"Noted." Tristan walked out, no gut feeling on Mason's innocence one way or the other. He hadn't shown any surprise at hearing someone had set her apartment on fire, but he hadn't acted guilty either.

He was halfway back to his house when Parker called. "Hey, you still at Skye's?" Tristan asked.

"Yeah. We found a camera that caught our man, but

it's not going to be much help other than knowing the time and estimating his height and weight. He wore black pants and a black hoodie. Kept his face down. Between his doing that and the dark, I don't think we'll be able to identify him."

"You're sure it was a male?"

"Pretty sure. The person is big, larger than the average woman."

"Well, that's a start. Could it be Mason, or can we rule him out?"

"It could be just about anybody, Mason included. I'm forwarding a copy to you. If we can estimate his height and weight, that could rule Mason out if he doesn't match."

"Okay. I just left his house." He recapped their conversation. "Unfortunately, I don't have feelings one way or the other."

"Well, we're finishing up here. I'll come back in the morning and look around in the daylight, but I don't expect to find anything. After that, the case is yours."

"Does it look like anything is salvageable?"

"Other than pots, pans, and dishes, not really. It's all either burnt, damaged by smoke and water, or cut up."

"I hate hearing that."

"Agree. See you at breakfast."

When he entered his bedroom, it was to find Skye asleep in his bed, her arms wrapped around Fuzz. Fuzz wasn't allowed on the bed, but this was one time Tristan would give him a pass.

Her beautiful hair was spread out over the pillow, one leg from the knee down was uncovered, and as he stood there, mesmerized by the sight of her in his bed, longing filled his heart. He wanted her in his bed tonight, tomorrow, years from now.

Chapter Twenty-Six

"You want a pickle, Miss Skylar?"

"Um…" Sky eyed her omelet, wondering how it would taste with a pickle. Not so good.

"You know we don't eat pickles for breakfast," Tristan said, his amused gaze meeting hers over Everly's head. "And remember, we use our quiet voices when we're inside."

"I forgot," Everly whispered. "But pickles would really make my eggs gooder."

Parker laughed. "Gooder, huh?"

"Yes!" she yelled.

"You can have pickles when you get home from school. Right now, you need to finish your breakfast so you can go get dressed or you'll be late."

"This omelet is delicious, Andrew," Skye said. It rivaled her Monday morning omelet at the Kitchen. Only thing missing was the buttered biscuits.

He blushed. "Thank you, Miss Skylar," he said to his plate.

She'd met Everly's manny when she'd come down to the kitchen, intending to make a cup of coffee. He had facial features associated with Down Syndrome and had a sweet personality. While her coffee brewed, he'd explained in detail and with pride in his voice what his duties were. He was a charming young man, and she liked him immensely.

They were seated around the large kitchen island, and it surprised her that she didn't feel like she was crashing the party. The family—and it was apparent that the Churches thought of Andrew as family—made her feel as if she belonged here at breakfast with them.

Everly dropped her fork, then threw her hands in the air. "Done!"

"Good job, kiddo." Parker stood. "Let's go get you ready for school."

"I go to kindergarten, Miss Skylar. Next year I go to the big girl's school. Daddy said when I go to the big girl's school I can take my lunch, and he'll put pickles in it."

The girl was adorable. "Well, that sure is exciting."

When Skye picked up her plate to carry it to the sink, Andrew vehemently shook his head. "That's my job, Miss Skylar."

"Give him your plate. He takes his job seriously," Tristan whispered in her ear.

How had he sneaked up on her like that? His warm breath caressed her skin, sending a shiver through her. His lips were so close to hers that she'd only have to turn a little for her mouth to touch his.

"Can I have your plate?" Andrew said.

She tore her gaze away from Tristan's mouth. "Here you go. Thank you, Andrew. Your omelet was as good as Katie's at the Kitchen."

He blushed again. "Miss Katie taught me how to make it."

"Well, you were obviously a great student." The people in this town really did take care of each other.

His smile was beautiful. "I can make it for you again."

"I'd love that."

"She means another day, Andrew," Tristan said when Andrew headed for the refrigerator.

"Oh, when?"

"We don't know. I'll tell you when Miss Skylar will be at breakfast again."

Everly's cat came flying through the doggie door, followed by Fuzz. They raced past, disappearing from sight. "He's not going to eat the cat, is he?"

"He hasn't so far." Tristan laughed. "If you could see your face. I'm kidding. They do this every morning. They're working off all the energy they stored up overnight. Watch."

Half a minute later, the two animals sped by—except the cat was now chasing Fuzz—and blew back out the doggie door. "They're hilarious."

"They're clowns, is what they are." He took her hand. "Come. While we're waiting for Parker to get back, I'll tell you what Mason had to say."

"Isn't this Parker and Everly's rooms?" she said as they walked down a hallway. "I don't want him to think I'm invading his space."

"Yep. We'll talk in his office since he'll be joining us," he said as he opened the door to one of the rooms.

A beautiful mahogany desk sat in front of a wall of windows, and a distressed brown leather sofa was against the wall. Instead of sitting in the two chairs in front of the desk, Tristan led her to the sofa. He waited for her to sit, then he sat next to her.

"Did I tell you how much I liked seeing you in my bed when I got home last night?" He took her hand again and linked their fingers.

When he said things like that, she turned all warm and fuzzy inside. Every single time. "I didn't mean to fall asleep. You should have woken me up."

"You had a rough evening and needed your rest. One of these nights, we're going to actually do more than sleep in that bed."

"One hopes." She didn't know how to explain it to him, but the fact he hadn't pushed her for sex did more to ease her doubts about being with him than any of his words.

He squeezed her hand and told her what Mason had said.

"So you don't think it was him?"

"Not saying that. We shouldn't rule him out, but we need to keep an open mind. One of your neighbor's security cameras caught our man." He took out his phone. "Recognize this person?"

She studied the video as it played. "It's too dark and he kept his face and hair hidden."

"He? That's your first impression, that it's a male?"

"From the build and the way the person is walking, yes. You don't think so?"

"No, I do. So does Parker. I think with the three of us agreeing, we can say it's not a woman."

"I don't think it's a kid either." The person's body was bigger and the shoulders too wide to be a teenager or even a young man.

"Play it again." He did, and she pointed a finger at the screen. "Right there. Did you see when he turned his face just a little and you get a glimpse of his cheek? He's a white male."

"Very good. We missed that. Is there anyone you've arrested who might have it out for you?"

"I thought about that last night while you were gone, and I can't think of a single person who'd be so set on revenge that they'd set my apartment on fire. None of the arrests the sheriff's department has made since I took over were serious enough to warrant that kind of retaliation. You know just about every resident in the county. Name one who would do something like that." They'd determined the person on camera was a male, and she'd considered and dismissed Danny. He never did anything that didn't benefit him, and what was the benefit in burning up her apartment? If caught, he'd go to prison, and he just wouldn't risk that.

"Yeah, I can't think of anyone besides Mason who'd be gunning for you."

It saddened her that a man who'd worked for her for a year could be so vindictive. "So, we prove it was him."

"If he's guilty, yes, but we still keep an open mind." Fuzz came in carrying his toy, and Tristan chuckled. "We usually leave about now, so he's telling me it's time to go to work."

"Such a dedicated officer." She scratched behind his ear. "I'm surprised the town council approved a police dog. They're expensive."

"He's not an officially trained dog. We pretty much trained each other." His smile softened as he gazed at his dog. "He showed up at the police station half-starved and filthy when he was about a year old. Stunk to high heaven. We tried to catch him to take him to the animal shelter, but he was wily. He stuck around, though, so I put water and food out for him every morning."

"How'd you catch him?"

"When I fed him, I'd stand back, but I'd talk to him. He started letting me get closer, then one day he let me pet him. The next day I had a leash ready. I fully planned to take him to the shelter, but halfway there, I just couldn't do it. Ended up at the vet instead. Left him there for a spa day. That evening, I picked up a sweet-smelling dog. Underneath all the grime was a beautiful, full-blooded German shepherd."

She smiled. "You have a soft heart, Chief."

He shook his finger at her. "Don't be going around town saying that."

"So, how'd Fuzz get his name, and how'd he end up being a police dog?"

"My officers named him. They like saying, 'Here come the Fuzz' whenever he's around. As for how he's a police dog, that's all his doing. If I left the house, he was determined to go with me. I tried leaving him home, but he'd show up at the station an hour later." He shrugged. "I finally gave up and let him ride with me. It's weird, but he seems to instinctively understand our job. He senses when someone needs a dog hug, and he knows when someone needs to hear a threatening growl."

"He growled at Mason when he threatened me." Now that she thought about it, he'd also growled at Danny. "Has he ever attacked someone?"

"No, but I have no doubt he would if those he loves are in danger, meaning me, my brothers, Everly, and his buddies at the station." His eyes locked on hers. "And I'm thinking now you."

Never would she have guessed how much it would

mean that a dog considered her a part of his family. As for the dog's owner, she'd never wanted a man as much as she wanted him. She was a little mad at him for stirring up this ache of arousal. The numb state she'd been in since leaving Florida had been working just fine.

Chapter Twenty-Seven

One expression after the other crossed Skye's face. Tristan clicked them off. Longing, followed by desire. Then an expression he didn't like. Was that doubt or resentment he'd seen in her eyes?

"Hey, you okay?"

Parker walked in before she could answer. He stepped around Fuzz, who was standing near the door with his toy. "Someone's ready to go to work."

Skye chuckled. "Wish all my deputies were as eager."

"Did Tristan show you the video?" Parker perched on the edge of his desk.

"He did, and between hiding his face and how dark it was, your guess as to his identity is as good as mine. I have no idea who he is."

"Can you rule out Mason?"

"Sorry, no. I really need to get to work." She glanced at him. "Can you take me to my apartment? I want to see the damage, and my cruiser is there."

"Of course." As soon as he stood, Fuzz raced out of the room. "He'll be at the door waiting for us."

"When we find the son of a bitch who did this, I'm going to…" Her eyes scanned her living room.

"You're going to what?" Tristan hated seeing the tears in her eyes. Parker had said everything was ruined, but he'd been hoping that wasn't true. It was.

She pinched the bridge of her nose. "I guess the sheriff can't torture someone."

"Probably not." He put his arm around her and pulled her next to him. "If you do, though, I won't rat you out." If nothing else, he'd coaxed a smile out of her. Fuzz leaned against Tristan's leg and whined. "I don't think he likes the smoke smell."

"I don't blame him. I'm not liking it so much either. What am I going to do? Everything I own is ruined. I can't stay here."

"Parker said your pots, pans, and dishes were salvageable."

"I guess that's something anyway."

"As for a place to stay, with us," he said. She wasn't going to stay in some motel for a week or two. "If you prefer, we have several guest rooms to choose from, or you can do what I want and sleep in my bed."

"I can't live with you. People will talk."

So let them. But he understood where she was coming from after learning what her ex had done to her. "Then we'll make sure they know you're staying in the guest room next to Everly…" He winked. "Even if you're not."

"You're a bad boy, Chief."

"Not yet, but I'm hoping to be." He looked around. "Is there anything here you want to take with you now? We can come back tonight with some boxes and pack up your kitchen."

"Yeah, I have a fireproof safe in the closet with my other guns and some paperwork." As she walked through her apartment with him following along, she fanned her hand in front of her face. "Stinks in here, and my eyes are burning." She stopped suddenly. "You know what? I don't see my laptop anywhere. I know it would be ruined, but it wouldn't have completely melted, would it?"

"Wouldn't think so." They both searched the rooms, but no laptop. "We have to consider the possibility that whoever did this took it."

"You think to sell it?"

"Probably. Or they thought something of interest to them might be on it. Was there anything in it that would be of interest to Mason?"

"I can't imagine what. It's password protected with one of those really strong passwords a computer assigns, so it'd be hard to get in it."

"I'll have Bentley check all the pawn shops here in town and the surrounding areas." Unfortunately, there wasn't reason enough to get a search warrant for Mason's house to see if he had it. "You ready to get out of here?"

"Yeah. It was nice of Parker or whoever did it to board up the windows."

"You can thank him at dinner."

"I haven't said I'll stay at your house."

"Sure you are. Why don't you take today off?"

"And just sit around and feel sorry for myself? No, I need to work."

"Okay. I'll take your safe back to the house." He put a finger under her chin, lifted her face, and brushed his lips over hers. "We'll find who did this."

"We better."

He liked her saying "we," as if they were a team. Fortunately, her cruiser wasn't damaged, and after seeing her off, Tristan went to his house to drop off the safe, then went to the station.

"Need a minute of your time," he told his captain. Matt walked into his office behind him. "Close the door."

"What's up, Chief?"

"You hear about the sheriff's apartment?"

"Bad business that. Any idea who did it?"

"Possibly. She fired Mason Culpepper, and he told her she'd be sorry."

"Mason's always had a hot temper. He wasn't happy he didn't get the sheriff's job."

"I talked to him last night. He swears he was home asleep and didn't go anywhere near her apartment. Right now, there's no proof he did it." He decided not to tell Matt that Mason had been at the resort. That would mean revealing he'd been out with Skye at the time. Not that he cared if anyone knew, but she did.

"Where do we go from here then?"

"Since this personally involves the sheriff, she's out of it. The investigation is ours. I want Mason watched. You, Vee, and Kyle take turns keeping an eye on him." Along with his captain, Vee and Kyle were the officers he trusted the most.

"How much can I tell them?"

"Everything I just told you but tell them to keep their mouths shut."

"Do you think Mason would do that? From what I've heard, if someone hadn't seen the fire, people could have died. Mason might be an ass, but he loves his ass. Would he risk life in prison or the death penalty?"

"I wish I knew the answer to that. Is Bentley around?"

"Saw him about ten minutes ago."

"Tell him I want to see him." Bentley Morrison was his only detective, and fortunately for the town, rarely had any serious cases. Crime in Marsville pretty much consisted of the Watters brothers getting drunk and starting fights, a few domestic calls—usually involving the same couples—occasional drug deals, and a few burglaries.

"And, Matt, the sheriff is staying in a guest room at my house until she makes other arrangements. If I hear anyone implying there's funny business going on between me and her, they aren't going to like the consequences."

"Gotcha, Chief." He stood. "But if there was something going on, who cares?"

Tristan couldn't agree more. Didn't matter what he thought. He wouldn't stand for Skye feeling like she was in the middle of a repeat of what happened in Florida.

Bentley stepped into the office. "You wanted to see me?"

"Close the door and have a seat." He filled Bentley in, including that Mason had been at the resort last night.

"You think he followed you there?" Bentley was a bored detective most of the year. He was going to want to go gung ho on this, so Tristan would have to keep him reined in and on track.

"Not me, the sheriff. Unfortunately, I can't be certain. You're the only one who knows we were there. Miss Mabel assigned us to a committee, and it was a business dinner. Since Mason threatened her, he might try to stir up trouble that we were there on a date."

"You're both single, so why would it be a problem if it was a date?"

Everyone seemed to get that but Skye. "She's new and still proving herself. She doesn't want people to get the wrong impression, so no one needs to know about the dinner. Unless we can prove he did follow her, then that goes in the file." At some point, he might have to tell Bentley about what happened to her in Florida, but not yet. "Mason made some threats, which she got on tape. I'll forward the recording to you."

"Can I interview him?"

"Not yet. For now, let him think he's convinced me he's innocent. Matt, Kyle, and Vee are going to keep tabs on him. You can start by talking to Parker. Get him to tell you everything he knows about the fire. One of her deputies talked to the neighbors last night but talk to them again. There's also footage from a neighbor's security camera I'll send you. See if you can get us height, weight, and any other identifying features."

Bentley's eyes were bright with excitement. "I'm on it, Chief."

"Also, her computer is missing, a MacBook Pro, the dark silver color. Check all the pawn shops in the county."

"Will do."

When he was alone, Tristan swiveled his chair to the side and stared out the window. There was one more obvious suspect, one he'd been waiting for Skye to volunteer the name. Had it not occurred to her, or was she trying to protect him? Did she still have feelings for Pretty Boy?

Chapter Twenty-Eight

As soon as she arrived at her office, Skye changed into one of the uniforms she'd picked up from the cleaners, then dug her spare badge out of her desk. Feeling like a sheriff now instead of a victim, she settled in to work. Thirty minutes later, sighing at the constant interruptions from her people asking how she was, she sent out a group text to her deputies to come in for a meeting. Those on patrol were to come in if they were able.

Johnny stepped into her office. "Did you still want to see me this morning, Sheriff?"

"Yes. Close the door and have a seat." She waited for him to get settled. "First, thanks for your work last night on my apartment fire."

"I don't need thanks to do my job."

She smiled. "Okay. Then thank you for not gossiping about what happened." She'd heard other deputies who knew he'd been there last night ask him about her apartment fire, and he'd given vague answers. She appreciated that, and it reassured her that she was making the right decision.

"The only answers to their questions would have been speculation. That's how rumors get started."

"And understanding that, among other reasons, is

why I want you as my chief deputy sheriff. I'm hoping you want the job. Randal's last day is a week from Friday, so if you accept the promotion, I'd like to make the announcement today."

"Yes, I want it. I won't let you down, Sheriff."

"I know." She smiled. "Otherwise, I wouldn't offer you the job. Starting today, you'll be spending your time with Randal."

"Sounds good."

"Send Randal in."

"I'm just glad you didn't let Mason bully you into giving him the job," Randal said when she told him who would be replacing him. "Johnny'll do a good job for you."

"He will." And there wasn't a chance of Mason bullying her into anything. "I think everyone's here, so let's go talk to them." She grabbed the small gift bag sitting on her desk, then followed Randal to the breakroom.

She scanned the room, noting who was here. All but three of her deputies had come in. The missing ones would hear what was said here soon enough. "Good morning, everyone. I have a few things to go over with you. I guess most of you have heard by now that there was a fire at my apartment last night. It was intentional." She waited for the gasps and comments to finish.

"We don't know who it was, so if anyone hears anything that might lead us to the culprit, I want to hear from you immediately."

"What evidence do we have?" Bradley Burns asked.

"There is no 'we' on this one. The police department is heading up the investigation."

There were some mutterings about that, which she ignored. She didn't blame them for wanting to be involved when someone was threatening their sheriff. It had taken a year, but she was finally feeling like she belonged here. It felt good. Really good.

"Quiet, everyone. I have some other things to talk about. One is that Mason is no longer with us." She still wasn't convinced Mason was behind her apartment fire, so that was all she was going to say about him.

"'Bout time," someone muttered.

She couldn't agree more. "Now to some good news. As you know, Randal is retiring. Johnny is being promoted to chief deputy sheriff."

There where whoops, slaps on Johnny's back, and congratulations. She could tell by everyone's reactions that she'd chosen well. When the hoopla died down, she pointed at Randal. "Come over here."

"Oh, you're in trouble now," Bradley teased.

Randal comically widened his eyes. "Should I be afraid?"

She laughed. "Be very afraid." She truly loved these people, and wasn't that just awesome? When he stopped next to her, she put her hand on his shoulder. "I took the job as an outsider, having no idea how I'd be treated. You welcomed me, told me my first day on the job that if anyone had a problem with me, they'd have a problem with you. I can't tell you how much that meant to me."

He gave her an aw-shucks grin. "That was me being all about me. I knew I was going to retire in a year, and I didn't want to get on your bad side."

"Well, whatever your nefarious reason, I appreciate it." She handed him the gift bag. "This is just a little thank-you for not making my life on the job miserable, which you easily could have." Her deputies had a going-away lunch planned for him on his last day, and she didn't want to take away from their celebration—why she'd made a spur-of-the-moment decision to give him her gift today.

His gaze snapped to hers at seeing the diver's watch she'd probably spent too much on, but what did she know about diver's watches? Her retiring chief deputy sheriff planned to spend his days diving shipwrecks. She didn't get how that was fun, but to each their own.

"Wow," Randal said. "This is awesome." He threw his arms around her. She froze for a few seconds—not a hugger, thank you very much—then she hugged him back. Hugging really wasn't so bad.

When everyone surrounded Randal to check out his watch, she stepped back. These people were her family, more of a family than her real one was these days. She'd found a home, and some faceless jerk wasn't going to run her off if that was the purpose of burning up her apartment.

Leaving the room, she'd taken a few steps into her office when her phone vibrated, an unknown number showing on the screen. "Sheriff Morgan here," she said.

Heavy breathing answered her.

The hell? "Hello?" She disconnected.

Her phone vibrated again, the same number appearing. She noted that the area code was local. "Sheriff Morgan speaking."

More heavy breathing.

"I'm tracing this call, so do me a favor and stay on the line." The caller disconnected. She pulled up recent calls and wrote down the number.

Tristan met her at her apartment that afternoon. He'd called earlier and told her that he'd picked up boxes, which was sweet of him. After he brought them in, she handed him a sticky note. "Do me a favor and call this number from your phone. See if anyone answers."

Without questioning her, he did as she asked. "Nothing's happening."

"It must have been a burner or a burner app. Someone called twice on my personal phone and just breathed in my ear. Do you think it's whoever set my apartment on fire?"

"That's certainly a possibility, especially if the call was from a burner phone." He took out his cell and made a call. "Bentley, I have a number I want you to check out. It might be a burner." He read off the phone number she'd given him. "Let me know what you find out."

"I'm not happy someone is messing with me," she said when he finished talking to Bentley.

"Understandable. I'm not happy about that either." He taped the bottom of a box, then handed it to her. "We'll figure it out, I promise. Let's get this done so we can get out of here."

"Yeah, the place stinks. I don't think I'll stay here." She looked around. "Maybe I'll look for a little cottage to buy now that I know I'm staying."

"Was that in doubt?" He paused with a pot in his hand and looked at her as if her answer really mattered.

"Yeah. I wanted to be sure I'd be accepted as sheriff before I bought a place. It was a relief that my deputies seemed to accept not only a woman but an outsider… well, except for Mason."

He set the pot on the counter, then stepped in front of her, invading her personal space. He slid his hand behind her neck and kissed her. It wasn't a gentle kiss

like the few they'd shared the past several days. It was
a kiss that claimed her. Tongues and lips and teeth. As
he kissed her, she realized she wanted to be claimed as
long as it was him doing the claiming. She gripped his
arms, digging her fingers into his skin.

Suddenly, he pulled away. "I need to stop."

Disappointment cut its way through her. "I thought
you wanted this. You changed your mind?"

"Believe me, I'm dying to get in your pants."

She snorted.

"Too crass?"

"Puzzling, actually. What's stopping you? I've already told you that I want this."

"With conditions."

"That you agreed to." She thought he'd understood
why she needed secrecy if anything happened between
them. He was a man. He wouldn't be talked about, but
she would be. There would be gossip, snickers, snide
comments—some to her face and some behind her back.

She couldn't do it again.

"Hey." He took her hand and pulled her back to him
when she tried to walk away. "It's okay. I did agree. I
don't like being your dirty secret, but I get it."

Was that how she was making him feel, that she was
ashamed of him?

Chapter Twenty-Nine

Tristan did get it, but she didn't. He would never stand for anyone disrespecting her. What she didn't understand about the people of Marsville, they wouldn't turn on her without a damn good reason. Dating him wouldn't have people talking about her.

He'd thought a lot about how to walk the minefield that was Skye Morgan. One wrong move, and he'd be relegated back to adversary status. The only way forward was slow and easy. Baby steps. Much like taming a wild animal, although he doubted she'd appreciate the analogy.

So, he'd abide by her conditions for a while, but he intended to ease her in to being seen with him. Supposed business dinners, lunch at the Kitchen once or twice a week, whatever else he could think of that would let her feel comfortable being seen with him.

The question he'd asked himself and still didn't have an answer: Why her? Why was he so determined to have her in his life? Oh, he knew they had chemistry, but it was deeper than that. There had been chemistry with women before her, and he had enjoyed their company, but there hadn't been this burning need to make them his, to belong to them.

All it had taken for him to fall hard had been one night with her. Even then, deep in his soul, he'd known she was *the one*. Not that he'd recognized it that night, especially believing she was passing through town. But he had known. Then, when she reappeared a month later, the new sheriff in town, his damn heart had landed at her feet without asking his permission.

And she had stomped on it. Sometimes gleefully.

For a year she'd given him a cold shoulder because of a night when they didn't know who each other was. Yet he kept coming back for more, a glutton for punishment, her distain better than nothing. If he'd understood the reason for her attitude toward him, the thing she feared the most, he would have done things differently.

He handed her another box. "Let's get this finished, then we'll go home, have some dinner. How's pizza and a beer sound?"

"Perfect. I just realized Fuzz isn't with you."

"He doesn't like the smell of smoke, so I dropped him off at home."

"Can't say I blame him."

It was on the tip of his tongue to ask her about her ex, if she'd considered the man might be responsible for setting her apartment on fire and the phone calls. He decided to hold off until after pizza and beer when she was more relaxed.

Once the boxes were loaded in their cars, he followed her home while keeping an eye on the rearview mirror. No one seemed to be tailing them. That was good. When they reached the house, he drove past her and motioned for her to follow him. He led her to the end of their property, stopping in front of the barn.

"You have a barn?" she said when they were both out of their cars.

"I'm impressed with your observation skills, Sheriff."

She punched his arm. "Smartass. Why are we here?"

"You can store your kitchen boxes here until you find a place to live."

"I was going to rent one of those mini storage units."

"No need when you have a big barn available."

"Thank you," she quietly said.

"That was hard, wasn't it?" Sometimes, he just wanted to shake her. "It's okay to accept help, Skye. It doesn't make you weak."

"Feels like it does."

"You would be wrong. The faster we get these boxes unloaded, the faster we get that pizza and beer I promised you."

It was going to take every bit of the patience he could muster to get her to the point where she admitted she wanted him in her life as more than her secret friend with benefits, and he was getting a little weary of trying.

Skye was in the shower, and his imagination was running wild. Water would be glistening on skin the color of pale honey, the drops drifting down her shoulders and over her breasts. Her long hair would be wet ropes hugging her back, her...

It was damn uncomfortable in his pants. He thought about joining her, standing with her under the water, his hands on her slick, soapy body. Would she welcome him? He stared at the closed door to his bathroom. Maybe she would, but maybe she wouldn't, so he didn't.

To get his mind off the beautiful and naked woman in his shower, he grabbed clean underwear and his sleep pants, then went upstairs and used Kade's bathroom to take a quick shower. That done, he headed to the kitchen to put the pizza in the oven. Because he and Parker sometimes had to eat on the run or arrived home late and hungry, they kept pizzas stocked in the freezer. They stored them by slices to make it easy to grab one or two for the microwave if they were in a hurry. Not sure how hungry Skye was, he got six assorted slices. He could eat three or four of those himself.

While the pizza was in the oven, he grabbed scissors out of the junk drawer and went outside. He chuckled when he almost looked behind him before snipping a perfect yellow rose. If his Aunt Francine was still alive, she'd skin his hide for touching her roses. It wouldn't matter that he was a grown-ass man. She'd still do it.

Back inside, he found a single flower vase in the butler's pantry. He also found a large silver serving tray he didn't know they had. "Perfect."

Fuzz came barreling in while he waited for the pizza to heat up. "You just now figure out I'm home?" He squatted and let Fuzz give him some doggie love. Once Fuzz settled down, Tristan washed his hands. When the cheese was bubbling, he slipped oven mitts on, took out the pan, and arranged the pizza on the plates, then added two ice-cold bottles of beer.

He critically eyed the tray. Pizza and beer wasn't the most romantic meal to offer a woman, but he knew his girl…or thought he did. She'd prefer pizza and beer over her fancy dinner at the resort.

He picked up the tray and went upstairs, almost tripping over his feet at the sight greeting him. "Good Lord Almighty," he muttered.

Fuzz had raced up ahead of him, and Skye, wearing a white camisole and white boy shorts, was bent over, her sexy as hell ass facing him as she petted his dog. She glanced over her shoulder and gave him a smile that said she knew exactly what she was doing to him.

She stood and faced him. He stepped forward until he was in front of her, his tray held out as if he was offering his queen all his worldly treasures.

And when had he turned into a whimsical fool?

"What have we here?"

"Dinner." He sounded like a croaking frog. He tried to keep his eyes on her face, but they refused to cooperate. The view was too magnificent. Her breasts, which he personally knew fit his hands perfectly and tasted sweeter than honey, were right there. The thin, silky camisole did nothing to hide those pert nipples. How was he supposed to not look? He cleared his throat and attempted to recover his brain. That might be impossible as long as she stood there in her barely there top and boy shorts.

Amusement danced in her eyes. "Shall we just stand here and admire it, or shall we eat it?"

"I… I…" He swallowed hard. "Pick one."

She laughed. "You're a funny man, Tristan." She looked up at him from under her lashes in that flirty way only a woman knew how to do. "A man who can make a woman laugh is one of the top desires on our what makes a man hot list."

"I know a lot of jokes." *Note to self: Add more jokes to your repertoire.* **Also, she'd said his name again. Big win!**

"Pizza, beer, a beautiful rose, and jokes. What more could a girl ask for?"

He could think of a few things he'd like her to ask for. "You okay eating on the couch?" Without answering, she went to the couch and sat. He set the tray on the coffee table, then sat next to her. "I didn't know what you like on your pizza, so there are three choices." She looked them over, then picked up a slice of Hawaiian. He shook his head. "You and Everly."

"What?"

"Pineapple doesn't belong on pizza." He went for one loaded with meat.

"Says who?"

"It's in the pizza rules." He picked up the remote. "What kind of music do you like?"

"Country."

He scrolled through the satellite music stations until he found one playing country.

"What do you like?" she asked.

"It's not so much that I like a particular kind. It's more about the artist. Some of my favorites are Kid Rock, Imagine Dragons, the Eagles… They're great. I have their Farewell Tour concert in Melbourne on my DVR. Best concert ever."

"Put it on."

"Oh, thank God." He laughed when she punched him. "You really have a thing for whacking on me, Sheriff."

She batted her eyelashes. "Maybe I just like touching you."

"In that case, my body is yours to abuse."

Ah, he liked the way her eyes darkened. They ate their pizza and drank their beers, talked a little about traffic lights and parking meters with some joking around thrown in. She was the most relaxed he'd ever seen her and seemingly enjoying herself. He regretted that he was going to have to ruin her good mood by asking her about her ex.

Chapter Thirty

"That was perfect for tonight," Skye said, rubbing her tummy.

Tristan smiled. "Pizza, beer, and good company. Can't beat that." He blew out a breath, and was that regret in his eyes? "We need to talk about who might have torched your apartment."

"Okay. I'm still having trouble believing it's Mason, but who else could it be?"

"Your ex?"

"I did wonder if he'd do something like that, but I don't know. I'm having trouble seeing it. It would take too much effort on his part, and he doesn't put much effort into anything."

"Revenge? Or he's trying to force you to go back to Florida? Maybe if he thought you didn't have a place to live, you'd move back. I don't know, just thinking off the top of my head."

"Danny doesn't even live here." She didn't want to believe Danny would hurt her like that, but there had been a lot of things she hadn't thought he'd do but had.

"It's what? About a nine-hour drive from here to Central Florida? He could have set the fire and been home by morning, no one the wiser." He took his phone, brought up the video, and handed it to her. "Watch this again. Could that be him?"

She brought the phone close to her face and watched the man in the hoodie jog across the lawn. "I just don't know. I can't say it isn't any more than I can say it isn't Mason. So, where does that leave us?" The phone vibrated in her hand, startling her, and she almost dropped it.

He took his cell from her. "Whatcha got, Bentley?"

Bentley was his detective, and she got nothing from Tristan's side of the conversation other than a few grunts and hmms.

"Okay, thanks. Let's meet up first thing in the morning and go over what we got so far," Tristan said, then set his phone on the coffee table. "It was a burner phone that whoever breathed in your ear used. It's turned off now."

"What else did he say?"

"The man on the video is a white male, approximately six feet tall and weighs in at around two hundred."

"Pretty vague. That could be Mason, Danny, or half the men in this county." It still bothered her that Danny had shown up here. She didn't believe it was only because he wanted to tell her he missed her. "My friend DeAnna is a police officer in Danny's department. I'll call her tomorrow, see if she's noticed anything going on with him."

"She won't tip him off that we're looking into him?"

"No, she hates him for what he did to me. She didn't even like him much when I was dating him."

"Ask her if he's missed any days, called in sick, or taken vacation time."

"I will." She scrubbed her fingers over her eyes. "I hate this so much."

He leaned over, put his hands on her waist, and pulled her onto his lap. "Okay, enough work talk tonight."

"Then what shall we do?"

"I have ideas, some really good ones."

"Hmm, I just bet you do." She turned and straddled him. Resting her arms on his shoulders, she leaned toward him until her face was inches from his. "What's your first idea?"

His eyes fell to her mouth. "That you should kiss me."

"Funny, I was thinking the same. Great minds and all that." She closed the distance between their mouths. Their breaths mingled, his feeling like a warm caress of feathers over her lips. She wanted to tease him, to play, but then she lifted her gaze to his, and mercy, the heat in his eyes as he looked back at her robbed her brain of anything but having her mouth on his. So, she did just that.

He made a sound low in his throat that curled her toes. It was primitive and needy, and her body responded to his need, to his arousal pressing against her sex. His spicy scent washed over her, and she breathed him in. Their tongues tangled, and his taste intoxicated her. She was drunk on the smell of him, the taste of him, on his touch.

"Skye." He whispered her name in the same raspy voice she remembered from a year ago.

"Please."

Without warning, he stood with her still wrapped around him. She laughed from the suddenness of it.

"Bed," he rasped.

That sounded wonderful. As he carried her to his bedroom, she buried her face against his neck. She couldn't stop smelling him, wanted to memorize his scent so when she dreamed of him, because she would, his smell would be there in her dreams, too. "Down," he said when he stopped at the edge of the bed.

She didn't want to separate from him, didn't want to lose his heat and his hands on her skin. He chuckled when she tightened her legs and arms around him.

"This isn't going to work if I can't take my clothes off."

In that case. Since she definitely wanted his clothes off, she let her legs slide down his body and unwrapped her hands from around his neck.

He stepped to the door, closed and locked it. "Don't want a surprise visit from Everly."

"Good thinking." His gaze was on her, hunger in his eyes. She lifted the hem of her camisole and pulled it over her head.

"There's not a place on that sexy body of yours, Skye, that I'm not going to taste, touch, make love to." He stalked toward her.

If you crossed paths with a jungle cat, you weren't supposed to run. Running would trigger a cat's love of chasing their prey. The man headed back to her with determined strides, his eyes devouring her was that cat, the one you weren't supposed to run from. But she wanted to, wanted him to chase her down, to catch her, to toy with her.

To never let her go. No, she couldn't think like that. What they had was just chemistry. He wasn't her forever; she wouldn't allow it. The chance of losing everything again wasn't worth the risk. As long as this thing between them lasted, and as long as it stayed their secret, she would enjoy their time together. When it was over there would be no regrets.

"You're thinking awfully hard there." He tapped her forehead. "No thinking tonight, no deciding this is a bad idea."

"I wasn't thinking this is a bad idea." A question popped into her mind, though, because of what he said, making her remember the night she'd broken up with Danny. He'd tried to force her to have sex with him, believing he could use sex to change her mind. She'd used her knee to put a stop to that idea. "If I did decide this was a bad idea, if I told you no, you'd stop, wouldn't you?" She was sure she knew the answer, but she had to hear it from him.

His brows furrowed, his eyes searched hers, and she wished she hadn't asked the question because he saw too much.

"It might kill me, but yes, I'd stop no matter at what point you told me no. Did he force himself on you, your ex?"

There was no use denying it, and again, she wished she hadn't brought it up. "He tried, but I made him sorry."

Rage filled his eyes then. "I'm sorry I didn't know that when I had him in front of me."

"I don't want to talk about him." Or think about him. She tugged on his shirt. "What I want is you naked. If that doesn't happen in the next few seconds, I'm getting dressed."

Well, that did the trick. He shed his clothes faster than she thought possible, tossing each piece on the floor as they came off. All but his boxer briefs. He gave her a sexy smirk as he snapped the waistband. "These come off when your panties come off."

She tried to keep her eyes on his face, but they refused to obey. Her gaze slid over his chest dusted with light brown hair, down to a trim waist, to the arrow of hair disappearing into his boxer briefs, his arousal impossible to miss.

"You keep looking at me like that, Sheriff, and I'm going to embarrass myself."

"Oh, I think you can control yourself."

He stepped forward until their bodies touched, then he lowered his mouth to her ear. "You'd be wrong. You want to know why?"

"Why?"

"Because I haven't been with a woman since you," he whispered into her ear as if telling her a secret. "Because I only wanted you."

She was stunned. How could that be?

Chapter Thirty-One

He'd shocked her. Good. Tristan shrugged. "It's true."

"Why? You're a man."

He glanced down at himself. "Glad you noticed, but what's that got to do with anything?" How had they gotten offtrack? By now, he should have his mouth on all the places on her he wanted to taste, to see if she was as sweet as he remembered or if his memory had played tricks on him.

"A man has needs."

"Let me guess. That's the excuse Pretty Boy gave you for cheating on you?"

She nodded. "He said—"

He put a finger over her mouth, stopping her. "Fuck what Danny said." For a strong woman, a woman owning her job as the sheriff, she sure was insecure about her worth. That couldn't stand. "If you judge every man by Pretty Boy, you're going to miss what's right in front of you." That would be him. Hopefully, she would see the light and soon. "Don't you get it, Skye? You're a beautiful, amazing woman. Pretty Boy is less than the scum on the bottom of your shoes."

"Danny can go to the devil."

"There she is, the woman who takes no prisoners."

He brushed his thumb over her bottom lip. "Nothing sexier than a strong, smart woman. Can we get back now to why we're in my bedroom almost naked? I really, really want to get back to that."

A beautiful smile appeared on her face. "Great idea." She hooked her fingers around the elastic of her panties, then pushed them down over her hips. "You said you'd take your boxers off when my panties are off. So, off with them."

That worked for him. Especially since it hadn't been easy keeping his attention on her face when they got sidetracked while she stood in front of him in nothing but her panties. It was okay to look now, thank you God, and he let his gaze roam over her, starting with those breasts that made his mouth water.

Had another man touched her breasts, slid his hands over her skin, held her close as their bodies joined together? Tristan had told her there had been no one else for him since his night with her, and he wanted to ask if it had been the same for her. Since she'd arrived, he hadn't seen her with another man, hadn't heard any rumors that she was seeing someone. He wanted to think that like him, there had been no one. That he was in her blood the way she was in his. He wanted to ask, but he wouldn't. If there had been someone else, he didn't want to know.

Instead, he wrapped his hand around her hair, still damp from her shower. Her eyes were warm and liquid as she looked up at him, and he could get lost forever in those eyes. His gaze slipped down to her lips, and he couldn't wait another second to have his mouth on hers.

She hummed when their tongues touched, and he remembered that about her, the little noises she made

and how she made him think of a cat purring its pleasure. It was music he wanted to hear all night long.
When she pressed her body against his, he lowered
them to the bed.

"I've waited so long for this, so I'm apologizing
ahead of time." He nipped her earlobe, and she rewarded
him with a whimper. "I need you now, Skye, and I'm
probably going to embarrass myself. I promise the next
time will be all about you."

"We have all night. We'll take turns being selfish."

"It's a deal." He reached into the drawer of his nightstand and grabbed a condom. How long had they been
there? Were they still good? He blew out a breath of
relief after checking the expiration date.

He spoke true when he said he needed her now, but
he wasn't an animal that would rut on her if she wasn't
ready for him. "I've dreamed of you so many times
since our night together. I'd almost given up hope we'd
be together again." He trailed his hand over her stomach, down to her sex, slipping a finger inside her. She
was slick and wet, ready to welcome him inside her. He
smiled when she moaned at his touch.

"I've dreamed of you, too." She circled a finger over
his chest. "So many times."

A year wasted when they could have been together.
It made him a little sad and a little angry that she'd
pushed him away because of her misguided belief that
the people of his town would turn on her. If he'd known
her reason, had known she wanted him, he would have
pushed harder. But he couldn't go back in time, so he
couldn't change that. They had the here and now and
the future. He was in her life now to stay.

"Then let's make our dreams true." They were on

their sides, facing each other. He hooked a leg over hers, pulled her to him, and slid inside her. *Home*, he was home. It was the oddest thought, but that was how he felt. As if with her was where he belonged. It wasn't the sex…well, not completely. It was the sense deep in his bones that he belonged to her. That they were fated to be together. It was a feeling he'd never had with another woman. It was as unsettling as it was… What was the opposite of unsettling?

She made one of her sexy noises as he moved inside her, and he forgot about words and opposite words. He'd warned her he was going to embarrass himself, and he did. Maybe that was what happened when one finally found his home.

He trailed his hand down her side to her hip. "I'm sorry."

"Don't be. My turn is coming up."

"It is. I'm going to taste every inch of you, starting now."

"Yes, please."

He worshiped her body until they were both sated, and when she fell asleep, he held her close. Would she wake up in the morning with a smile on her face or with regrets for tonight?

"Where's Skylar?" Parker asked after pouring half of the coffee in his cup down his throat. Guzzling coffee that way first thing in the morning meant he had stayed up half the night painting.

"Asleep." When Tristan had slipped out of bed, she hadn't moved and he'd stood for minutes, unable to take his eyes off her. They'd made love, slept some, made love again, slept some more, and then all of it again. His male ego had hummed with satisfaction as he'd stared down at her. He had her in his bed, he'd listened to her call out his name—a name she'd refused to say for a year—each time she came apart in his arms.

"By that smile on your face, brother, I'm guessing you had a good night."

Was he smiling? "A fantastic night, actually." Four times over.

"So, this thing with Skylar is serious?"

He met Parker's gaze. "As serious as it gets. For me, anyway."

"Not for her?" Parker gathered ingredients for one of his smoothies.

"I don't know. She has some issues to work through." Patience and baby steps were going to be the key. Patience wasn't one of his strengths, but for Skye, he'd manage.

"Don't you think it's a bit fast, getting this serious about her already?"

"If you want to call a year fast." Only Kade knew about his night with Skye, and that was only because Kade was both a nosy bastard and astute.

Since his middle brother never slept, he'd caught Tristan doing the walk of shame the next morning. Under interrogation by a highly trained Delta Force operator, Tristan had let Skye's name slip. When she'd arrived, the new sheriff in town, Kade had put the pieces of the puzzle together. Thus began Kade's game to amuse himself by flirting with Skye, then standing back to watch Tristan go a little crazy. His brother's years in Special Ops had apparently given him a wacked sense of humor.

Parker shut off the blender, then turned to him with a frown. "You've been seeing her for a year?"

"I wish, but no. I spent a night with her when she came for the sheriff's job interview. Not that I knew that. I thought she was just passing through."

"And you'd never see her again."

Tristan nodded.

"But then she shows up as the new sheriff, so why haven't the two of you been together all this time?"

"Her choice, not mine. And before you ask, the reason is not my story to tell."

"What's your plan then?" He brought his smoothie to the island.

"Romance her. I'm just going to have to do it slowly. Listen, whatever you do, don't talk about us being a couple to her or that you've heard anyone gossiping about us."

"Gotcha."

It was probably good Kade wasn't around. He wouldn't be able to resist playing matchmaker and meddling. Parker was the quiet brother, especially since returning from Paris. He was the one who didn't bother anyone and didn't want anyone to bother him. Well, the artist brother was like that. In his fire chief role, he was a different person. But Tristan trusted him to stay out of whatever was going on between him and Skye.

"Are you still investigating Skye's apartment fire?" Tristan asked.

"No. I gave my report to Bentley last evening. Our arsonist used gasoline in two different places to start the fire. That's the most commonly used accelerant by arsonists, next to impossible to know where it came from."

"I'll have Bentley check the security cameras at the

gas stations around the area. Maybe we'll get lucky and find someone buying a container of gas that matches the man on the video. By the way, Skye's going to be staying in the guest room next to Everly until she finds a new place to live."

"Why not just stay upstairs with you?"

"That would be my preference, but she doesn't want anyone to know we're seeing each other, and she doesn't want Everly to slip up and say something. Like Miss Skylar is sleeping in Uncle Tris's bed. Just so you know, I plan to sneak her upstairs as often as she'll let me."

Every night if he had his way.

Chapter Thirty-Two

Skye found Tristan in the kitchen. "I just talked to DeAnna."

"Nope. That's not how we start our day." He dropped the spatula he was holding on a paper towel. "This is the way we do it." He walked to her and cupped her face with his hands. After kissing her senseless, he grinned. "Good morning."

"Okay. Yeah. Good morning." Wow! She'd never started a morning with a kiss that turned her brain to mush. She could get used to it. But no, that was dangerous thinking. This thing with him was temporary, and she couldn't go falling in love with him.

He was a favored son. The people of Marsville loved him. If they were a couple and then at some point broke up, those people would blame her, not him. As soon as she found a place to live, she'd put distance between them. Until then, she'd let herself enjoy her time with him.

Just don't fall in love, Skye. I mean it.

"What did your friend have to say?"

She blinked, realizing she'd zoned out. "Oh, right. She said Danny's been at work every day. If he did set the fire, he drove straight back to Florida. She never really liked him, so she's all over spying on him. She said if he's the one who burned my apartment up, that she'll make his life miserable." The next time one of her friends said they didn't like a man, she was going to listen.

"So we don't focus on him, but we don't rule him out either."

"I guess that leaves Mason."

"Or someone we're not aware of." He'd been busy at the stove while they talked, and he brought a plate over and set it in front of her. "I know you love omelets, but how do you feel about French toast?"

She eyed the prettiest French toast she'd ever seen and the cup of mixed fresh fruit on the plate. "I feel amazingly happy about it." She glanced around. "Where are you hiding Andrew?"

He laughed. "Our aunt didn't appreciate having to feed three hungry and growing boys, and since I wanted more than a bologna sandwich thrown at us, I learned to cook a few things. Because Andrew loves feeding us and works hard at doing it, I don't take that away from him. But today's his day off, and that means I get to show off for you."

She didn't get it. He'd been abandoned by his mother, dumped on an aunt who didn't want him or his brothers, yet he was one of the most positive persons she'd ever met. "How do you do it? Have such a great outlook after the important people in your life abandoned you?"

"Eh." He shrugged. "A long time ago I realized I could feel sorry for poor old me because the people who should have wanted me didn't, and let that attitude rule my life. Or I could refuse to be a victim and live my life the way I wanted, which was to be happy. I chose happy."

"And your brothers? They both seem happy. Are they?"

"I made sure of it. Since I was the oldest, it fell on me to make certain they knew their worth. I like to think they're both happy, or as happy as they can be. For now anyway."

"What does for now mean?"

"Their stories aren't mine to tell. What I can tell you is that I want to kiss you again."

"Where's Parker and Everly?" She was all for more kissing, but not if one of them might walk in on them. She'd been surprised by how disappointed she'd been when she'd opened her eyes and realized she was alone in his bed.

"He's taking her to school, then he's headed to the firehouse." He comically waggled his eyebrows. "If you're worried about getting caught, the coast is clear."

"In that case, I—" At the same time the cat raced past, chased by Fuzz, both their phones chimed. They both groaned at seeing the text from Miss Mabel.

"We could ignore her," Tristan said.

"And have her track us down? Because she will. No thank you."

"I was afraid you'd say that." Fuzz and his cat returned, and Tristan snapped his fingers as they raced by. "Fuzz!" The dog skidded to a stop. "We have to go see Luther and Miss Mabel."

"Did he just wrinkle his nose?" At Tristan's nod, she laughed. "I'm with him on that."

Skye entered the mayor's office five minutes after Tristan.

"Morning, Sheriff." He stood, turning his back to Rebecca. "How's your day going?"

She narrowed her eyes at his smirk. "Fine, thank you, Chief." She stepped around him. "Good morning, Rebecca."

"Skylar, you poor dear. We all heard about your apartment fire. Because you lost everything, everyone's dropping off clothes and household items to help you get back on your feet." She waved a hand at the boxes lined up against the wall.

Speechless, Skye stared at the six boxes as tears burned her eyes. She'd never experienced kindness like this. Tristan, seeming to understand, came to stand next to her.

The phone on Rebecca's desk rang, and when her attention was diverted, he put his hand on her lower back. "I told you that you were one of us and that we take care of our own. Maybe now you'll believe it," he quietly said.

She was beginning to believe it. The boxes were also a reminder that she needed to find a place to live so she'd have somewhere to put all this stuff. She couldn't keep depending on Tristan to solve all her problems. Besides, she needed to distance herself from him before her heart went rogue and decided it wanted to keep him. As soon as she got back to her office, she'd call a Realtor.

Rebecca finished her call and came over. "Earl said he didn't have any clothes for you, but he wanted to give you this." She handed Skye a jar. "It's honey from his bees, and let me tell you, it's the best honey I've ever tasted."

Damn tears. She swiped at her cheeks. "I don't even know what to say. Thank you doesn't seem to be adequate."

Rebecca reached for her hand and squeezed it. "Oh, honey. Thank you is all you have to say. I made a list of who donated what so you can do just that."

"Okay then, thank you so much. I do want to let everyone know how much I appreciate this."

"What is this? A tea party?" Miss Mabel banged her cane on the floor.

Fuzz squeaked, snatched up his toy, and disappeared under Rebecca's desk.

"I'm sure you have plenty of things to do, Rebecca."

"Yes, ma'am." Rebecca scurried to her desk and shuffled some papers.

Miss Mabel scowled at her and Tristan. "You two come with me."

They followed her to Luther's office, and when they entered, he seemed surprised by their appearance. "Did we have a meeting this morning?" He put his finger on his desk pad calendar. "No, I don't have you down for an appointment."

"Shut up, Luther," Miss Mabel said.

Luther shut up.

"Good morning, Miss Mabel. You're looking mighty pretty today," Tristan said, smiling at the woman as if she wasn't scarier than a rabid dog. "I assume you want an update from me and the sheriff."

Skye gaped at seeing Miss Mabel preen. The old bat even fluffed her hair.

"I was going to say you looked very pretty, too, auntie," Luther said. "But he beat me to it."

"Oh, hush, Luther. You were not about to say that. It would do you well to take notes on how a true gentleman treats a lady. Maybe then you could actually find a lady."

Tristan stepped back, putting himself out of view of Miss Mabel, then winked at Skye. She covered her laugh with a cough. Between the bizarre comedy act happening and that they were here to talk about an alien museum, she had the urge to say, "Beam me up, Scotty."

Miss Mabel turned her attention to Skye. "Give me your report."

"Um…" Report? She didn't have a report. Skye eyed the door, wondering if she could get away with joining Fuzz under Rebecca's desk.

Chapter Thirty-Three

"We emailed you our findings and suggestions, along with cost estimates, Miss Mabel," Tristan said, stepping between the two, taking the matriarch's attention away from Skye. "You probably heard that Sheriff Morgan's apartment was destroyed by a fire."

"Bad business that, but what does that have to do with fulfilling her responsibilities?"

"Not a thing," Skye said.

Miss Mabel waved her off as if Skye was a pesky fly. "I wasn't asking you."

There was no reason for the rudeness, and Tristan was seriously tempted to grab Skye and walk out. Instead, he smiled. "We know you're busy and your time is valuable, but if you haven't had the opportunity to read our report, perhaps you can do that and then we can meet again at your convenience."

For some reason, Miss Mabel had always had a soft spot in her heart for him and his brothers. Probably because all three of them got a kick out of smiling when she frowned, telling her how nice she looked whenever she was grouchy, which was often, and refusing to be intimated by her, unlike most of the town. Most of Marsville's residents hauled ass or hid—much like Fuzz—at the sight of her.

Miss Mabel liked feeling important, and he and his brothers got that. It didn't hurt anything to feed her ego, and it kept them on her good side. He should have explained all that to Skye before now.

"We copied Luther on the email, so if you wish, he can print out the report now for you to read." He mentally crossed his fingers, wishing that she'd elect to read it later and they could get the hell out of here.

"I have an appointment I must get to. I'll study your report this afternoon."

Wishes did come true. He glanced at Skye and raised his brows, hoping she got the message that she needed to participate in this conversation. For her part, Miss Mabel needed to show the sheriff some respect, and she would if Skye demanded that respect. He realized he was getting attuned to Skye when he knew she wanted to roll her eyes. He swallowed a smile.

"We think you'll find we've covered all your concerns, Miss Mabel," Skye said. "After you go over our report, either one of us will be glad to answer any questions you should have."

"I'm sure I will." With that, Miss Mabel lifted her nose in the air and departed their company.

"It's always good to chat with you, Luther," Tristan said. Beside him, Skye made a noise that sounded a lot like a snort. He grinned at her. "Shall we go to work?"

"Yes, please," she fervently said. She smiled at Luther. "Thank you for your time, Mayor."

Luther gave them a wave, his attention already on other things. The moment he saw them, Fuzz rushed to the door, as eager as them to leave. Rebecca wasn't at her desk when they came out.

"How about I load up the boxes in my car and drop them off at home."

"If you don't mind."

"Wouldn't have offered if I did." He walked her to her car. "Here's the thing about Miss Mabel. She's a lonely old woman who grew up in a family that felt entitled. Her parents taught her that she was better than everyone else. If you treat her as if she is a very important person, while at the same time not letting her run roughshod over you, you'll find you might actually get along with her."

"I doubt I'll ever get along with her, but I see what you mean. I guess it's not really her fault for feeling superior to all us common people." She chewed on her bottom lip, then said, "You lied for me."

"How so?"

"You kept saying we. I didn't contribute to the report, and in full disclosure, with everything going on, I haven't even read it yet. You covered for me."

"And?"

"Why?"

"Do you really think I'd throw you to that she wolf?" If so, she sure didn't think much of him.

"Not really, but you've done all the work, and I've contributed nothing."

"It's not like you've been sitting around doing nothing." He glanced around and seeing no one was watching them, he trailed his fingers down her arm. "Go to work, Sheriff. I'll see you tonight."

She smiled as she got in her car. "You're a good man, Tristan Church."

"For you, I can be very good." He winked when she blushed. Maybe they'd taken one or two of those small steps forward today that he knew was the only way to insert himself into her life.

Grinning, he headed back to the mayor's office to collect the boxes of things his town had donated to Skye as soon as they'd heard she had lost everything in the fire. He'd seen the tears she'd tried to hide. His girl didn't know how to accept help, but she'd learn soon enough that an entire town had her back.

He was a few feet from the door of the municipal building, intending to load up her boxes, when Mason Culpepper walked out of the alcove of the jewelry store. Tristan noted the smirk in Mason's eyes and braced for trouble.

Mason glanced down the road where Skye's car had disappeared, then his gaze returned to Tristan. "Cozying up to the sheriff, eh? Can't say I blame you. She's a hot piece."

The only thing that kept him from putting his fist through Mason's face was giving the man what he wanted. A scene. The police chief getting in a fight over the sheriff. Still, Mason calling her a hot piece couldn't stand. If it meant a fight that ended with the sheriff arresting him, so be it.

"If you want to keep your teeth, you'll shut your mouth right now." Next to him, Fuzz growled.

"Just making an observation, Chief." Mason glanced down at Fuzz. "You really ought to keep that dog on a leash before he bites someone." He gave Tristan a mocking salute, then walked away.

"Feel free to bite him whenever you feel like it," Tristan told Fuzz. "Preferably in the ass."

He didn't want to believe Mason was responsible for setting Skye's apartment on fire, but he was their most likely suspect, and after that little confrontation, it was obvious the ex-deputy was out to stir up trouble. But if he had his druthers, it would be Pretty Boy. Nothing would make him happier than to see the man behind bars.

After dropping Skye's boxes off at home, he headed for the station. He went straight to Bentley's cubicle. "Tell me you have a lead on our arsonist."

"I might. I made the rounds this morning to all the gas stations in the area. Found a man filling one of those red gas containers the afternoon of the fire. Take a look." Bentley brought the video up on his computer. "I've never seen him around here before."

"Shit." He'd seen the man, had even given him a warning to pass on through town.

Bentley jerked his gaze to Tristan. "You know him?"

"Not his name, no. He was at Beam Me Up the same night the sheriff's ex showed up. I didn't like the way he was watching Skye, so I told him he wasn't welcome here."

"I thought the sheriff's name was Skylar. Does she go by Skye?"

Only to him. "No, it's Skylar."

Bentley gave him a funny look, which he ignored.

He tapped the screen over the man's face. "Run him through the facial recognition software, see if he turns up. That teardrop tat under his eye probably means he's been in prison, so I'm guessing you'll get a hit."

"On it. Too bad there weren't any prints in the sheriff's apartment we couldn't identify."

"Yeah, it would've been nice if there had been. Pull

up the video of our hoodie man." They watched that video, then the one with the man filling the container. "Same build and looks like the same height."

"It could definitely be the same man." Bentley frowned. "So we have a stranger who probably has a rap sheet. What does he have to do with the sheriff? Maybe someone she arrested?"

"If so, from her previous job. We'd know if this dude was arrested here." He pulled out his phone and called her. "Sheriff, how soon can you come by the station? We have a video we want you to take a look at." He could send it over to her, but he wanted to be with her when she watched it. "Great. See you in a few." He stuck his phone back in his pocket. "She's coming over now."

It seemed too much of a coincidence that the man had been at Beam Me Up the same night her ex showed up. It was time to do a little digging into Pretty Boy.

Chapter Thirty-Four

"I've never seen that man before." Skye studied the man Bentley had frozen on the screen. She'd remember that face if she'd ever seen it. "Just because he's filling a container with gas doesn't mean he set fire to my apartment."

"He's the same height and build as the man your neighbor's security camera caught," Bentley said.

"Do we know who he is?"

Bentley shook his head. "Not yet. I'm running his face through facial recognition."

"If he's in there, you'll get a hit pretty fast." Tristan touched her arm. "Let's go talk in my office. Bentley will let us know if he gets a name."

When they entered his office, he shut the door, then turned, put his hands on her hips, and backed her up to the door. He lowered his face until his mouth was an inch from hers. "I've never kissed a woman in my office before, and I have a sudden urge to correct that."

"I'm sure there are plenty of women who'd be more than happy to kiss you in here." It made her happier than it should that he'd never kissed a woman in his office.

His eyes darkened as he stared into hers. "There's

only one woman I'm interested in making that memory with."

"Who might that be?" The way he was looking at her, as if he wanted to eat her up, did funny things to her stomach.

"She might be the sexy sheriff I have pinned against the door."

"I see. Well, I think she'd probably be okay with that."

He chuckled. "Yeah, I think she might." He lowered his head and covered her mouth with his.

No man had ever kissed her the way Tristan did, as if she were his favorite treat that he couldn't get enough of. His tongue slid over hers, and he rocked against her, showing her what she did to him. She whimpered.

"Damn, Sheriff, those noises you make…" He gave her hips a squeeze, then stepped back and blew out a breath. "Those sounds coming from you makes me want to take you up against the door. Unfortunately, Bentley will be popping in any minute, and I figure you'd probably have a problem with him finding us going at it." He took her hand and walked with her to one of the chairs in front of his desk.

At least one of their brains was working. She'd forgotten where they were and had been ready for him to take her against the door. That couldn't happen again. They had to be careful, or the gossip would start.

After she was seated, he settled behind his desk. His gaze fell to the top of it, then his eyes locked on hers, and a sly smile crossed his face. "My imagination is running wild thinking of you naked on this desk and the things I'd do to you."

She glanced behind her, making sure the door was

still shut, then scowled at him. "You can't say things like that."

"I can and I did. Someday, Skye, against that door and on this desk."

Heat spiraled through her body as her mind went right to him going all alpha and doing things to her that involved a door and a desk. She clasped her legs together. "Stop it." He couldn't keep putting those pictures in her mind. It messed with her head.

"It will happen," he said with a satisfied smile on his face. Then his smile faded, and he propped his elbows on the desk and leaned toward her, all teasing and humor gone. "Until then, we need to talk about your ex. The man in the video Bentley showed you, he was at Beam Me Up the same night Pretty Boy was there."

"And?" If he was making a point, she was missing it.

"You don't think it's suspicious they both were there that night? The man you haven't seen for a year and a stranger who was watching you with a lot of interest?"

"He was watching me?"

"With more interest than was healthy. I chalked it up to his thinking you were hot." His gaze slid over her. "What any man would think at seeing you."

"I doubt he was looking at me like that. I was in my uniform, my hair in a bun, and no makeup."

"Exactly how you are right now, and trust me, Sheriff, you're hot in a uniform. That bun makes a man's fingers itch to pull out the pins so he can wrap that glorious hair of yours around his fist and hold you still so he can kiss you senseless. And you don't need makeup."

Wow! She swallowed hard. Secretly, his words excited her, but if he kept talking like that, she'd crawl up on his desk and let him at her, so she rolled her eyes.

"Every woman needs makeup. About this man, you think he's connected to Danny somehow?"

He shrugged. "I think we have to consider the possibility. As soon as we identify him, we can look into his background. I'd really like to know where he's from."

There was a knock on the door, then it opened, and Bentley stuck his head in. "Got a name for you, Chief."

"Great. Come in."

Bentley walked to the desk and handed Tristan some pages stapled together. "Made a copy for you, Sheriff." He gave her a set. "The man's name is Homer Drake, street name's Dagger. Name fits him since he likes knives, and he's not a man you want to mess with. As you can see, he's got a six-page rap sheet."

Skye skimmed through Drake's arrest record. "I'd say he likes knives." He'd put several people in the hospital using a knife, one almost dying. He'd been in and out of prison, should still be locked up, but like too many violent offenders, he'd served less time than his crimes warranted. She flipped back to the front, looking for his last known address, and when she saw it, she lifted her gaze to Tristan, who was watching her.

"Crap," she said.

He nodded. "Still think it's a coincidence?"

Bentley glanced between them. "What am I missing here?"

She'd been hurt by Danny, disappointed in him, and angry with him, but until now she hadn't hated him. He was messing with her life again, and along with being embarrassed that her past was following her to a job she loved and a town she adored, she was furious.

Tristan hadn't answered Bentley, and in his eyes she saw sympathy and a question. He was the only one here who knew what had happened, and he was silently asking if she wanted to be the one to explain it to his detective.

It was her mess to explain, and she appreciated that he was giving her the choice. She told Bentley what had gone down with Danny, including the rumors that she'd pocketed drugs and money during a joint sheriff's office and police department drug bust. When she finished, she tapped the sheets. "Homer Drake's last known address is Orlando. Your chief doesn't think it's a coincidence that he and my ex were here the same night at the same place."

"I'm afraid I have to agree." Bentley glanced at Tristan. "This lets Mason off the hook?"

Tristan shook head. "Not necessarily. We'll continue to keep an eye on him, but I want you to dig deep into Drake."

"What about the sheriff's ex?"

"Leave him to me and the sheriff."

Was Danny going to ruin this job for her, too? Maybe instead of calling a Realtor, she should start job hunting.

Chapter Thirty-Five

Take Skye out for dinner or stay in for a private meal? That was the question Tristan debated as he peeked in the oven to see what Andrew had left them. Okay, that made the decision even harder. He'd been leaning toward going out because he wanted Skye to get used to people seeing them together.

However, Andrew's assorted enchiladas dinner was one of Tristan's favorites. In that platter, there would be cheese ones for Everly, chicken for Parker, and steak for him. There were more enchiladas than usual, which meant Andrew had added some for Skye. Since he loved this dish, and because Andrew had thought of Skye, they'd eat here tonight. He made a mental note to tell Andrew that it would only be Parker and Everly for dinner tomorrow night.

Skye walked in, and he liked how his heart did a funny bounce at seeing her. He smiled as he headed for her, intending to give her a welcome home kiss. Affection from him was something he wanted her to get used to. He was halfway to her when he realized something was wrong. Her eyes were troubled, and she wasn't smiling back at him.

"What is it? Did something happen?"

She handed him a clear evidence bag. "This was under my windshield wiper."

He read the handwritten note printed in block letters. "What money?" He read it again.

WE KNOW YOU TOOK THE MONEY. IF YOU WANT TO LIVE YOU WILL RETURN IT. YOU HAVE TWO DAYS. BE READY.

"Do you know what whoever wrote this is talking about?"

"Maybe it's related to the rumor Danny started that I took drugs and money in that bust. If not that, I don't know."

"The note makes it sound like you should know what they're talking about." He wished he'd said that differently when she flinched as if he was accusing her of taking money. It never crossed his mind that she would steal anything.

Fuzz wandered in, lifted his nose toward Skye, and then went straight to her. He leaned against her leg as if giving her his support. Tristan wanted to punch himself in the face. Here he was grilling her, and it had taken his dog mere seconds to see what she needed. Since he was a fast learner—even if the lesson was from his dog—he took two more steps, until he was next to her.

"Here, let's sit." He slipped his arm around her waist and moved them to the bar stools at the kitchen island.

She swatted at his hand. "You don't need to treat me like a baby. I'm fine."

Not true, but he understood she needed the illusion that she was. "Of course you're fine. That's not in question." He set the evidence bag with the note in it on the counter. "We have two days to figure this out."

He called Bentley. "I need you to come by my house and pick up a note that was left on the sheriff's cruiser. There probably aren't any fingerprints but check anyway. Also, take a look at the cameras around the sheriff's building. One of them should have caught whoever left the note."

When he finished talking to Bentley, he took two plates from the cabinet. He'd thought they'd eat with Parker and Everly, but he doubted Skye was up for Everly's exuberant nature tonight.

"You're in for a treat. Andrew has enchiladas warming in the oven. We're going to fix a plate and take our dinner upstairs."

"Okay."

He hated how down she sounded. Not that he blamed her. It was looking like what had gone down in Florida had followed her here. If a dealer thought she'd taken his money, why had it taken a year to come after her? They needed to talk about that bust and who was involved.

"Beer, wine, or something else?"

"A beer's fine."

To give her something to do, he grabbed a bowl and a small salsa bowl, set those on the counter, then got the container with Andrew's homemade salsa from the refrigerator and a bag of tortilla chips from the pantry. "Set us up with chips and salsa."

A car pulled up, and seeing it was Bentley, he picked up the evidence bag. "Bentley's here. I'll be right back." He met his detective at the bottom of the steps and gave him the note. "This was on the sheriff's windshield."

Bentley read the note. "This isn't good. You think it relates back to what happened in Florida?"

"That would be my guess. Let's keep this to ourselves until we know for sure. Let me know if you're able to pick up any fingerprints from it."

"Gotcha. I talked to Vee before I left the station. She said Mason was at the Kitchen at lunch and bitching about the sheriff, that she didn't deserve the job and was in over her head. Then he said she'd get what was coming to her."

"Mason needs to shut his mouth." Or he'd shut it for him.

"Katie told him to shut up or leave. Vee said he stormed out."

"Tell Vee to write down everything that he said, especially that the sheriff would get what's coming to her." It was probably time to have another chat with the man.

"Will do. I'll talk to you in the morning."

He went back inside and found Skye sitting on the kitchen floor with both Fuzz and Jellybean in her lap. "I see you got some friends there."

She looked up at him and smiled. "I never had a pet. They're great therapy."

"That they are. You can borrow them anytime you want." He held his hand out to help her up. "Let's head upstairs." He wanted to be gone before Parker and Everly came in. Hopefully, he'd be able to convince Skye that since Everly didn't know she was here, she should spend another night in his bed.

After taking their dinner dishes back to the kitchen, Tristan returned to his floor, carrying two cups. He handed one to Skye. "Doctored it up a little."

"Looks delicious. What's in it?"

"Coffee, Baileys, whipped cream, and a little cinnamon on top." He sat next to her on the sofa. They needed to talk about her ex and what went down in Florida, but he decided to let her enjoy her coffee first. "You said you're thinking about buying a house. What part of town do you want to live in?"

She shrugged. "I really don't have a preference."

If he had his preference, she'd move in with him. If he told her that, she'd think he'd lost his mind. How could he want that already? She'd say it was too soon. But for him it wasn't. She was the only woman he'd wanted since their first night together. Although she'd pushed him away for a year—had seemed to barely tolerate him—he hadn't stopped wanting her even though he'd thought he'd never have her in his arms again. And even believing that, he hadn't been interested in another woman.

"I'll know it when I see it. A small place, maybe two bedrooms, two baths. Something cottagey."

"There's no hurry. We have plenty of room here, so take your time to find the perfect place." He was ready for a shower and some comfortable clothes, and he was sure she was, too, but first, they had to talk about Florida.

When she finished her coffee, he took her cup and set it on the coffee table. "Tell me about the drug bust. Was there money and drugs actually missing? Who was the target?"

She let out a long sigh. "I really thought I'd left that behind me. Okay, Thomas Grant ran a big operation. Everyone knew he was the top dog, but his people were extremely loyal to him, mostly out of fear. He had a reputation for being ruthless. The police department couldn't get any of his people to turn on him. Nor could they find the evidence they needed to prosecute. The little fish, yes, but Grant seemed untouchable. Finally, Vice managed to get a man inside the operation. It took the undercover cop a year to gather enough evidence to satisfy the prosecutor."

"I assume the sheriff's office was involved because multiple search warrants had to be served at the same time in various locations?"

"Exactly. There were warrants for nine locations, so the sheriff's department was asked to lend their support. I was on the team that hit Grant's main operation. His specialty was heroin and meth, but we also found cocaine, marijuana, and ecstasy. I never saw any money, but I heard later that one of the other teams confiscated over a million dollars."

"Was your ex on your team?"

"No." Her eyes widened, and she sucked in a breath. "He was a part of the team that found the money." She squeezed her eyes shut and shook her head. "He wouldn't... He wouldn't steal money and blame it on me."

"Are you sure?"

"No," she whispered.

"Were you still together at the time?"

"No, I'd broken it off with him a few weeks before." She covered her face with her hands. "Oh, God. What if Grant thinks I have his money?"

"Hey. Come here." He tugged her onto his lap so that she was straddling him. "We'll figure it out. A few more questions, then we won't talk about it anymore tonight."

She leaned into him and rested her head on his shoulder. "Okay. I want to get to the bottom of this, so ask all the questions you want." He trailed his fingers up and down her back, and she hummed. "That feels good."

He wrapped his arms around her, wishing they hadn't missed a year of being together. "One thing that puzzles me is the time between then and now. If Grant thinks you have his money, why wait a year to go after it?"

"I wonder that, too."

"Where is he now? I assume because of who he is and the severity of the charges against him that he hasn't gone to trial yet?"

"His bail was denied, so last I knew he was in jail. I haven't kept up with the case, though." She lifted her head and looked at him. "Honestly, I came here to start over and didn't want any reminders of the rumors and gossip about me."

"Understandable. We need to find out the status of the case, make sure Grant is still behind bars." If he'd managed to get bond or released on a technicality, that could explain why this was all coming back to haunt her now. "Would you be good with calling your old boss and seeing what he knows? Also, it might be a good idea to tell him what's going on."

"Yeah, I'll do that first thing in the morning."

"Ask him if the name Homer Drake means anything to him. You said you'd never seen him before, but you'd never heard his name or his street name before either?"

"No, but other than assisting in serving the warrants, I wasn't involved in the case. I'll also ask him if he'll talk to the prosecutor and the detectives handling the case."

"Good idea."

"I guess this lets Mason off the hook."

"Probably, but we'll still keep an eye on him. I don't trust him not to stir up trouble." He should tell her about his conversation with Mason, that her former deputy had been watching them, and what had gone down at the Kitchen today, but if he did, she'd spook. After a year of pushing him away, she was finally letting him in. He wasn't willing to give that up.

"I don't have Grant's money, Tristan. You believe me, right?"

"I never once thought you did." He loved when she said his name, especially since she'd refused to say it for so long. Also, he was done talking about this tonight. She'd taken off her shoes, socks, and utility belt soon after arriving home, but she still had on her uniform and her hair in a bun. "Hold your hand out." He pulled a pin from her hair and dropped it on her palm, then another and another until her beautiful hair was free and falling around her shoulders and down her back.

"You have a thing about my hair," she said, that smile on her face he loved seeing, when he gathered it up and wrapped it around his hand.

"I have a thing about you." He could imagine doing this every evening when they came home. Talking about their day, taking the pins out of her hair, slowly undressing her…the next thing on his list to do.

"I kind of have a thing about you, too," she said, sounding aggrieved by the admission.

He barely refrained from pumping his fist in the air and yelling, "Yeah, baby!" Instead, he slid his hands down to her ass. "Want to know what I noticed?"

She nodded.

"Your bottom is a perfect fit for my hands."

His girl giggled, a sound from her he really liked, and he vowed to spend the rest of his life giving her reasons to giggle.

Chapter Thirty-Six

While Skye waited to hear Dustin pick up or a beep to leave a message, her mind skipped to the way Tristan had taken care of her last night and how he'd made her laugh when that was the last thing she'd felt like doing. She needed to distance herself from him before she lost the willpower to do so.

"Anderson here."

"Dustin, it's Skye."

"This isn't a voice I was expecting to hear. If you're calling to ask for your job back, it's not available, but I can always use a kickass deputy. When can you start?"

She laughed. He'd always been a cool boss, and she did miss working for him. "I'm not calling to ask for a job, but thank you for the vote of confidence. I want to talk to you about Thomas Grant. Some things have been happening here that makes me think I'm on his radar."

"What kind of things?"

She told him what had been going on the last few days. "It's still possible that it's a coincidence Danny and Homer Drake were at the same place on the same night, but—"

"I doubt it. Drake is one of Thomas Grant's enforcers."

Her blood turned to ice. "I so did not want to hear that."

"You need to be really careful, Skye. The case against Grant fell apart on a ridiculous technicality. He was released three weeks ago. I'm sorry I didn't tell you, but you've been gone a year, and it didn't occur to me that he'd turn his attention on you."

"He's out?" she whispered.

"'Fraid so. There are murmurs that either the judge on the case was paid off or threatened some way."

"It pains me to say this, but if Danny was here the same night as Drake, then he's probably mixed up in this." She wasn't ready to accuse him, but she couldn't ignore the possibility he'd pocketed Grant's money and then started the rumor that she had it to divert attention from himself. If so, this was bad. Very bad. "The rumors that there was money missing from when the arrests were made. Do you know if that's true?"

"No one knows for sure, but I've heard that Grant claims so. I'll talk to Keenan. He's the lead detective on this. I'm sorry to say it sounds like they need to take a look at Danny. I'll call you if I learn anything new."

"I'd appreciate it."

"You be careful, okay?"

"I will. I have a great crew who'll help watch my back, and the police department is a good one. The police chief is aware of what's going on, and he's keeping his eyes open."

"Glad to hear it."

After finishing her call, she sent a group text to her deputies and Jackie to come in if they were able for a meeting at four. It was time to tell them what was going on and who they needed to be watching for. After that was done, she went online and printed out enough photos of Danny, Drake, and Thomas Grant to pass out to everyone.

She hated that she was bringing trouble to her new town. It wasn't fair, especially when she hadn't done anything wrong. "Damn you, Danny," she muttered as she headed for her car. She could call Tristan to tell him what she'd learned from Dustin, but she needed his calming influence. As she drove to the police station, she realized she wasn't doing such a good job of distancing herself from him. She'd get right on that as soon as this mess was over.

Bentley was in Tristan's office when she arrived, and although she wanted to close the door and crawl onto Tristan's lap and feel his arms wrapped around her, Bentley also needed to hear what she'd learned.

"Sheriff," Tristan said when she walked in. She wondered if Bentley picked up on how his voice had gone soft. "Come in. We were about to call you."

"Have you learned anything new?" She sat in the chair next to Bentley.

Tristan turned his monitor toward her. "Here's your note leaver."

She watched as a man wearing a hoodie that covered his head walked to her cruiser and stuck a piece of paper under her wipers. He kept his face down, but she was pretty sure it was Homer Drake. "Play that again." She leaned closer to the screen. "He's wearing flesh-colored rubber gloves."

"Yeah, so unfortunately, there aren't any fingerprints on the note," Bentley said.

"You think that's Drake?" She glanced between the two men.

Tristan nodded. "We do. Which means he's still around."

"I talked to Dustin, that's my former boss," she told Bentley. "Drake is one of Thomas Grant's enforcers."

"Hell," Tristan muttered.

"Thomas Grant?" Bentley asked.

She brought Bentley up to date on Grant. "He was released a few weeks ago on a technicality."

"That explains the question on why this is coming up now after a year," Tristan said. "He's out and wants the money someone stole from him."

"What I'm thinking." She handed him the folder she'd brought with her. "Here are photos of Danny, Grant, and Drake if you want to make copies to pass out to your officers."

He pushed the folder toward Bentley. "Make sure our people get a copy."

"I'll get it done today. Anything else?"

"Yeah, put someone on checking the hotels and motels in the area."

"On it. I'll also have them check with the rental agents, see if any one of these men have rented a cabin."

"Good. Anything else, Sheriff?"

"I think that covers it." After Bentley left, Tristan walked to the door and closed it, then came and sat in the chair next to her. "Until we catch these jokers, I don't want you going anywhere alone."

"I have a job to do, Chief. Sometimes it requires I go places, and I can't be dragging people around with me." After Danny, she'd promised herself no man was going to tell her what she could and couldn't do.

He pushed his chair around so that he was facing her. "These people are dangerous, Skye. You know that.

They're targeting you, so for my peace of mind, please don't go anywhere alone."

"Sorry. I guess I overreacted. It's just that I don't like being told what to do."

He took her hand, wrapping his around it. "I'm not telling you. I'm asking. I'm begging."

She didn't like the worry she'd put in his eyes. "Fine. I'll appoint Johnny my bodyguard." It annoyed her that she needed someone guarding her, but she wasn't stupid.

"Thank you. I'm also available if you need to go somewhere, and I'm prettier than Johnny." He winked.

"Oh, I don't know. Johnny has those sexy bedroom eyes."

"You better not be looking into his bedroom eyes."

She laughed. "You're silly." Fuzz rose from his corner bed, stretched as he yawned, then came to her. He sat in front of her and put his chin on her knee. "Hello, handsome. The chief working you too hard and you needed a nap?"

Tristan snorted. "That dog lives a king's life." He looked from her to Fuzz, then back to her.

She could see the wheels turning. "What?"

"How would you feel having him hang with you for a while?"

"A bodyguard and a guard dog? Don't you think that's a bit much?"

"When keeping you safe is in question, nothing is too much." He grinned then, and as often happened with this man, his eyes danced with amusement, warning her he was about to say something that would steal another piece of her heart. "Also, I only lend out my dog to special people. Full discloser, I've never lent him out before."

There you go, heart. Just jump right into his hands. How was she supposed to refuse him when he said things like that? "You play dirty, Chief."

He laughed. "With you, Sheriff, I'm good with down and dirty."

Lord help her. She leaned down and cupped Fuzz's face to hide her pleasure at his words. "What do you say, Fuzz, you want to hang with me for a few days?" He wagged his tail.

"Thank you again. He'll guard you with his life."

"Don't say that. I'd never forgive myself if something happened to him." Maybe this wasn't a good idea.

Tristan put his hand over hers. "You can't take it back. You already agreed."

"Fine, you win." She checked her watch. "I need to get back. I'm meeting with my people this afternoon."

He stood and pulled her up, then he put his hand behind her neck and brought her to him. "My mouth wants yours," he said as he lowered his head.

Her mouth was good with that. She was learning that Tristan liked to touch her and kiss her. Another thing she was learning…she liked his touches and kisses a lot. He rocked against her, letting her feel what she did to him, then he let go and stepped away. She reached for him, intending to pull him back, and he chuckled.

"You better go before we make my desk fantasy come true." He went to a filing cabinet and picked up a leash. "Fuzz, come." He clipped the retractable leash on Fuzz's collar. "I doubt he'll leave your side, but better to be safe and keep this on him."

"Hey, Fuzz, you want to go for a ride?" she asked. He snatched up his toy and headed for the door. "I guess he does."

"Keep your eyes open, and if Johnny's not available when you need to go somewhere, call me."

"Yes, Daddy."

He grinned as he gave her a little slap on her butt. "Go before I decide to lock the door and never let you leave."

"Promises, promises."

"Why is Fuzz here?" one of her deputies asked.

"The reason is why I called this meeting." She'd debated how much to tell them and had concluded that there was no way around it. She had to tell them everything. If she left them to wonder why a drug dealer, his enforcer, and possibly her ex might turn up in town, the speculation would probably be worse than the facts. They also needed to understand how dangerous Grant and Drake were. "Fuzz here is on loan for a few days doing duty as my guard dog."

She passed out Thomas Grant's photo first, then explained who he was. Next was Drake, and then Danny. That was the hardest part, telling them how Danny had started the rumor that she'd pocketed money and drugs.

"I know you're now asking yourself if I did that. I did not. There was an investigation, and I was cleared." She was thankful Mason was gone. He'd take all this and run with it, hoping she'd lose her job over it. He'd no doubt hear about it, but at least he wasn't around to start trouble. As for the ones in the room, other than a few wide eyes when she'd told them of the rumor, she couldn't read them. Did they believe her? "Drake has been spotted in the area, but Danny hasn't been seen recently, and Grant not at all. Doesn't mean they're not around. Keep your eyes open, and if you see one of these people, consider them armed and dangerous. I can't stress this strong enough. Call for backup. Johnny, got a minute?"

"You bet." He and Fuzz followed her to her office.

"A couple of things," she said after they were seated and Fuzz was settled on the floor at her feet. "As you know, the police department is heading up the investigation on my apartment fire, which appears to relate back to Thomas Grant and his missing money."

"It seemed that your apartment was searched before the fire. I guess they were looking for the money or evidence that you had it."

"Probably. Because Thomas Grant and Homer Drake are very dangerous men, the chief and I agreed that I shouldn't go anywhere alone until they're caught. So, you've been elected to be my shadow if I have to leave the building." She glanced down at Tristan's dog. "Well, you and Fuzz."

"Absolutely. I've not been on the patrol roster since I've been spending time with Randal, learning my new job, so I'm around whenever you need to go anywhere."

"Thanks." She glanced out the window, wishing she didn't need to ask her next question. Damn Danny and the problems he'd brought to her new home. She sighed as she turned her gaze back to Johnny. "I'm not asking you to spy on your coworkers, nor do I want you to pass on things they might be saying about me and this mess."

"Okay," he said with wariness.

"I just…" She blew out a breath. "Do you think they believe I didn't take a major drug dealer's money?"

"I think so. As I see it, doing something like that is really stupid, and you're not stupid, Sheriff. Besides, if you did, why aren't you sitting on a beach in Bora

Bora sipping rum cocktails and eating…do they have lobster in Bora Bora?" He grinned. "Instead of taking the sheriff's job in our little county?"

"You do have a good point there."

"If I hear anyone even hinting it might be true, I'll set them straight."

"Thank you." She'd really had chosen right when she'd picked him to be her new chief deputy sheriff.

Her phone chimed, Dustin's name appearing on the screen. "Hey. I wasn't expecting to hear from you this soon."

"It's not good news. Danny's in the wind. Yesterday he put in for immediate emergency family leave."

Her stomach took a sickening roll. "And no one knows where he is?"

"Unfortunately, no. I talked to Keenan. He's going to take a close look at Danny. His finances and his phone records."

"What about Grant and Drake? Does anyone have eyes on them?"

"No."

They were here, all three of them. She could feel it in her bones.

Chapter Thirty-Seven

Tristan walked into Skye's office at five. She usually left around six, but he didn't want to risk missing her if she decided to leave early. His dog would protect her with his life, but Fuzz didn't carry a gun. He did. He'd thankfully never had to end a life because of his job, but he wouldn't hesitate to do so to protect his girl. She probably wouldn't appreciate his thinking of her as *his girl,* but that was what she was in the same way he was her guy. She just wasn't ready to admit that yet.

The plan was to take her straight to the Kitchen for dinner. The reason he wanted to go from here to dinner was that she'd have her uniform on, and he could convince her that it wouldn't look like a date. Although it was definitely a date. He chuckled. He was dating her without her knowing it.

He poked his head around her office doorway. "Sheriff."

"What are you doing here?"

"I'm here for you." He walked to her desk and perched on the edge. He glanced around. "Where's Fuzz?"

"Johnny took him for a walk out back. Why are you here for me?"

"To give you a ride home after we stop at the Kitchen for dinner." Wait for it...

She scowled. "My cruiser is fully capable of getting me to your house. And since when are we going out to dinner? That's not a good idea."

"Remember the part about not going anywhere alone? That includes to and from work. And since when is food not a good idea?" He probably shouldn't tell her that scowl and the fire in her eyes had him wondering how fast he could get her home and in his bed.

"I need my car to get to work in the morning."

"Negative. I'll bring you to work."

"Tristan—"

"Skye." He laughed when she threw a pen at him. "Look, there are two dangerous men possibly here wanting something they think you have. It worries—"

"Three. Possibly."

"Three?"

"My former boss called this afternoon. Danny suddenly put in for emergency leave yesterday, and now he's nowhere to be found."

That was not news he wanted to hear. "He's involved in this up to his eyeballs, and he's probably headed this way, if not here already."

"I know."

"Then you understand why you can't be alone." Even if she didn't, too bad.

"I hate this so much. I came here to put Danny and his lies behind me. Why can't he leave me alone?"

"Because he's scum and doesn't care who he hurts." Fuzz ran in, coming straight to him. "You miss me, boy?" His dog had never been one to jump on people, but he could sure wag his tail like no one's business.

"Mission accomplished. Fuzz was a good boy and

did his thing," Johnny said, following behind Fuzz. "Oh, hi, Chief."

"Johnny. How goes it?"

"Good. Well, except that there are people messing with our sheriff. We're not liking that much."

"Me either. These men are some very bad actors, so keep your eyes open."

"Yes, sir. And I'll stick to the sheriff like glue whenever she has to leave the building."

"Good, and if she tries to sneak out on you, tackle her." He was only half kidding.

"Hey, I'm right here, guys."

"Sorry," Johnny said. "Well, now that the chief's here, I'll call it a day." He was halfway to the door when he stopped. "Should I pick you up in the morning, Sheriff?" He scratched his head. "Where are you staying, anyway?"

"I got it covered," Tristan said, saving her from having to tell her deputy where she was spending her nights.

"Oh, okay. Well then, see you in the morning."

Tristan was smiling as he turned to Skye. "He's a good man." He stood. "Ready to go?" At hearing the word *go*, Fuzz grabbed his toy and raced to the door.

She rolled her eyes. "Never let it be said that I kept Fuzz waiting."

At least she hadn't put up too much of a fuss about him showing up and organizing her life. He'd decided not to mention that to make sure she returned safely, he'd followed her back to the sheriff's department this morning when she'd left with Fuzz.

When they walked outside, a young man Tristan recognized got out of a car. Ray Latimer was a junior attorney at Hines, Jericho, and Mahoney. He stopped in front of them and handed Skye a white envelope. "You've been served, Sheriff." He darted a glance at Tristan, then quickly returned to his car and left.

"What now?" She pulled sheets of paper from the envelope. "You've got to be kidding me. If I had a spaceship, I'd put all the men in it and send it to the moon. No, the moon's too close. A black hole would work." She thrust the papers at him, then stomped to his car.

He scanned the top sheet. Damn Mason. The man was suing her, the sheriff's department, and the town of Marsville for age discrimination. Tristan hit the remote to unlock the car so she could get in. Normally, he'd open the door for her, despite the scowls that got him because she was perfectly capable of opening her own doors, but he wasn't getting anywhere near her right now. He was a man, guilty by default.

"In you go," he told Fuzz after opening the rear door. When he slid into his seat, he dared to reach over and put his hand on her balled-up fist. "I know you were smart enough to document all the problems you had with Mason, so he's whistling in the wind."

"What does that even mean?"

Although annoyance was in her voice, her fist opened, and her fingers curled around his. He considered that a win. "It means he doesn't have a chance to win this lawsuit. It means he's a fool."

"Well, bless his heart."

He laughed so hard that Fuzz stuck his muzzle between the seats and licked his face.

"I'm also learning to say y'all." She peered at him and grinned.

How was he supposed to not love this woman?

* * *

"Told you it was no big deal." They left the Kitchen with a go box, a slice of chocolate cake for him and red velvet for her. No one had blinked an eye at seeing them having dinner together. Probably because they were still in their uniforms, but he didn't mention that.

Outside, he groaned at seeing Miss Mabel parking her turquoise Cadillac next to his SUV. He cringed when she almost hit his bumper.

"I say we make a run for it," Skye muttered.

Without thinking, he grabbed her hand. "This way." Fuzz, recognizing Miss Mabel's car, shot ahead of them. They fast walked down the sidewalk, laughing like kids. At the end of the block, Fuzz stopped and glanced back. Satisfied Miss Mabel wasn't chasing after them, he sat and waited for them to catch up.

Skye checked behind them, too. "He really doesn't like her, does he?"

"It's not so much that he doesn't like her, but that she scares the daylights out of him."

"Same."

"Two scaredy cats, both of you. Her bark is worse than her bite."

"Easy for you to say. She likes you."

"What's not to like?"

"Arrogant much? Hey, you can't be holding my hand in public." She jerked hers away.

He'd wondered how long it would take her to realize they were still holding hands. "No one cares but you, Sheriff." She didn't say anything, and he didn't push the issue. "It's safe to go back now. Miss Mabel went inside the Kitchen."

As they walked to his car, he sensed they were being

watched. He scanned the area around them and spotted Mason on the other side of the street. After giving them a smirk, he walked away. Trouble was brewing with that one.

Chapter Thirty-Eight

Aside from the tension of waiting for Grant or Drake or Danny—or all three together—to show themselves, it had been a blissful four days. Especially the nights spent with Tristan. Skye chuckled to herself as she slipped into his bed. Her vow to stay in the guest room next to Everly hadn't lasted from the first night.

She did sneak downstairs at dawn each morning, giving the impression that was where she slept. If anyone asked Everly where Skye spent her nights, the girl would say in the room next to her, and that was all that mattered. But oh, those hours spent with Tristan's arms around her, the way his body moved when inside her, the places his mouth found to pleasure her…how was she supposed to walk away from all that?

Maybe she didn't have to. Other than his lawsuit, Mason wasn't causing trouble. It still concerned her that if things didn't work out with Tristan, the town would side with him. As for Tristan spreading lies about her if they did break up, that no longer worried her. She could enjoy her time with him as long as she didn't fall in love with him.

"Miss Skylar!" Everly jumped onto the end of the bed. "Are you awake?"

Skye laughed. "I am now." This had become a morning ritual, and she was going to miss starting her day with Everly's enthusiasm. How could you not begin your day with a smile when this one was your alarm clock?

"Good. Let's go sneak some pickles." She jumped across the bed, flopping down next to Skye. "We have to do it before my daddy and Uncle Tris catches us."

Who knew how much fun it would be sneaking pickles under the noses of the men in the house? "We have to be quiet, okay? Use our whisper voices."

"Okay," she whisper-yelled.

Holding hands, they giggled all the way to the kitchen. Everly pulled her to the refrigerator. "I want five."

"Two."

"Four."

"Two."

Everly sighed. "Okay, three."

"Two and we'll share one, so how many will that make?"

"Two and a half!"

"Shhh. Remember, whisper voices." This routine was repeated every morning, much to Skye's amusement.

"I forgot."

"Because pickles make you excited?"

"Yes! Sooooo excited!"

As they ate their pickles, Everly talked, jumping from one subject to another. The new sneakers she was going to wear to school today, a boy in her class who picked his nose ("Gross!"), her teacher who sneezed a lot because she was allergic to cats, and her best friend, Brandy, who always had cat hair on her clothes.

Jellybean strolled in, making a loud and drawn-out yowl, which Skye had learned meant *feed me now!*

Everly scooped her cat up. "You can get Jellybean's food, Miss Skylar."

"Oh, I can, huh?" She wondered how much cat hair Everly took to school with her every day on her clothes. Poor teacher. After opening a can of cat food and putting it in Jellybean's bowl, Skye started a pot of coffee, then put the pickle jar away, hiding the evidence.

When Jellybean finished her breakfast, Everly scooped her up again. "I have to wake my daddy up now. Don't tell him we ate pickles, 'kay?"

"Wouldn't dream of it." She was pretty sure Parker wasn't clueless about his daughter's pickle thievery.

She leaned against the counter, waiting for the coffee to finish brewing. "I'm going to miss this," she murmured. Her morning ritual with Everly, her nights in Tristan's bed. She was going to miss Parker's teasing and Andrew's shy smiles and delicious dinners.

She'd called a Realtor and was supposed to look at a few houses this afternoon. Her good mood vanished, an ache in her heart taking its place. She'd found the home of her heart, and she couldn't keep it.

Shaking off her sad, she filled two cups with coffee and carried them upstairs. Tristan was asleep on his stomach, one naked butt cheek and a leg outside the covers. He'd stopped sleeping in his pajama bottoms since they were now keeping the door locked, and she appreciated the view. After setting the coffees on the night table, she returned to the door and locked it.

She sat on the edge of the bed. "My, my, what a pretty sight." He grumbled something, making her chuckle. "Did someone wear you out last night?"

"Mmm-hmm." He turned over, sadly hiding her view of his tush. One eye peeled open. "There was this pretty lady in my bed. Don't know why she can't stay put." He scrubbed his hand over his eyes, then his nose twitched. "Is that coffee I smell?"

"It is. What would you do to that pretty lady if she was still in bed with you when you woke up?" If her time with him was limited, and it was, she wanted every minute with him she could get.

"The answer to that question is best shown, not told." He snaked an arm around her waist and pulled her down next to him. He kissed her, then chuckled. "How many pickles did you and Everly eat this morning?"

"Can't get nothing past you, Chief. Do I have pickle breath?"

"Uh-huh. Have I told you how much I love pickle breath?"

"I believe you've been remiss in sharing that."

"How neglectful of me." He slipped his hand under her sleep shirt and cupped a breast. "Mmm, look what I found."

She never knew what to expect from him in bed. Sometimes it was what he called sweet lovin', and when he made love to her like that, it was dreamy. Sometimes he liked it a little on the rough side, and he'd warn her it was going to be hard and fast. She loved it like that because it felt like she had the power to make him a little crazy with needing her. Then there was his playful side, and it seemed that was what she was getting this morning.

"If you look hard enough, you might discover a second one." Sex had always been a serious act, never a fun one, and it turned out laughing and sex went great together. Who knew?

He scooted down a little, then pushed his head under her top. "By God, you're right! There is another one." He rubbed his face over the newly found breast.

She giggled. "Your scruff tickles." When he sucked the nipple into his mouth and swirled his tongue around it, she moaned.

"Killing me, Sheriff, with those noises you make."

Because she liked killing him, she moaned again. He answered with a growl.

"I wonder what other treasures I might find if I look hard enough." He trailed his tongue down the middle of her stomach, into her bellybutton, then to the waistband of her silk lounge pants. "What have we here? A magic gate guarding the treasure?" He hooked a finger under the elastic and let it snap back into place.

"Yes. You have to know the secret words to open the gate." She loved his playful mood.

When it was hot and heavy between them, her blood sizzled, and her sex throbbed with need. When he was of a sweet lovin' mind, she would close her eyes and float away on a fluffy white cloud while her body was worshiped by this man. He made her feel cherished. This playful side of him gave her laughter and oh so good feels.

"I know the magic words. Ready?"

"Yes. So ready."

He chuckled. "All right, here they are. I'm going to make you come so hard that you're going to forget your name. Stars are going to dance in front of your eyes and—" he slipped a hand inside her pants and a finger through her folds "—you're going to drench my tongue with your delicious juices."

"Ohhhh." She lifted her bottom. "That's them. The magic words. Take my pants off!" He face-planted on her stomach and laughed so hard that his shoulders shook. "Whaaaat? Why aren't you taking my pants off?"

He laughed harder, and apparently it was true. Laughter really was contagious. Tickling bubbles erupted in her stomach and made their way out her mouth, first in a snort, which tickled even more, and then she was gasping for breath along with him.

I would love a lifetime of this with him. The stray thought dropped into her mind like an exploding bomb that changed the course of one's life. She couldn't think like that, couldn't wish for it. Their laughter died off, and she was glad for that. Sex with him was just that. Sex. Nothing more, and she didn't need to learn that she could love a man who made her laugh.

"What was that all about?" She didn't even know what she was asking, but she felt like she was walking a tightrope without a safety net, and she didn't know how to balance herself.

"Can I get back to you on that?" He lifted his head and grinned at her. "I have more important things to do first."

As she stared down her stomach and into his eyes that were somehow still laughing yet filled with heat, another bomb dropped. *I love him.* No! No, she did not love him. Liked him a lot, yes. Respected him, yes. Trusted him, yes. But she could not love him.

"Skye?"

There he went, being him again. Calling her by the

name she'd grown up with—the one that only the people special to her used—refusing to call her Skylar like everyone else here did. She knew why. Because his doing that was a constant reminder that they'd clicked from the beginning in a way neither had expected or experienced before. She should have told him her name was Skylar the night they'd met.

"Yes?"

He moved up until his face was next to hers. "You're clicking off all the reasons in your mind why you shouldn't like being with me. Please don't do that."

She pretended not to know what he meant, but how did he know her so well? "Did you forget you said the magic words to get into my pants?" She closed her eyes against his sad smile. How did they go from laughing to her wanting to cry?

"I didn't forget," he softly said, a touch of sadness (or was that disappointment in her?) in his voice. He touched his lips to her nose, then he dropped kisses on his way back down her body. He slid her sleep pants down and off and made good on his promise that stars would dance in front of her eyes, but there was a heaviness hanging over them now.

Chapter Thirty-Nine

Still on for house hunting?

Tristan hit Send on the text. Last night had been incredible, and then this morning had started great when Skye returned to his bed. She hadn't had much laughter in her life the last few months in Florida, or here for the past year, and he loved giving her that. It was one of the many sounds he loved hearing from her. He was a firm believer that sex didn't always have to be serious. Hot and heavy serious sex was awesome for sure, but sex and laughter were fun, and he liked seeing her having fun.

It was the first morning that she'd come back to him after sneaking off to the downstairs bedroom at dawn. That had made him happy, had put him in a playful mood. Then something had happened. He wasn't sure what exactly, but she hadn't denied it when he'd said she was thinking of all the reasons they couldn't be together. It all went back to what her ex had done to her, and Tristan didn't know how to get her past that, for her to believe he would never be the reason she'd have to leave another job and town she loved.

Dots appeared on his phone screen, and he felt like

a fifteen-year-old boy waiting to see if his crush liked him back. The atmosphere had been tense when he'd driven her to work. She hadn't said anything about that, but he knew she resented the loss of her freedom to go and come as she pleased.

If U R busy Johnny can go with me.

Not busy. See U at 4.

K

She was retreating, putting those damn walls back up. He wanted to shake some sense into her, wanted to tell her he was in love with her. Falling in love with her hadn't been a sudden thing where he blinked his eyes and said, "Oh my God, I'm in love with this woman." It had happened slowly, beginning the night they met. He wasn't sure how she'd managed it, but she'd made a home for herself in his heart.

Yes, he hadn't expected to see her again, but within minutes of leaving her, he'd known he'd made a mistake not getting her phone number. He hadn't even paid attention to her license plate to know what state she lived in.

He'd almost gone back to the hotel. As the police chief, he could have gotten her information. But she'd been the one to insist on first names, and he had to respect that. For the month between then and when she'd shown up as the new sheriff, he'd thought about her constantly. In the year he'd spent being around her, wanting her, being impressed by her, he'd fallen in love with her. So no, it wasn't overnight, and it wasn't a passing fancy.

Maybe he was a fool.

Chapter Forty

That bomb blast going off in her mind was a wake-up call. She couldn't let herself be in love with Tristan. *Too late, kiddo.* Skye refused to listen to that voice in her head. There were too many complications, therefore she was not in love with him. It was time to put distance between them before she really did fall in love with him.

The first thing she needed to do was find somewhere else to stay until she had her own place. It was impossible to resist him when she was living in his house where he was free to touch her, to send her those heated looks. Tonight, she'd check the *Marsville Observer* classifieds to see if there was a rent by the week or month apartment available.

She glanced at the clock. Twenty minutes before he was supposed to be here to go house hunting with her. He'd ignored her offer to let him off the hook, but she tried again.

Don't want to disrupt your day. Johnny's free to go with.

"No need to tie up Johnny's time. I'm here," Tristan said as he walked into her office, his eyes on his phone.

He lifted his gaze to her. "Side note. There's no one else on earth I'd rather have disrupt my day than you."

She ignored the way her heart fluttered at his words. "You're early."

"I am. Didn't want you to skip out on me." His mouth quirked up in an *I've got your number, Sheriff.*

He was too good at reading her mind. Fuzz trotted around her desk, his tail madly wagging in his excitement to see Tristan. She'd told Tristan when he drove her to work that Fuzz didn't need to stay with her, but the bossy man refused to listen.

Tristan squatted and scratched around Fuzz's ears. "Were you a good boy for Skye?"

"He was a perfect gentleman." Afraid her heart would audibly sigh at the sight of the two of them loving on each other, she locked her desk, gathered her purse, and stood. "Ready?"

"When you are."

He followed her to his SUV, both of them scanning the parking lot for strange men. This waiting for something to happen was getting to her. She was jumpy, and although she wouldn't admit it to anyone, a little scared. The tension she'd put between her and Tristan wasn't helping.

"Where to?" he said when they were on the road.

She pulled the Realtor's text message up and read off the address.

"That was the Radfords' house. Cute one, but it'll probably need work."

It was in her price range. If she liked it, any work it needed, she could do over time. She gazed out the window, noting the scenery she'd pass by each day if she bought the house. It was a two-lane country road, and the houses they passed were spread out. Although it was a pretty area, she wasn't sure she wanted to live this far from town. She'd prefer easy access to takeout, the grocery store, and her office.

"What happened this morning, Skye? What did I say wrong?"

"Nothing happened." This was why she'd tried to get out of his coming with her. Well, that and it hurt to be near him now that she'd made the decision to end their brief affair. Because that was what it was, an affair. Nothing more.

He swerved the car to the right, onto the shoulder, then slammed on the brakes. She yelped at the sudden move. "What? Did we almost hit a deer? A dog?"

"No." He turned off the engine, then unbuckled his seatbelt, and turned toward her. "What's going on in that head of yours? What did I do to deserve your silent treatment? Tell me, and I'll make it right."

This man was determined to break her heart. Stupid tears burned her eyes, and she turned her face to the window. "It's not you."

"Worst breakup line in history, Sheriff, the it's not you, it's me excuse." He reached across the console, put his fingers under her chin, and turned her face toward him. "At least do me the courtesy of looking at me when you stomp on my heart."

"I'm sorry," she whispered.

Sensing the charged emotions between them, Fuzz stuck his face between the seats and whined. Tristan pushed him back. "Not now, Fuzz."

He was right, he did deserve an explanation, but she didn't know how to explain her fears.

"You have it so together and you're so sure of yourself." As she said the words that had come from the top of her head without thinking, she realized that was a part of it.

His shoulders lifted in a shrug. "I had to be." When she didn't say anything, he sighed. "I'll make a deal with you. I'll tell you my worst fears if you'll tell me yours."

"Okay." But only because she couldn't imagine him fearing anything, so she really wanted to know what his fears were.

"I'll go first, and no going back on our deal, yeah?" She nodded.

He stared out the window for a few moments, then his gaze returned to hers. "I was still a boy myself when I had to step into the role of father and mother to Kade and Parker. Our aunt sure as hell didn't want the responsibility of us. I guess I should be grateful she let us stay when it became obvious our mother wasn't coming back, but I don't have that much generosity in me."

"She was that bad?"

"She was. It didn't take long for me to realize that keeping my brothers alive and well fell to me." His eyes took on a distant look, as if he was remembering, and he chuckled. "Kade was a handful, a boy on the fast lane of self-destruct." He chuckled. "With him, I understood why parents drank."

"He seems to have turned out okay."

"Yeah, miracle of miracles." Love for his brother was clear in his voice. "The Army saved him. Two days after he barely graduated high school, he and some friends stole a car, took it for a joyride, and got caught."

"He went to jail?"

"Almost. I went to the judge and begged him to give

Kade a choice of jail or the military. Judge Sorenson is dead now, but I'll always be indebted to him for doing just that. Kade decided the military was more appealing than jail. I think he's questioned that decision a few times, but he knows as much as I do that Sorenson's offer turned his life around."

"And Parker?"

"Yes, Parker. The sweetest and most sensitive one of us. For a year after our mother left, he barely spoke. It was Parker who I believed she would come back for. He was her baby, her favorite. She never did. One day I walked up behind him, and looking over his shoulder, I saw an amazing drawing of the three of us. As soon as he realized I was there, he slammed the notebook closed, then refused to show me any of his drawings."

"What did you do?" She was enthralled by the story of him and his brothers.

He gave her a sly grin. "I sneaked into his room that night after he was asleep, found his notebooks, slipped out with them, and spent hours turning the pages, marveling over art he'd drawn that was better than the last one."

"And then?"

"And then I found him a private art teacher. After he graduated high school and told me he was going to Paris to learn from some dude whose name I can't remember, I didn't stop him as much as I wanted to. He was too innocent, too naïve, too sweet to be off in another country where I couldn't keep watch over him."

"But you let him go?" The way he'd stepped up for his brothers wasn't helping her resolve to walk away from him.

"I did, and he came home a few years later with a

beautiful baby girl. As much as I love my niece and wouldn't trade her for anything in the world, I'm not sure I did him any favors. He hides it, but he's incredibly sad and lonely."

Did Kade and Parker appreciate how special their brother was? "What about you? Who takes care of you?"

"Your turn," he softly said instead of answering her.

Everything he'd told her made her fears seem selfish, like she was only thinking of herself when he thought of everyone but himself. But he hadn't answered the one thing he'd said he would. "You said you'd tell me your greatest fear."

"I was hoping you'd forget that part." He gave her a sad smile. "My greatest fear? It's this. I gave the years that were supposed to be my greatest to raising my brothers. I don't regret it, and I'd do it all over again, but now I want my turn. And I want it with you. My fear is that you're not going to give us a chance."

He was right.

Chapter Forty-One

When she shut down, Tristan didn't know what else to say. He'd put it out there in the hope that she'd tell him what was going on in her mind, because something was. A myriad of emotions sat heavy in his chest. A sense of loss for what could be, hurt that she didn't respect him enough to be honest with him, and a bone-deep sadness. Then there was the resentment. He'd offered her his heart only to have it stomped on.

He settled back in his seat and clipped on his seatbelt. His finger was on the start button when she put her hand on his wrist.

"I'm sorry."

"Me, too." He wanted to ask her what she was sorry for exactly, but what was the point?

"I'm afraid."

There was vulnerability in her voice, and he hated it. Skylar Morgan, the Skye he knew—that he loved— was a strong, independent woman. She wasn't a woman afraid and vulnerable. He turned his hand over, and with their hands palm to palm, he lowered them to the console between them. "What are you afraid of, Skye?"

"I lost myself in a man, and that cost me everything.

I can't do it again." Tears pooled in her eyes, and she blinked them away. "I'm afraid it would be too easy to lose myself in you."

She still didn't believe he would never do anything to hurt her. He'd grown up in Marsville, knew the people, and not a one of them would turn on her simply because they broke up if it ever came to that.

Was he willing and did he have the patience to prove to her that she was safe with him, no matter how long it took? If not, then he needed to let go for both their sakes. As he roamed his gaze over her, he knew he couldn't walk away without trying.

"Here's the thing. I'll never ask you to lose yourself in me. I don't want you to change who you are. It's never made sense to me why a man wants to change what attracted him to a woman in the first place."

"I think I believe you. I want to."

Because she'd been deeply hurt and betrayed by a man she thought loved her, he tried not to let her words hurt. They hurt anyway. But those were her feelings, and he had to respect that. Her fear was putting a name to what they were to each other—a couple, boyfriend, girlfriend—so for her, he'd take that off the table, even though he wanted every living soul in Horace County to know she was his girlfriend.

He'd told himself it was going to be baby steps with her, so baby steps it was. "How about this? We don't put a name to us or any expectations. We just enjoy each other's company, whether it's dinner, UFO text jokes, or you in my bed…" He did a mental fist pump when she tried not to smile. "It stays our secret."

"Okay."

Just okay? That was all he got? Apparently, it was.

* * *

"It's cute," Skye said.

Tristan snorted. She was being nice. The house was a horror. Ralph Radford had lived another twelve years after Ethel had died, and looking around, it was obvious he hadn't known how to take care of the place without her.

"It has potential," Leigh, Skye's Realtor, said.

With a lot of elbow grease, even more money, and vision—which he did not have—it probably did have potential. He'd pass on it, but it wasn't his decision. If he had his way, Skye wouldn't need to be looking at houses.

He stayed in the living room with Fuzz while the women walked through the rest of the house. He just couldn't see Skye living here. It wasn't her. She walked back down the hall with Leigh following behind her.

"I don't think this is the one." She glanced at Leigh. "Do you have anything closer to town?"

"Actually, there's a loft on Main Street I think you might like." Leigh took out her phone. "Let me call the owner and see if I can show it now."

There was only one loft Tristan knew of, and he was surprised it was for sale. "The one above Sweet Tooth Bakery?"

Leigh nodded, then stepped outside as she spoke to the owner. Tristan almost told Skye who owned it but decided to wait until after she saw the loft. She might like it enough to deal with Miss Mabel.

"Have you seen it?" Skye asked.

"Once." When he'd had to evict the occupant. "It's pretty nice."

"I think I'd like the convenience of being able to

walk to lunch or dinner, and imagine how good it would smell, being above a bakery."

"All pros." And one big con.

"If it is nice, and in my price range, I might jump on it before someone else takes it." She walked over to him. "Leigh asked if we were dating. I guess because you're looking at houses with me. Then she said you were her boyfriend in high school."

"For about two weeks, and it was actually the summer after we graduated. She dumped me for—" he grinned "—Sherrie Adams."

"She's gay?"

"Well, since she's now married to Sherrie, I'd say yes."

"Is there anyone in this town you don't know?"

He thought about it. "I guess I'd say if I don't know them, I know of them."

"I should get out more. Meet people. The only ones I know are people we've arrested."

"You know me."

She smiled. "True that."

Tristan could tell by the excitement in Skye's eyes that she wanted the loft.

"I love it," she said as she trailed a hand over the granite countertop. "This is perfect for me. It's at the top of my price range, though. Is anyone else interested in it?"

Leigh shook her head. "Not that I'm aware of. It just went on the market."

"Okay, let me think about it. And if you come up with any other options, let me know."

"Will do, and if someone makes an offer on this one, I'll call you so you can put one in if you want."

"I'd appreciate it, and I'll call you with my decision on this one in a day or two."

The best option was his house, which would cost her nothing. If she didn't want to live there, they could find a place they both liked. Not that she wanted to hear that. His gaze followed Fuzz as the dog trotted around the room with his nose to the floor, then to sniffing the furniture. He whined as he dropped his tail between his legs, went to the door and pawed it.

"He's acting strange," Skye said, coming to stand next to him.

"I don't think he likes the smell." He guessed that Fuzz had caught Miss Mabel's scent in the place and wanted to be gone before she came back.

They left Leigh to close up the loft. "You really liked this one?"

"I like it a lot. I just wish the price was a little less."

"You could offer less." Although he doubted Miss Mabel would negotiate. "If you're serious, it might be worth it to pay for an appraisal. Personally, I think it's a little overpriced, and if an appraisal agrees, that would give you bargaining power."

"Good idea. I just might do that."

They reached the sidewalk, and he stepped to the street side of her. "Let's grab a bite at the Kitchen since it's about dinnertime."

"Okay. I think I really would love living there, having the Kitchen steps away and a bakery below me. Sweet Tooth has the best coffee. I'd have to figure in daily trips to my monthly budget."

She was still excitedly chattering about the loft when

they reached the Kitchen. As much as she already loved it, maybe it wouldn't matter who she'd be buying it from. Fuzz took his usual position right outside the door when they entered.

"Hey, guys." Katie glanced between the two of them and grinned. "Take a seat wherever you want."

"What was that grin for?" Skye asked as he headed for the back booth, away from the windows.

He dared to put a hand on her back, considering it a win when she didn't slap it away. "Beats me." He wasn't about to tell her Katie knew he was interested in Skye.

"I want the wall behind me," she said when they reached the booth.

"Then slide in and over because I want the wall behind me, too."

She scowled. "People will talk if we're sitting on the same side."

"Don't care." He wasn't turning his back to the door where he couldn't see someone coming at her. "You can slide over or sit on the other side."

"You think I can't protect myself?"

"I think you can protect yourself just fine, Sheriff. Still going to sit on this side with you either next to me or across from me. Your choice." He glanced around. "We're getting a lot of attention, which doesn't bother me, but probably does you," he quietly said. "So pick your seat."

He laughed when she growled, sounding like a snarling kitten. She shot him a glare as she slid into the booth seat and then over, giving him room next to her. He was a sucker for her glares and sounds, even growly ones.

Katie bounced over. "It's so great to see you two together." She set two glasses of water on the table.

"Together?" Skye said.

"Aren't you—" Katie waggled a finger between him and Skye "—like dating now? I know the chief's had the hots for you for a long time."

He groaned. "What's tonight's special?"

"Wait." Skye leaned forward and peered at Katie. "He told you that?"

"Uh…" Katie glanced over her shoulder. "I think I smell something burning in the kitchen." She took off.

"Tristan."

"Skye."

"You talked to her about me?"

"Not exactly."

"Then what exactly."

He sighed. Guess it was confession time.

Chapter Forty-Two

If Tristan wasn't blocking her exit, she'd bolt. Skye tapped a finger on the table, waiting for him to answer. This was what she was afraid of, being talked about. People would give her the side-eye, gossip about her, and snicker when she walked by. She'd lived it, refused to go through it again. He'd sighed already, but he did it again.

"Stop noise delaying and spit it out, Chief."

"Noise delaying? Is that a thing?"

She picked up her fork. "I'm going to stick this in your eye if you don't answer me. And stop being amused."

"All right. It's not a big deal. Remember the first night you came to dinner, and I promised you lasagna?"

"It was good. I was impressed."

"Great. Katie will be back in minute. What do you want to eat?"

"I swear I'm going to stab you with this fork. What did you tell Katie?" He was still amused and enjoying this.

"Just that you were coming to dinner."

"Why would you tell her that?"

He shrugged. "Because she wouldn't help me make

the lasagna until I told her who I was making it for." He glanced at her and winked.

"What am I going to do with you?" She wanted to snatch the words back at seeing the mischief lighting up his eyes. "Don't answer that."

"Pity. I had some really good answers to that question." He pressed his leg against hers.

She just bet he did.

"Y'all decide on what you want?" Katie said, returning to the table. "The special tonight is spaghetti and meatballs."

"I was kind of hoping for lasagna. Since I already know how good yours is." Skye smirked when Tristan, in the process of drinking water, choked. She patted him on the back. "That go down wrong, Chief?"

"She knows," he muttered, glancing at Katie.

Katie's eyes widened. "I swear he made it. I only guided him a little."

"Just a little?" Skye raised her brows.

"Okay, maybe more than a little, but only to tell him what to do. He actually did make it."

"Well, it really was good, so thanks for helping him," she said, letting Katie off the hook. Not Tristan, though. She wasn't done with him. "I think I'll have the ham and cheese wrap, a side of sweet potato fries, and unsweetened tea."

"A hamburger, everything but onions, a side salad, and coffee will do it for me," Tristan said.

After Katie left, Skye leaned back in the corner of the booth. "I don't know whether to punish you for talking about me to Katie or reward you for the effort you put in to making me lasagna."

"Both could be good if done right." Heat flared in his eyes.

"Stop looking at me like that."

"No."

"That's it? Just no?"

"Yep. See, it's my eyes." He pointed at said eyes. "They look at you, and it just happens. Nothing I can do about it."

"You're impossible." And adorable and sexy and... everything she wanted in a man. All those bricks she'd piled up to make a wall no man could penetrate again, well, he was sneaking in and stealing those bricks, one by one. And doing it with smirks, smiles, and winks. With treating her as an equal and the way he listened to her. With lasagna dinners, kisses that melted her, and laughter. She thought she loved...liked the laughter best. Or maybe it was the kisses and the things he did to her body in the quiet hours of the night.

"The wheels are spinning, Sheriff. What's going on in that mind of yours?"

Another thing. He saw her in a way no other man had. "I was thinking about the loft." It was the first thing to come to mind because she sure wasn't going to admit her brain was stuck on him.

"So, you're really thinking about it?"

"Yeah. It's perfect for me. You said you'd been in it once before?" There had been something in the way he'd said it that had snagged her attention. And now the wheels were turning in his mind. "What?"

"Not sure you want to know."

"That only makes me more curious." There was nothing he could say that would change her mind about the loft. The more she thought about it, the more she wanted it.

"It was Luther's love nest."

The fork she was playing with clattered to the table. "What?"

"Told you that you didn't want to know. If it helps, that was about nine years ago. I was a rookie at the time, eight months on the job, when Miss Mabel grabbed me by the front of my shirt as I was walking into Sweet Tooth. She demanded I go upstairs and evict the—" he made air quotes "—hussy living there."

"Miss Mabel owns my loft?"

"'Fraid so. Change your mind about wanting it?"

"Not sure. Tell me the rest." Would she be able to live there knowing it had been Luther's love nest? Just eww!

"Luther lived there at the time, and he'd installed a lady of…well, to quote Miss Mabel, 'loose morals,' and she wanted the woman gone."

"Was that true?"

"I so didn't want any part of whatever was going on, but you don't say no to Miss Mabel. I went upstairs and a woman with long bleach blond hair and wearing nothing but a sheer negligee came to the door. She looked me up and down and said in a sultry voice, 'A man in a uniform with a gun on his hip is my fantasy. Are you my birthday present?' Then she grabbed my belt and tried to pull me inside."

Skye burst out laughing and slapped a hand over her mouth.

"It's not funny, Sheriff."

"Oh, it is funny—hilarious, actually, and your lips are twitching. You're trying not to laugh. Don't stop now. What did you do?"

"I told her she couldn't stay. Big crocodile tears rolled down her cheeks, and she launched herself at me, wrapping herself around me like a spider monkey. That was how Luther found us."

Skye lost it, laughing so hard that she gasped for breath and her eyes teared up. "I wish…" She waved her hand in the air as she tried to catch her breath. "I wish I could have been a fly on the wall for that. What did Luther do?"

"He fired me."

"What? Obviously, you managed to keep your job."

"Miss Mabel unfired me when she found out."

"This is the funniest thing I've ever…" She stuttered to a stop when Mason walked in.

"Ignore him." Tristan reached under the table and squeezed her leg. He shifted his body toward her. "Tell me, still interested in the loft?"

"I'm going to have to think about it. It might be a little too creepy living in Luther's love nest." Her gaze darted to Mason. "He's coming this way."

"Don't give him the satisfaction of letting him get to you."

Easy for him to say.

Mason slid into the seat across from them. "Isn't this cozy. The police chief and the sheriff snuggled up together." He smirked at Tristan. "Finally got in her pants, did you?" He'd raised his voice, making sure the people around them heard him. "Rumor is there's a drug dealer after her. Seems she stole his money."

She gasped, as did several others. Everyone was looking at them now, and she wished for the ground to open and swallow her. It was Florida all over again.

Chapter Forty-Three

"Mason, you say one more word, and you'll regret it."
Tristan leaned toward him. "Leave. Now."

All eyes in the place were on them, and you could
hear a pin drop. Tristan knew Skye was embarrassed
and humiliated by such a public scene. She'd relate this
to what happened to her because of her ex. He resisted
the urge to pick her up in his arms and carry her out of
here. She'd never forgive him if he did that.

Katie brought their dinners, and after she set them on
the table, she glared at Mason. "You get out, and don't
come back. You're not welcome here."

"Just having a friendly chat with my old boss and
her squeeze." Mason slid out of the booth. "See you in
court, Sheriff."

As he walked by the counter, Earl lifted a gnarled
finger, pointing it at Mason. "That weren't a nice thing
to do, Mr. Mason. A man's not supposed to be mean
like that to a lady."

"Crazy old coot," Mason snapped as he marched
out the door.

Tristan glanced at Skye. All the color was gone from
her face, and his rage at Mason burned through his

blood. He touched Katie's shoulder. "Stay with her until I get back."

He was done with standing passively by while Mason toyed with her life. They were about to come to an understanding if Mason wanted to stay in Marsville. And if they didn't come to an understanding and Mason stayed in town anyway, it was going to be a miserable existence for the man. Tristan would make sure of it.

Mason was unlocking his car door when Tristan caught up with him. Mason crossed his arms and smirked. "I'm thinking you have something to say, Chief?"

"Just this. You never talk to the sheriff again. You never come near her again. You see her walking down the sidewalk, you go the other way."

"And if I don't?"

"You'll wish you did."

"She's brought you this low, huh? Has you making threats on her behalf. I used to respect you, but she's turned you into a pussy. Got no respect for pussies."

What he wanted to do was put his fist through the man's face, but that was what Mason wanted. Then he could file assault charges. Tristan wasn't about to play into the asswipe's hands. "You might want to seriously consider relocating, but if you aren't smart enough to see that, consider this the only warning you'll get. Stay the fuck away from her."

"It's a free country, meaning I'm free to walk down any sidewalk I want." He opened the car door and gave Tristan a mocking salute, knowing he'd achieved his goal. "Been nice talking to you."

Tristan's breaths came in harsh waves as the car disappeared. It had been by sheer force of will that he hadn't decked Mason, and truthfully, he regretted he hadn't. He was also angry at himself for playing into Mason's hands. The man had set out to embarrass Skye in front of everyone in the Kitchen, and he had. She'd be the center of gossip now, something that would humiliate her.

"Well, that was enlightening."

He squeezed his eyes shut at hearing Miss Mabel's voice. *Just perfect. The icing on the freaking cake.* He took another deep breath, then faced her. She stood in the alcove to the stairs going up to the loft.

"Miss Mabel, you're looking lovely tonight as usual." How much had she heard?

"Cut the bullshit, Tristan. What was that about?"

He almost laughed at her cursing. Anytime she heard someone curse, she banged them across the leg with her cane. "Just a misunderstanding."

"Humph. Sounded a bit more than that. Mason's always been a self-centered boy, too lazy to work for what he thinks he deserves."

Tristan blinked at her spot-on assessment.

She chuckled. "You think I don't know what goes on in my town?"

"No, ma'am. I'm pretty sure nothing gets past you."

"Exactly. Like this thing you have going on with our sheriff…carry on." With that, she walked away, the echo of her cane tapping along the sidewalk filling the air.

Tristan shook his head. It felt like his and Skye's relationship had been blessed by the queen or something. He'd left Skye alone too long with all those curious eyes on her, so he strode back to the Kitchen.

She was gone.

* * *

Where was she? From Katie he'd learned that she'd left with Old Man Earl. She wasn't at home, at her old apartment, at her office, wasn't anywhere. He'd gone home first, thinking that was where she'd have Earl take her. Parker said he hadn't seen her, and her stuff was still in the guest room. That was a relief. She hadn't packed up and cleared out.

He'd left as soon as he determined she wasn't there. "You got any suggestions where to look next, Fuzz?" Unfortunately, Fuzz didn't. Out of desperation, he headed for Earl's place. Earl would tell him where he took her.

But Earl refused to say where Skye was. How many times had he sat with the old man in his jail cell and listened to him cry? How many times had he loaded Earl and his goat in his car and driven him to Beam Me Up to get his riding mower? Enough that you'd think Earl would feel some loyalty.

Apparently not.

He tried again. "I just want to talk to her, make sure she's okay."

"I reckon she don't want to talk to you. Not after you left her all by herself and everybody looking at her like that."

That was a shot straight to his gut. "I wanted to warn Mason to leave her alone." A poor excuse for leaving her to the thing she feared the most, people whispering about her.

Earl waved a hand as if shooing away a fly. "Who cares about Mr. Mason? You shoulda cared about her instead."

Regret landed heavy inside him. Earl was right; he

should have stayed with her and not gone chasing after Mason. He hadn't accomplished a thing by doing that other than lose Skye. Fuzz gave a yelp, then took off for Earl's barn. That was a happy bark, and Tristan assumed he'd picked up Billy's scent. Except there was Billy, coming out the open door of Earl's house. He hopped down the porch steps, then took off for the barn.

Suspicion eased into his mind. "Who's in the barn, Earl?"

"Ain't nobody in there."

"I think I'll take a looksee."

Earl stepped in front of him. "She don't want to talk to you. Not tonight."

"I know you're trying to take care of her, and that's a good thing. But I'm not leaving without seeing her." The old man meant well, and Tristan could appreciate that, but he wasn't leaving Skye to build up what happened and make it bigger than it was. He put his hand on Earl's shoulder. "You're right. I made a mistake tonight, and I need her to know I'm sorry for that."

"You tell her you're sorry, then if she still wants you to go, you do it."

Stubborn old man. "I promise if that's what she wants, I'll leave."

"All right, but only 'cause you promised." He stepped aside.

When Tristan reached the entrance to the barn, he stopped. Skye sat on the floor while a half dozen kittens climbed on her. Fuzz was on his belly next to her, his attention on the little things. Hay bales were piled up behind her, and Billy and a cat he assumed was the mama stood on top of the bales, watching the goings-on below. A donkey or a mule, he wasn't sure which, had his head over a stall door, also observing.

It was like a scene out of a fairytale, the princess and her devoted woodland creatures. He took out his phone and snapped a picture of her surrounded by the assortment of animals. How could he not? "I see you're making friends."

"They're so innocent." She didn't seem surprised to see him. "They don't know how mean people can be."

"That's a good thing." He eased down and leaned against the stall. "I'm sorry, Skye."

She finally looked at him. "For?"

"For leaving you alone. It was stupid to chase after Mason. I should have stayed with you."

She shrugged, returning her gaze to the kittens. "You did what you thought you had to. The thing is, I'm not some fragile woman you have to take care of."

"I know that." But she was, or maybe it was more that he wanted to take care of her. No doubt she was being talked about after the scene at the Kitchen. People liked to gossip. What she wasn't getting was that Mason would come out on the wrong end of his stunt before it was all over.

She had nothing to be ashamed of, no reason to be embarrassed or humiliated, yet she was. As he sat across from her, the silence between them heavy, her eyes avoiding his, all he could think was that he was losing her. He thumbed through the words going around in his head, trying to find the ones that would bring her back to him.

He chose to start with the ones he thought might show her the town wouldn't turn against her. "Miss

Mabel called Mason a self-centered boy, too lazy to work for what he thinks he deserves."

Her gaze darted up to his. "When did she say that?"

"Tonight, after Mason left. I know you feel like you're back—"

"You don't know what I feel." Her attention returned to the kittens.

"Fair enough. Listen, Mason's been building up to pulling a stunt like he did tonight."

"What do you mean?"

"He's been watching you...us."

"You didn't think that was something you should tell me?"

"I was keeping an eye on him. You had enough to worry about with your apartment fire and a drug lord targeting you."

Her lips thinned and her eyes narrowed. "That wasn't your decision to make. He was my deputy, my problem."

"If I told you he was watching us, you would have spooked. I was hoping with enough time, you'd see that no one has a problem with us dating."

"We're not dating, Chief, we're...we were having sex. Nothing more."

"Lie to yourself all you want, but what's between us is definitely more than just sex." He didn't like the "*were* having sex." He leaned toward her and put his hand on her knee. "We have something, Skye. Something good. Don't walk away from us. Don't give Mason that kind of power."

"I don't know what you mean." She gently set the kittens aside, then pushed up. "Would you mind giving me a ride back to your house? I'll get my stuff and get out of your hair."

As he stood, he forced himself to swallow his anger. "You're not in my hair." Okay, that had sounded as angry as he felt. He sighed. He had one last card to throw on the table, and he hoped it was a winning one. "I'm in love with you, Skye. Have been for a while."

"I don't want you to love me." She walked away, taking his heart with her.

He dropped his chin to his chest. How was he supposed to live without a heart?

Chapter Forty-Four

He loved her.

The words to tell him she loved him, too, had burned on Skye's tongue. Thankfully, she'd managed to hold them back. Unable to sleep, she slipped leggings on over her boy panties and a hoodie over her camisole. She slid her feet into the rhinestone-encrusted flip-flops Fanny had talked her into. She looked down at her feet. Glittery things were so not her, but she liked them. Maybe she didn't know who she was anymore.

He loved her.

She couldn't get his words out of her head. It would be so easy to walk upstairs and slip into his bed. The longing to do that almost brought her to her knees. She'd hurt him in the worst way possible when she'd walked away after he'd opened his heart to her.

Not just once, but after leaving him in the barn when she'd slung her hateful words at him, she'd done it again when they'd arrived back at his house after a silent car ride. He'd walked beside her to the guest room.

"Give me ten minutes to get my stuff together, and I'll be gone." She'd had no idea where to go, but that wasn't his problem.

He'd put his arm in front of her, bracing his hand on the doorjamb. "You're not leaving tonight."

"Says who?" She focused on her shoes so he couldn't see the longing in her eyes, wishing he'd ignore her ridiculous bravado and carry her upstairs to his room. That he would wrap his arms around her and make her forget this night.

"Me." He scrubbed a hand over his face. "It's late. If you leave, I'll follow you to make sure you're safe. Stay, even if it's only for tonight. Here, in the guest room." He dropped his arm to his side. "Please."

So she'd stayed, but she couldn't stay in this room, in the silence of it, with her thoughts. She needed fresh air, then maybe she could breathe. She let herself out the back door. Clouds covered the moon, stealing the light. The darkness suited her. She walked to the steps and sat on the top one.

If Mason had only dropped the bomb that she and Tristan were together, even if it had been the way he'd said it in front of everyone, she would have shrugged it off. Tristan had said no one cared if they were in a relationship, and she was beginning to accept that was true.

But Mason had made sure they believed she'd stolen money from a drug dealer and was now screwing their beloved police chief. That they did care about. She'd seen it in their eyes, had heard their whispers, and Tristan had chased after Mason, leaving her to face them alone. The only people who'd talked to her were Katie and Earl.

Would she have reacted differently if Tristan had stayed by her side? Not slipped out the back door with Earl, her tail tucked between her legs. She didn't know, but it didn't matter now. She'd made a home here, had been happier than when she lived in Florida, and what had she done? Brought along dangerous drug dealers.

The two-day warning they'd given her was up, and she wished she could believe Thomas Grant had decided she didn't have his money and had left, taking his enforcer with him. He hadn't, though. She could feel danger in the air. The best thing she could do for Tristan and for the town was leave before someone got hurt. And if it was Tristan, she would never forgive herself.

There was nothing stopping her from leaving. Just get in her car…right, a problem with that. She didn't have a car. The vehicle she drove belonged to the sheriff's department. Besides, she didn't have it in her to walk out on her deputies.

She brought her knees up, wrapped her arms around them, and lowered her face. She wished she could believe she'd made a mistake walking away from Tristan. Then she could go upstairs, tell him she'd been wrong, and he'd hold her and tell her everything would be okay. But she couldn't do that. Who knew how this mess would play out, and she wouldn't allow him to tarnish his reputation by association with her.

He loved her.

Stupid tears burned her eyes, and she squeezed them shut. He loved her, and she loved him, too, but that was her secret. If she told him, he'd move heaven and earth to have her. That was the kind of man he was.

"I love you, too," she whispered into the black night. "So much." And it hurt…so much.

He loved her.

Those were the worst and the best words anyone had ever said to her.

* * *

"It's pickle time!" Everly screamed as she jumped on the bed, then landed on Skye.

"Omph." Skye put her hands on Everly's waist and lifted her to the side. "Girlfriend, you're a pickle." She goosed her under her arms. "A ticklish pickle." Everly laughed so hard she got hiccups, and Skye wrapped her arms around the little girl she'd grown to love. She swallowed past the lump in her throat. "Let's go eat pickles."

"Yay!" Everly bounced up, then jumped off the bed.

This would be their last pickle morning, and Skye never would have dreamed how sad she would be over such a silly thing. She glanced out the kitchen window as she poured a cup of coffee. A light fog swirled around the distant Blue Ridge Mountains, making them appear mystical.

That was another thing she loved about North Carolina, the landscape. Maybe it was because she'd grown up in the flat lands of Florida, but even after a year of living here, she was still in awe of the mountains. She'd considered herself blessed to have those views to enjoy every day.

"Let's eat our pickles on the porch." If her time here was going to end soon, she didn't want to miss a minute of feasting her eyes on the beauty surrounding her.

"Like a picnic? Please, Miss Skylar, can we have a picnic?"

She smiled at the little girl's excitement. "We sure can."

They made plates of pickles, toast, slices of cheddar cheese, and cookies. When they decided on root beer to drink, Skye poured her coffee out. Why have coffee when you could have a root beer for breakfast? She put everything on the tray Tristan had used to bring her breakfast in bed.

"Stand by for a minute." She went to the bedroom and pulled the comforter from the bed. If it got grass stains, she'd buy them another one. A breakfast picnic with a sweet and amusing little girl was more important than worrying about ruining a bed cover.

"I know where we can have our picnic, Miss Skylar," Everly said, dragging the comforter along the ground. "Follow me."

Carrying the tray with their feast, she trailed after Everly. The spot Everly led her to was under a large magnolia tree, its plate-size flowers scenting the air with a sweet fragrance. Fat bumblebees buzzed from flower to flower.

"Ah, that's a lot of bees."

"Those are bumblebees, Miss Skylar," Everly said, walking under the tree. "They won't hurt you if you don't touch them. My daddy said so."

"You promise?"

"Cross my heart." She made an X over her chest, then set about spreading out the comforter.

Skye had sat in a tire swing that had a wasp nest in it when she was a little girl. She'd been stung so many times on her bottom and the back of her legs that her parents had taken her to the hospital. She did not trust anything that had a stinger. But she wasn't about to disappoint her little friend, even if it ended up in a hospital visit.

"What should we eat first?" Skye asked after they were seated with the tray between them.

"Pickles!"

Skye laughed. This girl and her pickles. "What made you love pickles?"

"I don't remember it. I was just a baby, but my daddy said I cried and cried and cried when I was getting my teeth." She leaned toward Skye as if about to share a secret. "Did you know we was borned without teeth?"

"Yes, I did know that." She didn't know how she managed not to laugh.

"I wonder why." The little girl shrugged. "So, I was crying and crying one day when my daddy was holding me, and he was eating a sandwich he got from Sandwiches, Soups, and More. Do you eat there, Miss Skylar?"

"I do. Their sandwiches are great."

"Uh-huh. They give you a sour pickle with your sandwich. My daddy said the strangest thing happened. See, I was crying 'cause my new teeth hurt, then he picked up a pickle to eat and I grabbed it with my little baby hand. He let me put it in my mouth, and he was sure I'd make a funny face 'cause I wouldn't like it. But guess what?"

"What?"

"Surprise!" She threw her hands up. "I liked it. Daddy said I gummed it and stopped crying. What does gummed mean, Miss Skylar? I asked my daddy, but I don't think he splained it real good."

"It means to chew on something when you don't have teeth." Skye didn't think she'd ever been as entertained as she was by this child.

"But I had teeth. I was crying 'cause they hurt."

"You didn't really. Your teeth were trying to grow, but they weren't there yet. They were just starting to come out, but mostly you just had gums. So, your daddy's right. You gummed the pickle."

Everly clapped her hands. "You splained it better than my daddy. You're so smart."

"Why thank you. So, he'd let you gum a pickle when your new teeth hurt, and you'd stop crying?"

"Yes! And that's how I love pickles."

"That's a wonderful story, Everly."

A big grin appeared. "I know." Her eyes widened. "Look, Miss Skylar. A butterfly! I love butterflies. My best friend…my other best friend, 'cause Brandy's my best friend, too. So, her name's Brianna, she loves butterflies, too. Do you love them?" Without waiting for an answer, she went off on an explanation of how caterpillars turned into butterflies.

It was the best picnic Skye had ever had. She had never given much thought to having kids. Maybe someday in the future if she found a man she wanted to spend her life with and he wanted them. If not, she was okay with that, too. Now, though? An image of a little girl with Tristan's eyes and…

Stop it.

Her heart was already breaking. Wishing for something that would never happen would only make it harder to do what she had to do for his sake.

Chapter Forty-Five

He was done. A man could only handle so much rejection before his heart decided enough was enough. Didn't mean he wasn't going to worry about her, like this morning when he'd come downstairs to find Skye was gone. Since everything she owned was also gone from the guest bedroom, she wasn't coming back. Apparently, he wasn't important enough to even get a note saying it's been fun or whatever.

Tristan sat at the kitchen island, hunched over his coffee as he tried to temper his anger. The woman had no business taking off on her own when she had dangerous men gunning for her. If Kade was home, Tristan would have him shadow Skye. His brother could be a ghost when he wanted. She'd never know he was tailing her.

Parker walked in after taking Everly to school. "Morning."

Tristan grunted.

"What rained on your parade? Or should I say who?"

"The who would be right." He'd missed her in his bed. Why couldn't she see it was where she belonged? He knew why she was pushing him away. It was a misguided attempt to protect him from the fallout of the gossip that would spread like a wildfire thanks to Mason. Skye was a smart woman, but in this she was being just plain stubborn. Tristan wanted to shake some sense into her. With him by her side, they could stare down anyone who dared point a finger at her.

Parker brought his smoothie to the island. "Marion Benetti cornered me when I was dropping off Everly. She wanted to know if it was true that the sheriff was dirty."

The anger he'd calmed somewhat amped up again. He added Marion Benetti to his list of people he was going to make miserable. "What'd you say?"

"I told her I was pretty sure the sheriff bathed every day."

Tristan snorted. "Good answer."

"Where's Skylar? She's usually down here having coffee with us."

"Beats me. She's gone. Took all her stuff with her."

"And she didn't say anything? She was here this morning. Everly said they had a picnic under the magnolia tree."

"Not a word. She spooked."

"How so?"

"Fucking Mason ran his mouth at the Kitchen last night when we were there." He told Parker what Mason had said. "I messed up." He scrubbed a hand through his hair. "I was furious with Mason for running his mouth, and instead of staying with Skye to face everyone, I chased after him. When I got back to the restaurant, she was gone."

"And you what? Just came home and cried in your beer?"

"No, I did not. I found her at Earl's. We talked, and

she said we were over. She thinks the town is going to turn on her, and she's protecting me. She doesn't want me to be guilty by association."

"I have to respect her for that, but she's wrong. You don't need protecting. So what now?"

"Now I take Fuzz to her. That's providing she's at the sheriff's office. Then I pass the word to all her deputies and my officers to keep an eye on her. I wish those men from Florida would show their faces so we can put an end to their threats."

"And then you'll go after your girl?"

"Why? So she can push me away like she's done for the past year? She wasn't willing to fight for us, and I can't go down that road again." Someday, this pain in his chest would stop hurting. He prayed that was true. And when his eyes burned with unshed tears, he squeezed them shut. He didn't want to cry in front of his brother.

Parker came to him and wrapped his arms around him. "You know, men are allowed to cry. I did."

As if his heart had been given permission to mourn, he pressed his face against Parker's shoulder and let the tears come. "Sorry," he said a few minutes later.

"What good's a brother if you can't slobber all over his shirt? Just don't make a habit of it."

As Parker intended him to do, he laughed. "Promise." He grabbed a paper towel and wiped his face. "You ever going to tell us what happened in France that made you cry?"

"Someday, when it doesn't hurt so much to talk about it."

Was that what he had to look forward to? Years of the kind of sadness in his eyes that he saw in his brother's?

* * *

Tristan steeled himself as he and Fuzz walked into the sheriff's office. He ignored his relief at seeing her safely at her desk. "Sheriff."

"Chief. What can I do for you?"

So this was how they were going to play it. If she could pretend his hands had never touched her skin, that his mouth had never explored her body, and he'd never been inside her, then so could he. Another layer of ice coated his heart. That was good. The thicker the ice, the deader that organ would be.

"You forgot to take your sidekick with you when you left this morning." He put Fuzz's leash on her desk. "Keep him with you." He wanted to ask where she was staying, but he didn't. It was no longer his business. "Stay, Fuzz."

"Tristan, I…"

He stopped at the door, then turned and waited.

"I wish…" She shook her head.

Either he was fooling himself, or that was regret in her eyes. "I wish, too," he softly said, then left.

Johnny arrived as he was walking to his car. "Morning, Chief."

"Johnny. Glad I caught you. You're still sticking by the sheriff's side when she has to leave the building, right?"

"I am, whether she likes it or not."

"Good. Remind everyone to keep their eyes open when they're out patrolling. These people, if they are in the area, aren't going to wait much longer to make a move."

"I'll do that. If any of us notices any strangers that seem suspicious, I'll let you know."

"Appreciate it. Catch you later."

Before he drove away from the sheriff's department, he called Kade and got his voice mail. "Hey, brother. I don't know if you're at the base or out of the country. Wish you were home, though. We have some shit going down that would be right up your alley. If you're around, call if you get a minute. Wherever you are, you better keep your ass safe."

Shortly after he left the parking lot, a black pickup truck crossed the no-passing line and blew by him. Tristan lit his blue lights and turned on his siren. The pickup pulled over, and before approaching the driver, he called in the plate number.

He walked up to the driver's door, and staying back behind the handle, he tapped on the window. "Roll it down." The man wore a ball cap and had his head turned away but obeyed. In the instant that the man showed his face and Tristan recognized the driver and reached for his gun, Homer Drake leaned out the window and tased him.

That hurt was his first thought as he fell to the ground. His second was anger that he'd let Drake trick him. It pissed him off that the asshole knew to avoid his bulletproof vest. But he had to get up before Drake got out of the truck.

He willed his hand to pull the darts out of his upper arm. God help him, he tried. If they took him, they'd use him to control Skye. He couldn't let that happen, but he couldn't make his hand work fast enough. Drake slapped a cloth over his face, and his world turned black.

Chapter Forty-Six

Be at 3244 Laurel Lane in three hours with my money.
Come alone.

Skye stared at the text. At last, Thomas Grant was making his move. He was a fool if he thought she'd come
anywhere near him alone. It seemed stupid of him to
give her his location and a three-hour window, and from
what she knew of him, he wasn't stupid.

She logged on to Google Maps and entered the address. Laurel Lane was a rural area, mostly cabins and
mobile homes. The aerial view of the address showed a
small cabin set back in the woods. She texted him back.

I don't have your money. Never did.

Three hours, Sheriff. That's plenty of time to get my
money from the bank or wherever you have it hidden.

Well, it was worth a try. What did Grant have up his
sleeve? Before his deadline, her deputies, Tristan's officers, and his SWAT team would have the house surrounded. At least now they knew where the man was.
She called Tristan's cell and got his voice mail. She left

a message to call her, that it was urgent. She was calling the police department main number when her phone dinged with another text, one containing a photo. When she opened it, her heart fell to her stomach.

"Oh, God. Tristan." He was tied to a chair, one eye was swollen shut, and his lip was bleeding from a cut. Someone standing out of range of the camera held a Glock 22—the kind of gun Tristan carried—to his head.

This was her fault. She'd brought these people here. The text accompanying the photo sent an ice-cold chill through her.

In case you need a reminder to come alone.

How had they gotten him? She had no choice but to go, and without backup. Her phone chimed with another text, and, God, she didn't want to open it. But she had to.

"Oh, no. No. No. No."

The photo was of her and Everly having their picnic that morning. Someone had been watching them, and her stomach took a sickening roll at the thought of those bastards involving Everly in this.

"Please God, tell me what to do." Fuzz got up from his bed and came to her. He put his paw on her leg and whined. "We have to sneak out of here." She couldn't have Johnny involved in this. If she showed up with him, with anyone, they'd shoot Tristan.

She collected supplies: an extra box of ammo, a Taser, the tactical knife Dustin had given her. He had one like it, and she'd admired it once, so he'd gifted one to her for her birthday one year. The knife went in her boot, the ammo and Taser in a pocket of her pants. She turned off her police radio.

"Let's go, Fuzz. Hope you're good at being sneaky." She clipped the leash to his collar. Fortunately, her office was at the back of the building, near the rear door. She peeked out, and seeing no one in the hallway, she stepped out, then closed her office door. Hopefully, her people would think she was in there but didn't want to be disturbed.

Fuzz, seeming to pick up on her tension stayed close to her leg, and they slipped outside unnoticed and were able to get around the building and to her car without being seen. As soon as she was out of the parking lot, she turned her radio back on.

She had three hours to come up with a plan. But first she had to call Parker. Above all else, Everly had to be protected.

"Hey, Skylar. To what do I owe the pleasure?"

"Is Everly at school?"

"Yeah, why?"

"Don't panic, but I need you to go get her. Don't go home. Go…" Where? *Think, Skye. Where would they be safe?* "Um, take her to the firehouse. Both of you stay there."

"What's going on? Is something wrong with Everly?"

"Just go right now. I'll meet you there. And don't say anything to anyone, okay?"

"I won't, but only because I trust you. If it involves my daughter, I want to know what's going on."

"Get her so I know she's safe, then we'll talk."

Was anyone following her? She kept her eyes on the rearview mirror as she headed to town. So far, she hadn't seen anyone suspicious, but she wasn't taking any chances. Her first instinct had been to figure out how to rescue Tristan by herself, but that would be a reckless thing to do. She didn't know how many men she'd be facing, and she doubted Grant had any intention of letting her or Tristan go.

Parker deserved to know his brother was being held hostage by a drug dealer. She wouldn't let Parker involve himself in the rescue. His job was to keep his daughter safe. But like his brothers, he was smart, and she valued his input. Grant or Drake or someone she didn't know about could be watching her, so she went straight to the bank, parked her car in their lot, then she and Fuzz went inside. If she was being followed, let whoever it was think she was getting Grant's money.

The two tellers had customers and weren't paying attention to her. So far, so good. The loan officer was in his office on the phone, and she waved as she passed by. He smiled and waved back. Annie, the bank manager, was in her office by herself.

Skye stopped at her open door. "Annie, I need you to let me out the back."

"The back door?"

"Yes." She would have preferred to pass through the bank unnoticed, but the rear door was alarmed. "It's official police business. I'll also need you to let me back in in a little while."

"Can I ask what this is about? Is the bank going to be robbed?"

"No and no. I can't tell you now, but I promise when the situation is taken care of, I'll tell you. There's nothing for you to worry about."

"Okay." She opened her drawer and took out a ring of keys. "You really have me curious." She frowned at Fuzz. "Why do you have the chief's dog? Those two are never apart."

"Fuzz is on loan to me for the day. I don't know how long I'll be, but I'll call you when I need you to let me back in. Do you have a direct line?"

"No, but call my cell phone."

Annie gave her the number, and Skye put it in her phone. When they reached the door, Annie put the key in the exit alarm mounted on the wall. "Okay, you're good to go."

"Thanks. And keep this between us, okay? It's more important than you can imagine."

"I will."

After the door closed behind her, Skye walked down the alley until she reached the Baptist church. All she had to do was get to the other side of the church without being seen, and she'd be at the firehouse. She and Fuzz crossed the alley and skirted around the church. They walked into the firehouse as Parker, driving his fire chief's vehicle, pulled into a bay.

"Miss Skylar," Everly yelled after Parker unbuckled her seatbelt. "My daddy picked me up in his fire car and it didn't have a booster seat, so I got a seatbelt like a big person."

"Well, aren't you special?"

"I am." She beamed. "And I got to leave school before the bell, and I get to come to work with my daddy." She noticed Fuzz. "Fuzz!" She wrapped her arms around his neck, giggling when he licked her chin. "Is Uncle Tris here, too?"

"Not right now, sweetie," Skye said. She had to save Tristan. She would not be the reason this little girl got her heart broken.

Parker put his hands on his daughter's shoulders. "What's going on, Skylar?"

"Is there someone here who can watch her while we talk?" Everly didn't need to know her uncle was in trouble.

"Yeah. Wait for me in my office."

"Make sure you tell your people not to let her out of their sight."

His lips thinned and his eyes turned cold. "Someone messes with my daughter and it will be the last thing on this earth they do."

"Who messed with me, Daddy?"

He kneeled in front of her, and those eyes that were ice-cold a second ago turned soft. "No one, baby girl. I'm going to let you play with the guys for a little while."

"Yay! Can we cook something?"

"I think you can probably talk them into that."

While Parker took Everly to the back, Skye took Fuzz with her to his office. What if she couldn't rescue Tristan? She'd had a higher-than-a-kite druggie point a gun at her once. She hadn't been as scared then as she was now. If she failed to save the man she was in love with, she didn't know how she'd live with herself. That was if she did manage to live through this.

She'd been so stupid to worry that people would gossip about her. Who cared? She would either keep her job or she wouldn't, but losing Tristan would devastate her. She wanted to find a bed, climb in, pull the covers over her head, and have a good cry, but she didn't have the luxury of doing that. Somehow, she had to save her man.

Please, God, don't let it be too late.

Parker came in, closing the door behind him. "Start talking. Why is my daughter in danger?"

"They have Tristan."

"Who has him?"

"The drug dealer who thinks I took his money." She brought up the texts, then handed him her phone.

He grimaced at the picture of Tristan. "The hell? They beat him."

"Scroll down."

"I'll kill them." He handed her phone back. "No one threatens my daughter. Let's go."

"No. You can't. If they see you, they'll kill him. I have to do it. You need to stay with Everly. Make sure they don't get to her." She blew out a breath. "I don't know how, but I'll get him away from them."

"How much did you supposedly take?"

"I have no idea how much Thomas Grant thinks I stole."

"Take a guess."

She shrugged. "It had to be enough for Grant to come looking for it. But we're wasting time. I need to make a plan."

"Pay them."

"What? I don't have that kind of money, however much it might be."

"I do. Think a hundred thousand would do it? I can get my hands on that right now. More, it would take some time." He paced to one end of his office, then back. "Actually, it might be good if it's more. You can tell Grant, or whoever's collecting his money, that that's all you could get this fast. If it's not enough, then they need to give you more time."

"That might work, but if it doesn't, I don't see Grant letting either one of us go." She doubted Grant intended to let either one of them go even if it was enough money.

Parker's phone played "Secret Agent Man." He pulled his cell from his pocket. "That's Kade. There's no one better to help us come up with a plan. I'll put him on speaker."

"Wish you were here, brother," Parker said. "We have a situation."

"Tristan called a while ago, said about the same thing, but he's not answering his phone."

"He's not answering because some assholes are holding him hostage. They beat him up, Kade."

"Tell me everything," he said, his voice turning hard and menacing.

"Skylar's here with me. I'll let her fill you in." He handed her his phone. "I need to check on Everly. Make sure the boys are keeping her close."

"I'm so sorry, Kade. This is my fault."

"How so?"

She told him about Danny, the rumors, and Grant's demand today for his money. Her phone rang, Johnny's name coming up. "Hold on a minute." She switched phones, leaving the line open on Parker's phone. "I can't talk right now, Johnny."

"Where are you? I'm supposed to be with you at all times if you leave the building."

"I know, but it couldn't be helped. Listen, I'm with Parker, so I'm safe, but I have to go."

"The chief's missing." She put him on speaker so Kade could hear. "Vee called, wanting to know if he was with you. His car's on the side of the road about three miles from here, and he's nowhere to be found."

He must have stopped to help someone or made a traffic stop, except it was Grant or one of his people. "Johnny, I know, and I'm handling it."

"Not by yourself you're not. Where are you, Sheriff?"

"I'm sorry, but I have to go." She disconnected.

When this was over, she'd explain why she couldn't include him. Hopefully he wasn't one to hold a grudge.

"How long now before you're supposed to meet Grant?" Kade asked.

She checked her watch. "Two hours and twenty-five minutes."

"I'll see you in about an hour and a half."

"Wait, what?"

"Are you at the firehouse?"

"Yes, but—"

"Stay there, Skylar." He disconnected.

Huh?

Chapter Forty-Seven

The next time Tristan saw Kade, he was going to give his brother a big smack right on his lips. Kade had taught both him and Parker how to get out of zip tie handcuffs. For that, he would be forever grateful.

The first mistake Drake had made was to cuff Tristan's hands in front of him. He still could have broken the ties if his hands were behind him, but it would have been much harder. Unfortunately, they'd roughed him up before he had a chance to break the ties, or he would have fought back. Now his hands were free, but his legs were duct taped to a chair. He couldn't do anything about that unless they left him alone.

They were in a rental cabin about ten miles outside of town, one of the many the Mackel family owned around the area. Tristan found that darkly amusing. If Miss Mabel knew a major drug dealer, his enforcer, and a dirty cop were using one of her vacation cabins for criminal activity, she'd march in and vanquish all three with her cane.

Since Miss Mabel wouldn't be coming to the rescue, maybe he could stir things up, get them to turn against each other. "Skye didn't take your money, Mr. Grant."

It left a sour taste to be polite to a major drug dealer, but it probably wouldn't be smart to call him dirtbag.

He focused his attention on Pretty Boy. Yeah, he was here. Whether by choice or force, he didn't know. "If I had to guess, I'd say Danny was the one with sticky fingers. What's your last name, anyway, Pretty Boy?"

"Shut the fuck up." Danny punched him, and the ring he wore sliced open Tristan's bottom lip.

It took every bit of his control to keep his hands on his lap, the severed zip ties hidden, and not strike out at the man. His right eye was already swollen shut from when he'd tried to fight Drake taping his legs to the chair.

"As I was saying, Mr. Grant, you might want to ask Danny here where he was during that raid." Tristan lifted his shoulder and wiped his bleeding mouth over his shirt. "I say that because there was an investigation, and Skye was cleared by her department of having sticky fingers. Did Danny tell you that?" He glanced at Pretty Boy, who was shooting daggers at him.

He turned his attention back to Grant. "No, I don't think he did. Members of her team were with her at all times, and they all said they never saw any money at their location." He didn't know if that was true, but it sounded good.

"Another thing you might want to think about. Sheriff Morgan was engaged to your friend here but broke up with him a few weeks before the raid on your property. Caught Pretty Boy cheating on her." He gave Danny a disgusted look. "Doesn't sound like such an honorable man, does he? Want to know what I think?"

"By all means, share your opinion," Grant said, sounding a bit bored.

"I'd bet serious money that Danny boy's ego didn't take that well and he wanted revenge on her. What better way to get it than to put her in your line of sight? Added benefit of that, it takes attention away from him and his sticky fingers." Tristan decided it was time to shut up and let all that sink in with Grant.

Grant eyed Danny, and Tristan could see that the drug dealer was considering the possibility that Danny had been lying to him all this time. Passing Thomas Grant on the street, one would peg him as an accountant or maybe an attorney. He was tall and thin, blond hair and blue eyes, and wore a button-up blue shirt and gray pants. He did not look like a man who headed up a large drug operation. Tristan decided the man was very smart and surrounded himself with mean-ass enforcers like Homer Drake.

"He's making that up." Danny took a few steps back, distancing himself from Grant. "I know for a fact Skye took the money. She told me she had it."

"You're a lying piece of shit." Tristan shook his head, disgusted with the man. "Nothing worse than a bad cop." He glanced at Grant. "How much you missing, anyway?"

Grant turned to Drake, who had been leaning against the wall with his arms crossed and his gaze focused on Danny. "Take Mr. Church's picture." Then Grant raised his hand and pressed the barrel of Tristan's own gun to his head. "Smile for the camera, Mr. Church."

Not likely. He stared straight into the lens, refusing to flinch from the press of the gun to his head. There had been suspicion in Drake's eyes as he looked at Danny. His hope was for Grant and Drake to turn on Pretty Boy. Maybe beat the truth out of him.

Grant nodded when Drake held up the phone, showing him the picture. "Send that and the one you took this morning to our lovely sheriff. Give her this address and tell her she has three hours to bring me my money."

Which she did not have. And what picture had they taken this morning? It wasn't of him, so what did they have—along with one of him sporting a closed eye and split lip—that would make sure she'd appear? He knew, and she knew, that she didn't have Grant's money.

It wouldn't matter to Skye that she couldn't arrive bearing a briefcase full of thousand-dollar bills, and it wouldn't matter that she'd ended things with him. She'd take one look at that photo of his battered face and mount a rescue. And if he knew her as well as he thought he did, she'd come alone after getting that message.

"Think this will get your girlfriend's attention," Grant said, showing him the phone screen.

Tristan saw blood boiling red. "You touch one hair on that little girl's head, and I swear on all I hold holy that you'll live to regret it. I will come at you with everything I have." He prayed he lived through this so he could follow through on that threat.

"You especially should fear her father. He'll tear apart with his bare hands everything in his way of getting to you. And if that doesn't scare you, my brother Kade should. He's the one you won't see coming until it's too late. Smirk all you want, Mr. Grant, but you do not want to be on a Delta Force operator's radar. I promise you that." He turned his gaze on each man in turn. "None of you do, and he will come after all of you. Never doubt that."

The three men shared uneasy glances. He didn't

think they were afraid of him, but if he got out of this alive, they should be. As for Parker, a father's rage and thirst for revenge knew no bounds. He hoped they realized that. But it was the threat of having a Delta Force operator coming at them that had them apprehensive. They were smart to be worried.

"You know, thinking about it, Kade's still going to be pissed that you messed up his brother's pretty face. You might want to consider letting me go and crawling back under your rock. We'll just call today a misunderstanding."

"You're a funny man, Mr. Church, but if you think you're scaring me, you'd be wrong. I'm not leaving without my money." Grant pointed the gun at Tristan. "Bang."

Tristan stared him down, refusing to flinch. His most fervent wish right now was for Kade to have been home. This would all be over now.

Chapter Forty-Eight

When Parker returned to his office, Skye grabbed his arm. "Your brother's on the way."

"They let Tristan go?"

"No, Kade. He said he'd be here in an hour and a half."

"Thank God."

"I don't know how he's making that happen, but I agree."

Kade could be a ghost when he wanted. She'd watched him in action at their drills. Too many times when she had thought he was at one end of their fake town, he'd materialized right in front of her. It was spooky.

"Knowing Kade, he'll commandeer the fastest helicopter on the base."

She wouldn't put it past him. "Okay, we have a little over an hour before he arrives, and we need a plan. I've been thinking, what if we get a dye pack from the bank and put it in a briefcase? When Grant opens it to make sure all his money is there, it explodes in his face."

"Does our bank have them? I can't remember there ever being a bank robbery here."

"I don't know." She took out her phone and called

Annie. "Question, do you have dye packs?" She nodded at Parker, letting him know they did. "Great, I'm going to need one." She cut Annie off. "No, the bank isn't going to be robbed, and yes, I'll tell you why I need it when I can." Okay, that wasn't what she wanted to hear. "Their dye packs are triggered by a sensor at the bank door and are set to go off twenty seconds later," she told Parker.

"Maybe we can retrigger it somehow. Kade would probably know."

"Annie, I'll get back to you." That was disappointing. If the pack exploded in Grant's face, they could use the diversion to take the men down and rescue Tristan.

"On the off chance the dye pack's trigger can't be reset, I'm going to go ahead and get the money," Parker said. "I hope they can come up with a hundred thou."

"I don't think we need that much. Twenty-five thousand in hundreds and twenties or whatever denominations they can come up with will work. Even ten thousand if we put ones, fives, and tens under hundred-dollar bills will look like a lot. We just need it to buy me some time once I'm inside."

Parker was pacing again, and the tension in the room was agitating Fuzz. Fuzz knew something was up and was pacing right along with Parker.

"I'm going to take Fuzz with me," she said. "If Grant or whoever is with him goes for me or tries to hurt Tristan, he won't like that." And please don't let her get Tristan's dog killed, but Fuzz could be the difference between success or failure. He could give her the few seconds she might need to win this war. Because that was what it was…a war.

"I don't like this, Skylar."

"Tell me about it, but we don't have a choice. Go get the money. Ask Annie if she has a briefcase you can use."

"I have one here." He stopped his pacing, planting himself in front of her. "Don't get some idea to be heroic and go deal with this yourself. You be here when I get back." He stared at her for a moment, then said, "If you haven't figured it out yet, my brother loves you."

"I know," she whispered. And she did. But would he forgive her for not believing in him?

While Parker was at the bank, Skye called Dustin. She told him what was going down and what she was going to do. If she died, she wanted to make sure that Danny didn't walk away unscathed. "No matter what happens, don't let him get away with this," she pleaded.

"I promise you, Skye, his life as he knows it is over. As soon as we hang up, I'm calling his captain. I wish I could order you to not go through with your plan, but I'm not your boss now, and even if I was, you'd do it anyway. Stay safe, you hear me?"

"Yeah, I hear you." They signed off. Her legs refused to hold her up anymore, and she planted her butt on the floor. Fuzz didn't waste any time landing on her lap. "I know," she said, burying her face in his neck fur. "I'm worried, too." What if…

No! She couldn't think like that. They would rescue Tristan. Everly would have her uncle, and Parker and Kade would have their brother. Nothing less was acceptable.

The thought that she'd been trying to keep out pushed its way in. This was all on her. She was the reason

Tristan's life was in danger. If the worst happened, she would never forgive herself. Dangerous men who didn't blink at killing someone were here because of her. She already didn't forgive herself for that.

She didn't know how long she and Fuzz cuddled, taking strength from each other. Well, her taking strength from Fuzz. She wasn't sure what she was giving him other than her fears and tears.

At some point, Parker returned, carrying a large bank bag. "Why are you on the floor?"

Because she and Fuzz were having a moment? She lifted her hand, and he helped her up. "Fuzz and I were making rescue plans. How much do you have there?"

"Annie was able to come up with twenty thousand without us giving her prior notice. I had to tell her what it was for, but she promised to keep quiet."

"Good." She glanced at her watch. "Kade should be here soon."

"I'm here." Kade walked in and right behind him were two men who, like Kade, were made of muscles. All three wore black T-shirts and black cargo pants, and one of them was covered in tattoos. They each had sidearms at their waists, carried duffel bags, and one had a long gun slung over his shoulder. Danger radiated from the three men.

Kade came straight to her and wrapped his arms around her. "We're going to get him back, Skylar." He then slung an arm over Parker's shoulders. "Big brother was always getting us out of trouble. It's our turn to return the favor." He pointed to the man with the tattoos. "That's Viper. He's our sniper." He lifted a chin toward the other one. "This dude here is Cupcake. He can make anything out of nothing."

"Cupcake?" Really?

"Don't ask," Cupcake said, amusement in his eyes.

Kade rolled his eyes. "A girl he was dating when he joined the team used to say he was sweeter than a cupcake."

"I keep telling you, dude, I'm not sweet."

They might call him Cupcake, but he was no less dangerous looking than Kade and Viper. "How'd you get here so fast?"

"Better not to ask that, darlin'," Viper said. "Deniability and all that." He winked.

"Bring me up to date," Kade said.

Parker showed them the money. "We don't know how much this Grant person expects, but this will get Skylar in the door. She had a great idea to put a dye pack in the briefcase."

"It would be the perfect diversion when it exploded, but there's a problem." She told them how it was triggered by a sensor at the bank's door. "We were hoping it could be set to go off when the briefcase is opened, but I guess that's out."

Kade shook his head. "Not necessarily. Cupcake, you think you can rig something up?"

"Affirmative, but I'll have to go to the bank and disarm the trigger. Then I can bring the pack back here and rig something up. How much time do we have?"

Skye glanced at the clock on the wall. "I'm going to have to leave in about thirty-five minutes to get there by the deadline."

"No problem," Cupcake said.

"The three of us need to beat feet in twenty, so we can get set up before Skylar arrives at the target house." Kade put his hand on Parker's shoulder. "Take Cupcake to the bank while Viper and I go over with Skylar how this is going to go down."

After the two left, Kade said, "Here's the plan."

Chapter Forty-Nine

Where were they? Skye resisted searching for Viper, who was supposed to be set up in a tree with his sniper rifle. The small log cabin set back in the trees was cute. She could imagine honeymooners sitting in the swing on the front porch as they enjoyed a glass of wine. Normally, she'd like this kind of isolation if she was on vacation, but not today when knowing who was waiting for her inside. Kade said he'd be somewhere near the front of the house, and Cupcake would be at the back.

She grabbed the briefcase, then exited the car. Fuzz followed her out. Cupcake had attached a thin blade to the bottom of his pink collar, the color intended to catch Tristan's attention. Kade said the collar would tip off Tristan that he was here because he had once, as a practical joke, painted Tristan's fingernails and toenails pink while he slept. How Cupcake acquired a pink collar in such a short time was a mystery. The plan for Fuzz was that he would go straight for Tristan as soon as he saw him. Hopefully, Fuzz was onboard with that plan.

In the photo Grant had sent of Tristan, his hands weren't visible, so they didn't know if they were free or cuffed. Kade said if Tristan's hands were bound, he'd be able to free them. She hoped that was true and that he'd manage to find the blade hidden in Fuzz's collar.

Because they knew her weapons would be taken away as soon as she arrived, she wasn't carrying her gun or the Taser. She sure missed having them, but along with the knife she'd put in her boot, the boys had given her a clever necklace that had a long turquoise tube. One end of the tube was a nozzle and inside the cylinder was pepper spray. Another Cupcake invention.

She was also wearing comms in her ears and one of her shirt buttons had been replaced with a listening device, both of which she greatly appreciated since they could hear what was happening inside the house and she could hear them if they needed to give her direction. The comms were the smallest she'd ever seen, and she was also wearing her hair down. Hopefully, no one would think to look in her ears.

Parker and two of his EMTs were in an ambulance a half mile away. She hoped they wouldn't need them, but this could easily go south. She also understood Parker's need to be close to his brothers should one of them get hurt.

It was showtime.

You got this! She took a deep breath, steeled her nerves as she headed for the door. All she had to do was follow the plan and this would be over in a matter of minutes.

Drake stepped out of the house. "You're late."

"Three minutes is barely late. It took time to get the money."

He eyed the briefcase. "I'll take that."

"No, not until I see the police chief with my own eyes."

"You think I can't take it away from you?"

"I'm sure you can, but do a girl a favor and let her feel she has some control over this situation."

He rolled his eyes. "Whatever. The dog stays out here."

"The dog's a big baby, and he suffers from separation anxiety. He'll raise hell trying to get to me. I doubt you want that kind of attention from the neighbors." Not that there were neighbors close enough to worry about, but it was what they'd decided to say, knowing Fuzz would be objected to. Hopefully, they wouldn't want to chance getting any attention.

"If he tries anything, I'll shoot him. Come up here."

Fuzz let out a low growl, and she put her hand on his head. *Not yet, boy.* He quieted, and she walked onto the porch.

"Give me your gun."

"I don't have one. You'd only take it from me, and I'm partial to my gun."

"Hands on the wall."

She'd known one of them would frisk her, but she hated the thought of his hands on her. She almost warned him not to touch her inappropriately, but that would only cause him to do just that. When his hands were on her, she stared so hard at the wall to keep from shuddering in disgust that she half expected to burn a hole in the wood. Her biggest worry was that he'd find the knife in her boot. He did run his fingers around the inside, at the top, and not finding an ankle holster, he stood.

"Go inside."

There were two windows each on the front and left walls, and the kitchen was to the right with a smaller window over the sink. Viper, after studying the house on some top-secret Army site, had told her not to stand in front of any of the windows, especially the two on the left wall. She paused inside to get her bearings. The cabin was a rental, the furniture the kind that wouldn't cost much to replace if vacationers ruined something.

The man she assumed to be Thomas Grant stood next to a stone fireplace with his arm resting on the mantel. Danny, the lying bastard, sat on the couch and had his feet up on the coffee table. That was her laptop next to him. At least she knew for sure now who'd set fire to her apartment. She glared at him, then her gaze sought out Tristan. He sat in a dining room chair that had been pushed against the wall. Good. He wasn't in front of a window. By his scowl, he wasn't happy she was putting herself in danger.

Fuzz was instantly aware that Tristan was in the room. She'd expected him to be excited at seeing Tristan, and that had worried her. She didn't want him to bark his excitement and race to Tristan. It seemed, though, that he understood this was an unusual situation, or at least he sensed the tension in the room. With his ears back and after a quick glance at Thomas Grant, then Danny, he took a few steps toward Tristan.

"I don't recall including a dog in my invitation for you to visit," Grant said.

Doing her best to appear unafraid, she snorted. "One can refuse an invitation. What I received from you was a command to appear."

"Told you she had a smart mouth," Danny said.

"And you're a lying bastard and the biggest mistake of my life." She turned her attention back to Grant and gave him the same excuse for bringing Fuzz that she'd given Drake. As they talked, Fuzz had eased over to Tristan. "He knows the chief," she said.

Tristan stared at the pink collar, then lifted his gaze to her, a question in his eyes. *Kade's here?*

Well, Kade sure knew his brother. She gave him a minuscule nod. The relief in his eyes was instant. To keep the attention away from Tristan and Fuzz, she stepped farther into the room. Drake had positioned himself behind her, against the wall. She repositioned herself where she could see all three men.

"Exactly how much do you think I took, Mr. Grant?"

"Well, since you took his money, you would know," Danny said.

She ignored him. She wanted to know how much Danny had stolen because, assuming she would walk out of this house alive, she was going to make sure his captain and his fellow officers knew what a slimeball thief he was.

Grant's gaze landed on Danny for a moment, and it seemed to her that he was trying to work out a puzzle. Was he starting to be suspicious of Danny? Grant wasn't at all what she'd expected. She'd had an image in her mind of thug, a rough bully-looking man. This man could be mistaken for a businessman, maybe a banker. Although he wasn't scary looking like Drake, she sensed Grant was the more dangerous one, a venomous snake you didn't see until it was too late.

"To answer your question, Sheriff, there had better be a half million in that briefcase." He glanced at Danny again.

She almost gasped. *You stupid fool, Danny.* "Well, I wasn't able to retrieve it all in the time you gave me, so you'll have to allow me one more day."

"Put the briefcase on the coffee table, then step away from it," Kade said in her ear.

It would be a miracle if her heart didn't pound itself right out of her chest, she thought as she set the briefcase down. "It's all yours."

Chapter Fifty

What was the plan? It was reassuring to know Kade was here, but Tristan wished he'd left Skye out of it and had just come in, guns blazing. There would be a plan, though, that much he knew. Other than a brief glance and slight nod to confirm Kade's presence, Skye had ignored him.

He didn't know what the strategy was, but they weren't going to all smile at each other as he and Skye traipsed out of here. That was a fact. For one, there was no way there was a half million in that briefcase. If he had to guess, it would be that Parker had contributed to however much was in it.

Was Parker here, too? He hoped not. His baby brother was one hell of a fire chief, but a warrior he was not. Not that Parker would agree to stay out of it knowing Tristan's life was at stake.

Kade, who *was* an elite warrior, and also devious, had sent a message with the pink collar. All Tristan had to do was interpret it. While no one was paying attention to him, he ran his hand over the collar, startling a little when he pricked a finger on something sharp. He caught himself before he grinned. *You really are a devious bastard, brother.*

While everyone's attention was on Skye and the briefcase she was setting on the coffee table, Tristan palmed the blade he found in Fuzz's collar. Using Fuzz as cover by pretending to pet him, he slipped the hand with the blade down his leg and sliced the duct tape binding him to the chair. Then he freed his other leg. Now to be ready for whatever was about to happen, because something was. Since he wasn't privy to the plan, his only objective was to protect Skye when the bullets started flying.

The first thing he'd noticed when she'd walked in was that her hair was down. Her hair wouldn't be down unless there was a reason, and the only thing he could think of was that she was hiding comms in her ears. If so, that made him feel marginally better, as she would be taking direction from Kade.

She'd set the briefcase on the coffee table and was now backing away from it. He eyed the briefcase, then her. She didn't want to be anywhere near the thing. Suspicion grew, and he wondered what surprises Kade had planned for them.

Grant was watching her, too, and he narrowed his eyes. The man wasn't a fool, and he was coming to the same conclusion Tristan was. The briefcase was rigged somehow. Tristan measured the distance between him and Skye and how many steps it would take to get to her.

Pretty Boy reached for the briefcase, and as he lifted the latches, Grant yelled, "No!"

His warning came too late. The briefcase exploded in Pretty Boy's face, and red smoke swirled around him. Then chaos erupted as everything happened at once.

Pretty Boy screamed.

Tristan dived for Skye as Drake reached for her with a wicked-looking knife.

A window exploded, and Drake's knife flew out of his hand.

The front and back doors of the cabin slammed open and two men in all black, their faces covered, entered, guns drawn. Tristan recognized one of the masked men as his brother and assumed the man who'd come in from the back was also an operator.

Grant got to Skye before Tristan could. He put a gun to her head and pulled her against him as he backed the two of them to the wall.

The situation was a powder keg ready to blow, and Tristan didn't want Grant to get a twitchy trigger finger.

"I told you that you should be afraid of my brother, Mr. Grant. He even brought a friend, who I'm guessing is just as deadly," Tristan said. "You won't walk out of here a free man, so the best thing you can do right now is let her go."

"Not happening. She's my ticket out of here." His gaze darted from Kade to the other man. "Move away from the door, or I'll shoot her."

"Dead man walking," Kade's partner muttered. Neither man moved.

When Drake put his hands on the floor to try to push up, Tristan stomped on his wounded hand, causing Drake to scream. "Freeze, asshole." Drake froze.

"You okay?" Tristan asked Skye. Where he'd expected to see fear in her eyes, all he saw was a pissed-off woman.

"Just peachy." She was playing with a green cylinder hanging from a thin chain, an odd necklace he'd never seen her wear before.

"I'll take it from here," Pretty Boy said, standing up, his face red from the dye pack. His face was probably hurting like hell, too. Good.

"Excuse me?" Skye glared at him. "You'll take what from here?"

"The prisoners. I've been working undercover."

"You're a big fat liar, Danny." She glanced at Kade. "Do me a favor and put a bullet between his eyes."

"I will if you want me to."

"While this is highly entertaining, all of you shut up," Grant said.

"No." She huffed an irritated breath. "You burned my apartment up, and now you're threatening to put a bullet through my brain. I think I'm entitled to have my say. I did not take your money. Danny did, then started the rumor that it was me to throw off suspicion from him."

"That's a lie!" Pretty Boy yelled.

"Funny, but I believe her." Grant turned the gun on Danny and shot him in the chest, then whipped the weapon back to her head. "No one steals from me."

A beat of shocked silence followed as the dirty cop fell to the floor, then Skye said, "Well, Mr. Grant, not only was your trip here wasted, but now it looks like you're going to be a guest in the chief's jail for murder. Or you could end this farce, let us get him to a hospital, and maybe save his life. Then you might avoid the electric chair."

What was she up to? Grant was getting angrier by the second. She caught Tristan's eyes and slowly caressed the cylinder, and all he could think was that she was walking around with a bomb of some sort around her neck. He might put his fist through his brother's face for that. What if it blew up on her?

"Shut the fuck up," Grant yelled, finally losing his cool.

"Okay. Shutting up." She yanked on the tube, breaking the chain. She winked at Tristan, then she lifted the green thing over her shoulder and pointed it at Grant's face.

Tristan had no idea what she did, but Grant stumbled as he slapped a hand over his eyes. Tristan pushed her away from the man, and he and Grant fell to the floor as they wrestled for the weapon, Tristan trying to get the gun away, and Grant doing his damnedest to point it at Tristan.

Fuzz, the dog whose dislike list was growing, added another person, clamping his teeth down on the back of Grant's leg, his growls the most vicious Tristan had ever heard from him.

"Get him off me!" Grant screamed a second before his gun went off. Unfortunately for him, Tristan had won the strength contest and the gun was pointed back at Grant.

Minor problem, though. His other arm was pushed against Grant's chest, and the bullet traveled through his forearm before tearing its way through Grant's heart. Damn, that hurt. Still tangled up with Grant, Tristan met Skye's gaze. He didn't know what he hoped to see in her eyes, but it wasn't there.

Her face paled of all color, and she shook her head as she stepped back. "You're bleeding."

"A little." He pushed up from Grant...and looked down at the man. A dead Grant. Even though the drug dealer had probably caused many overdose deaths, Tristan would have preferred to see the man face justice and life in prison.

A flurry of activity ensued. A third man, also

masked and dressed in all black, and with a long gun slung over his shoulder, rushed in, pulled Drake to his feet, and took him out of the cabin.

Fuzz, who'd lost interest in Grant—apparently his dog wasn't impressed with dead people—decided Kade's teammate needed his help. He nipped at Drake's heels, making the man double step to keep his ankles away from the vicious dog.

When had his dog become vicious?

Kade's other teammate went to Pretty Boy, kneeled, and put his fingers on the man's neck. "He's alive."

Over it all, he heard Skye screaming for Parker.

"Parker and his EMTs are pulling up now." Kade grabbed him in a tight hug. "I leave, thinking you're the police chief of a town where the most excitement a police chief gets is finding new places to hide from Miss Mabel." Fear flashed in his eyes before he hid it. "Do me a solid and not scare me like this again, yeah?"

"Can't promise, but I'll try. Why are you here? How did you know to be here?"

"Parker and Skylar."

"Where is she?" In all the commotion, he'd lost track of her.

Kade grabbed Tristan's arm. "Is that your blood or Grant's?"

"Mine. Where's Skye?"

Before Kade could answer, Parker and two of his EMTs came in. Tristan wasn't surprised Parker was nearby. Baby brother would have insisted on it, knowing Tristan was in trouble. One of the EMTs went to Pretty Boy and one to Grant.

Parker came straight to him, and he got another tight

hug. "This is too much excitement for me," he said. "Don't do it again."

"Uh, okay?" Where the hell was Skye?

"This one's dead," said the EMT kneeling at Grant's side. He then joined his partner working on Pretty Boy.

"He's been shot," Kade told Parker.

Tristan held up his arm for Parker to see before he freaked. "Just a minor wound. In and out. No bone or muscle damage or it would hurt more than it does." It hurt like the devil.

"You don't know that without an X-ray." Parker took his arm and poked at it.

"Ow. You have a lousy bedside manner, little brother."

Parker snorted. "Joe, come over here and wrap the chief's arm. I'll help Ty load your patient up." He poked Tristan in the chest. "Then you will go to the hospital and get it X-rayed."

For the next few minutes, Tristan impatiently waited for Joe to clean and wrap his arm. When Joe was finally done with him, he turned on Kade, suspicious that his brother was avoiding answering his question.

"Where. Is. Skye?"

Kade sighed. "She and Cupcake are taking Drake to the jail."

She was gone? Without a word to him? The part of his heart that thought she would run into his arms now that this was all over decided it couldn't take any more disappointment. It hurt too much.

"Who the hell's Cupcake?"

The teammate of Kade's that Tristan thought must be a sniper, since he wore the long gun on his back like it was a second skin, walked back inside. He stepped next to Parker as he helped lift Pretty Boy onto a spinal board. The man was covered in tats, and he had the coldest eyes Tristan had ever seen.

"You the artist?" he said to Parker.

Parker darted a glance at the man, startled a bit, then nodded. "Yeah."

"We need to have a beer someday, talk art."

"Uh, yeah, sure."

Parker sounded doubtful that would ever happen, and Tristan blinked, trying to clear his head. He'd stepped into another universe, one where his dog had morphed into a caped crusader, his brother—who he'd thought was in some foreign country doing his special ops thing—was magically here, where a man with killer eyes was talking art with his brother, and where the woman he loved was able to disappear right in front of him.

"I need to sit down," he said. He must have lost too much blood, and nothing was as it seemed. "Who's Cupcake?" Had he already asked that question? He wasn't sure.

"A teammate. He and Skye are taking Drake to jail. She said she'd send the coroner and Bentley Morrison this way."

"Cupcake?" he said again.

Kade chuckled. "Yeah, that's what we call him. He's like MacGyver but on steroids. Dude there bonding with Parker over pictures is Viper. Don't get on his bad side."

"Trust me, I intend to stay on his good side for all my days."

Parker stopped next to them as the EMTs carried Pretty Boy out on a stretcher. "You gonna be home anytime soon?" he asked Kade.

"Probably."

"Good. Keep yourself in one piece, okay?"

"I plan on it." They hugged, then Parker left.

"How'd you get here so fast?" Tristan asked.

"Stole a helicopter and its pilot," Viper said, as he came over to them. "No biggie." He laughed. "We should probably get that helo back to base before someone notices it's missing, eh, Ace?"

They stole a helicopter *and* a pilot? Because of his brother, he knew operators were a bit wacked. He hadn't realized just how wacked, though. "Why Ace?" Kade rarely talked about his job, and Tristan had never thought to ask what his team called him.

"Because your brother always has an ace up his sleeve. He's the thinker, Cupcake's the inventor, and I'm the muscle."

Kade snorted. "There's nothing between his ears, though."

"But I'm really pretty," Viper said.

"So you always say." Kade bumped Tristan's shoulder. "We really need to beat feet, brother. We still have to pick up Cupcake. You need a ride?"

"I'd love a ride, but I'm going to have to stick around and wait for my detective and the coroner." He should order Kade and his friends to give a statement before they left, but… "Ah, does it have to be a secret that you three were here?"

"That'd be great if you can manage it, but if not, don't sweat it."

"Are you going to get in trouble over the helicopter?"

"It's cool. Viper's just messing with you. Our captain wrote today up as training." He grinned. "As long as we didn't kill anyone, then he said he'd swear he's never seen us before in his life." Kade gave him another hug. "Try to stay out of trouble, brother."

"It's been some serious fun, man," Viper said, then he followed Kade out.

Fun. Right.

Chapter Fifty-One

"This is movie stuff," Tristan's detective said as he took a seat across from Skye's desk. Bentley was here to take her statement, which she'd already prepared. "You, the chief, and Fuzz take down three bad guys, a dirty cop, a major drug dealer, and his enforcer. Should the main character be the hero, the heroine, or the dog? People love dog movies."

She laughed. "I vote for the dog." She'd heard from Tristan once since yesterday, and she'd read his text numerous times, looking for a hint as to his feelings. There wasn't one.

Can you live with not revealing Kade and friends were here? If not, no problem. Kade will deal.

No, she did not have a problem keeping Kade and his teammates' involvement out of her report. She and Tristan might not have come out of that house alive if it hadn't been for those guys, and she had no interest in causing them problems with the military. So, the statement she'd prepared made no mention of Kade and friends. She handed it to Bentley.

"How's Danny Peterson doing?" Not that she cared.

She only asked because it seemed like she should inquire after a man she'd once been engaged to.

"He's still in a coma. I talked to his captain before I came over. They're sending a medevac plane for him tomorrow."

She knew that. Dustin had called this morning to tell her they'd found Grant's money in a bank safety deposit box that was in Danny's name. He'd said the police department wanted Danny back where they could keep a guard on him while they filed charges against him.

Maybe when he came out of the coma, he'd explain why he didn't just take off for some remote island with the money he stole instead of joining up with Grant to go after her. She thought it likely that Danny didn't consider a half million enough to last the rest of his lifetime. That he saw teaming up with Grant as a way to get his greedy fingers on more of the pie.

He probably pointed the finger at her in the beginning to divert any suspicion away from himself, and for revenge. His ego couldn't take her breaking up with him. He would have thought he could control the situation with Grant and didn't know how to deal when he'd found himself in over his head.

Whatever his warped reason, it was over, and she really didn't care anymore. A part of her wanted to keep him here and charge him with kidnapping, but honestly…good riddance.

"The chief is letting Peterson go back to Florida, but he's going to file kidnapping charges against him," Bentley said. "At some point, if Peterson lives, he'll have to stand trial here, too. That's probably a few years down the road since Florida wants him first. The chief refused to turn Drake over, though. He said Florida could wait their turn on that one."

The chief. The man she loved and had walked away from. Again.

"I do have a question off the record," Bentley said.

"Hmm? What's that?"

"Drake insists that there were some ninja men there. Three of them. Know anything about that?"

"Not a thing. Apparently he suffers from delusions. Either that, or he can't admit that one man, a girl, and a dog got the best of them."

"No doubt it's the man, girl, and dog one." He stood. "By the way, when you see Kade again, give him my regards." Bentley winked.

She managed to keep a straight face. "You bet." This was why she loved her adopted town. They took care of their own. Tristan had tried to tell her that. She hadn't listened, and now she wasn't sure she could stay. She wasn't sure she could handle seeing him on a regular basis.

She picked up her phone and read the text again. It hadn't magically changed. There were no encouraging words, no hint that he missed her or even wanted to talk to her. That was made clear by the text. He could have called her but didn't. Not that she blamed him after she'd pushed him away.

It probably didn't help that she'd left the cabin without talking to him, but because of her, he'd been shot and could have been killed. It had been too much, and she'd almost burst into tears. So, with her heart breaking, she'd walked away from him again. Her mistakes were piling up.

After delivering Drake to the jail and Cupcake to

the firehouse, she'd checked into the Marsville Motel. Thankfully, the room was better than she'd expected, so she'd booked it for the rest of the week. It hadn't taken long after moving to Marsville to feel like she had found her home, but she didn't belong here. Not anymore.

It was funny. She'd thought Danny had broken her heart, but compared to the godawful pain in her chest, Danny's betrayal was a mere pinprick. It hurt to breathe. The burning in her throat hurt.

Everything hurt.

Food was the last thing she wanted, and the frozen pasta dinner she'd nuked was about as appealing as eating mud. Would probably taste about the same. Thankfully, there was a microwave and mini fridge in her motel room. She couldn't bring herself to walk through the door of the Kitchen or any other place in town, so she'd picked up a few frozen dinners and bottles of water at the grocery store in the next town over. Yes, she was a coward. Couldn't even shop in Marsville's grocery store. What if she ran into Tristan? Or Parker? Or anyone?

She forced herself to eat the pasta, and when she finished, she wondered what to do with herself for the rest of the night. Three days had passed since she'd walked away from Tristan. Three days of fighting back tears at work, of forcing food down her throat, of sitting in a room at night where the loneliness was so heavy that even breathing hurt. Three nights of crying for what she'd lost and regret for her mistakes. The regret haunted her dreams.

This couldn't go on.

A decision needed to be made, but she was incapable

of deciding anything. It was as if she'd stopped being a person and was a thing. An inanimate object without a brain capable of thinking. If only that were true, then she wouldn't hurt like this.

The loud knock startled her. Tristan? She tried not to hope as she walked to the door, but her foolish heart dared to hope. "Oh, Parker." Tears burned her eyes at seeing the wrong brother. She blinked them away. She was so tired of crying.

His smile was soft and kind. "Took a while to find where you were staying. Can I come in?"

"Oh, sure. Sorry." She stepped back. There was only one chair in the room, and she waved a hand at it. "Have a seat. Would you like a water? It's all I have to offer."

"I'm good, thanks."

When he sat, she perched on the edge of the mattress. "Um, what can I do for you?"

His gaze roamed over her. Not in a sexual way, but as if he was checking on her well-being. She could tell him her well-being wasn't so great. His eyes were so much like his brother's that she couldn't bear looking at them. She dropped her gaze to the floor.

"How are you, Skylar?"

Terrible. Heartsick. Dying inside. "Fine. I'm fine."

"No, you're not. You're not any more fine than my brother is."

Her eyes snapped up to his.

"Ah, I caught your interest, yeah?" He leaned forward and rested his elbows on his knees. "What are your plans for your future?"

The lump in her throat doubled in size. He was hoping she planned to leave, to get out of his brother's life. She swallowed hard, and when she was sure she could speak without her voice trembling, said, "Dustin, he's the sheriff and my previous boss, said he'd hire me back. As a deputy, though, since my chief deputy sheriff's job was filled when I left."

"Now why would you want to do that?"

"Wouldn't that make you happy? I'd be gone. Tristan can move on with his life. I know he'll be glad to see the last of me."

He shook his head in a way that said she was a child he didn't know what to do with. "I don't know which of you are more stubborn. Not to take sides, but I think he has a bit more reason for his stubbornness where you're concerned."

She couldn't argue with that. "I don't understand why you're here."

"He's miserable, Skylar. Do you love him?"

She tried to tell him no, but as she looked into Parker's kind eyes, she couldn't lie to him. "Yes."

"So what are you going to do about it?" He stood and walked out, not waiting for her answer. She didn't have an answer.

The room grew dark as night moved in, and she sat in that dark as his question sat heavy in her mind. What was she going to do about it?

Something or nothing?

Chapter Fifty-Two

"Bath," Tristan said. A week after getting shot, his arm was only a little sore. He'd been lucky that it had only been a flesh wound. The bullet hadn't hit muscle, bone, or an artery.

Fuzz yelped with excitement, snatched up his KONG, and raced to the bathroom. Tristan shook his head. He probably had the only dog in the world that loved baths. He tried to find the amusement he always had with Fuzz and his baths. It wasn't there.

It wasn't Saturday, Fuzz's bath day, but Tristan was grasping for anything that would keep his nights busy and not give him time to think. He'd washed his car, Parker's car, cleaned the house from one end to the other, and then had started over, cleaning until Parker put a stop to it. Apparently, he was upsetting Andrew since the house was Andrew's domain. You'd think Andrew would welcome the help, but no.

He'd been kicked out of the kitchen when he'd decided to prepare and freeze meals for the following week. Andrew hadn't liked that either. At least no one had complained when he'd mowed the lawn twice in three days. He hadn't fared much better at the station. No one was talking to him anymore. They were, in fact, scattering like rats when they saw his snarly ass coming their way.

Whatever.

At least his dog still liked him. Fuzz loved baths because the silly dog would drop his toy in the water, then go diving for it, over and over and over. By the time Tristan could coax him out, the bathroom would be a mess. That was good. It gave him something to do.

Fuzz clean, the bathroom clean, and with nothing left to do, Tristan showered, then warily eyed his bed. Maybe he could sleep tonight. He'd give it a try, and if his mind insisted on thinking about Skye, he'd sneak downstairs and clean something. Andrew had gone home, and Parker would be asleep, so no one would yell at him.

What a surprise, he couldn't sleep. His mind refused to obey his demand that it not think about Skye. He glanced at the bedside clock. He'd given it an hour. Sleep just wasn't going to happen. The books in the library could probably use a good dusting. Hell, he bet there was a better way to arrange them than how they were now. How were they arranged anyway? By author or book titles? Whichever it was, they needed to be the other way.

As he was getting out of bed, his phone chimed with a text. He took it out of the charger and stared at the message.

What did the astronaut cook in his skillet?

How did she do that…make his heart beat so fast he could hear the thump of it in his ears? And what did she mean with this text? Answer her or not? Not…he had a library to rearrange. He was halfway down the stairs when he stopped, turned, and stomped back up to his room. The only reason he was going to answer the text was because if he had any hope of sleeping at some point, he needed to know what the astronaut cooked in his skillet.

I give up.

With the intensity of a hound dog eyeing a juicy bone, he watched bubbles dance on the screen.

Unidentified frying objects.

He snorted. More bubbles appeared, then…

Can we talk?

Did he want to? No…yes…maybe. No, he had a library waiting for him. He put the phone back in the charger, stared at it, then picked it up again. The library could wait.

If U want.

I do. When?

Why did she keep asking these hard questions? He supposed now was a good time. Maybe if he talked to her, he could finally sleep.

Now. Where?

Ha! He could ask hard questions, too.

I'm parked down the street from your house.

He'd been thinking a neutral location would be best, but she was down the street. So close. He fisted his hand and pounded his chest. "Stop it!" Stupid thumping heart. Might as well talk here. But not in the house, not in his rooms. He'd cleaned his rooms from top to bottom and washed his sheets to get rid of her scent. She was banned from the second floor.

He drew in a deep breath, annoyed as hell that she was messing with his head. Still.

"You're losing it, brother," Parker had accused him when kicking him out of the kitchen.

Maybe he was. Even his dog had tired of his craziness and had removed himself to Everly's room. He'd talk to Skye, get all these thoughts that were keeping him from sleeping off his chest, then he could move on with his life without her in it. After a year of pining after her, it was time. He texted her.

Meet U on the porch.

He considered exchanging his sleep pants for jeans, but nope. He'd put on a T-shirt. That was the extent of his civility because he wasn't feeling very…well, civil right now. Barefoot, he headed for the porch.

The night was comfortably warm, the three-quarter moon was high in a cloudless sky, a soft breeze blew, and the honeysuckles filled the air with their sweet perfume. He bet he could sleep out here. The lights from her car lit up the driveway, and he crossed his arms as he waited for her to park and get out.

When she walked in front of the car's headlights, which hadn't automatically clicked off yet, his breath caught in his throat. The Skye walking toward him was the Skye he'd met the night he couldn't forget no matter how hard he tried.

Her hair was down, the long strands lifting and falling with the wind. She wore a sleeveless blue top and white shorts, and on her feet were those glittery flip-flops.

She was his fantasy. The girl in his dreams. He shook his head, mentally pushing those thoughts away. When she reached the bottom step, she looked up at him and gave him a shy smile.

A few days ago, he would have fallen all over himself for that smile, but no longer. He turned without speaking, went to one of the Adirondack chairs, sat, and waited.

He refused to be curious as to what she had to say. Correction, he refused to let her see he was curious.

Chapter Fifty-Three

Skye knew this wasn't going to be easy. But she'd earned his indifference, if that's what it was. It could be that he hated her now. She prayed he still felt something for her. He hadn't invited her to sit, hadn't looked at her with warmth in his eyes, hadn't given a hint that he was happy to see her. Her mind blanked, the speech she'd rehearsed in her motel room and on the way over forgotten.

"May I sit?"

He shrugged as if he couldn't care less what she did. Tears burned her eyes, and she was so tired of that happening. She almost walked back to her car. *He's worth fighting for,* her heart reminded her. That was what she'd grabbed on to as she'd sat in that dark motel room after Parker left.

If she sat in the chair next to him, it would be too easy for him to ignore her, to refuse to look at her as she offered him her heart in her trembling hands. So she moved to the section of the porch rail in front of him, then leaned back against it.

"I…" She cleared her throat. "I had this speech prepared that would… I don't know. Sweep you off your feet?"

He made a noise that sounded like disbelief.

Again, she was tempted to run, but she'd been doing that since she'd met him, and where had that gotten her? Miserable and lonely. "Forget prepared speeches. I came here to say this in a roundabout way, but I'll just say it straight out. I love you."

"You have a funny way of showing it."

Still no warmth in his voice. She wasn't giving up, though. Not yet. "I know, and for that, I'm sorry. If I could do everything over, do it differently, I would."

"I can't keep doing this with you, Skylar."

Skylar. She was Skye to him, not Skylar. Or she had been from their first night together. She knew what he was doing with the Skylar nonsense. He was building walls to keep Skye out. Walls were her specialty, and she wouldn't let him get away with that. "You can tell me to leave, Tristan, or you can tell me to go to hell, but I'm Skye to you. I have been her to you since we sat next to each other at a bar with a ridiculous name."

He finally looked at her, and the pain in his eyes was almost enough to make her leave for his sake. She'd put that pain there, not once but often. Maybe leaving was the best thing she could do for him.

"You left without a word." There was accusation in his voice, but when was he referring to? She'd left him without a word more than once.

"When?" she whispered while knowing she wouldn't like his answer.

He sighed, and there was a lot of hurt in that sigh. "I can't do this with you. You should go."

No! She wasn't leaving until she bared her heart to him. If he still wanted her to go after that, she would, even knowing she'd never love another man after him.

There was a part of her that was getting mad, though. There was a little voice saying, *Oh, poor him. What about what you went through? Is he even trying to understand that?*

She shushed that voice. She might listen to it later if he dug in his pig-headed heels, but she'd give him a chance to listen to her.

"You pushed me away for a year," he said. "Then when I think you're finally seeing what we have, something that was fucking amazing, at the first sign of some ridiculous gossip, you were like a ghost I could never catch."

"I almost got you killed." If there was anything she wished she could unsee, that was it. "I looked at you bleeding there on the floor, and I ran out to call for Parker. Then when I told him you'd been shot…" She shook her head. "You didn't see the pain in his eyes, and it was because of me. Everly, your brothers, they almost lost you because of me, and all I could think was that I didn't deserve you."

"You didn't deserve me? What kind of bullshit is that?"

"I know," she whispered. She had to touch him, to be near him. She moved away from the railing and kneeled in front of him but kept her hands to herself. That was such a hard thing to do. "I should have believed in us."

"But you didn't."

"No, and that's my greatest regret." She glanced to the side, trying to gather her thoughts, to say the right thing. What was the right thing, really? The truth was all she had to give him. "When Danny started those rumors about me…" She turned her gaze back to him. "No one trusted me anymore. Even after Dustin's investigation cleared me, the rumors persisted. I thought once I was cleared things would go back to normal, and I could do the job I loved. I was so naïve. The whispers behind my back that I was meant to overhear, the side-eyes and snickers didn't stop."

"I'm not Danny, Skye. How many times do I have to say that?"

"No, you aren't, and I knew that. Maybe not at first. I didn't trust my judgment, so I did push you away as soon as I realized who you were. I'd made a promise to myself that I'd never let another man use me like that, especially a cop. And you were not only a cop, but the chief. You had the power to ruin me."

It seemed his eyes were softening. She hoped that was true, but she needed to finish. "I managed to keep you at arm's length, but then after the fire, you were there for me in a way Danny never had been. I finally accepted what I'd known all along. You weren't him. You'd never hurt me that way."

"So, what changed? Because you let me in, then you kicked me out again."

"I panicked. After Mason spewed his lies, it was Florida all over again. Only this time, I was dragging you down with me. Before I could figure out that was the nonsense it was, you were kidnapped. I stood in that cabin after, saw you bleeding, and I just couldn't stay where you might have died because of me, so I left."

"If I had, it would have been because of Grant, not you."

"If it hadn't been for me, Grant would have never come here."

"Pretty sure Grant was here because of Pretty Boy's lies."

She needed to touch him. If he slapped her hands

away, she'd leave. She put her hands on his legs and stilled, waiting to see what he would do. He did nothing. Maybe it was a small win that he didn't push her away.

"I love you, Tristan. So much it hurts my heart. What happens next is up to you. If you want me to leave… from here or from Marsville, I will. But I'm praying that you'll give us another chance."

"And the next time something spooks you? I can't keep doing this. One day I have you in my life, and the next you run. I just can't."

"It will never happen again. I know you don't trust me right now, and I can't tell you how sorry I am for that, but I understand. Just tell me what I need to do. Do you want me to beg?"

"I'd never ask that of you, Skye." He leaned forward and put his hands over hers. "I don't need you to beg, and I'm not ready for your promise, because you're right. I don't trust you."

"Oh." Sadness was heavy in her heart. "I'll go then. I don't think I can stay in Marsville and—"

"The thing is, I'm in love with you, too. Have been since you dragged me to your motel room."

"I dragged you?"

He gifted her with the hint of a smile. "That's the way I remember it."

"I think your memory is faulty. So, what happens now?" She was afraid to hope, but oh, she wanted to.

"We take our time. We date…openly. No sneaking around. Teach me to trust you again, Skylar."

"For you, I'm Skye."

"I thought you preferred Skylar. I only called you Skye to aggravate you."

She smiled her first smile in days. "And you did, but

not for the reason you think. I've always been Skye. I only insisted on Skylar, which you ignored, because every time you called me Skye, it was a reminder of our night together."

He smirked. "That was why I did it. To remind you. Also, if I couldn't be with you, the next best thing was to aggravate you, Sheriff."

"Well, you did that, Chief." Over the past year, his calling her Sheriff had become a bit of an endearment because of the soft way he'd say it. Hearing it from him again sent her heart soaring with happiness.

"Well, Skye Morgan, do you agree to the terms?"

"Oh, yes, I sure do."

"Seal it with a kiss?"

"Yes, please."

"Come up here, then."

Epilogue

Tristan let himself and Fuzz into Skye's loft. The past five months had been the best of his life, and he was ready to take the next step. He thought Skye was, too, so he and Fuzz had gone to Asheville and bought an engagement ring.

"Remember, our trip today is a secret," he reminded Fuzz as they walked into Skye's home. He really liked the loft, and when the time came for them to live together, he was good with it being his home or her loft. She could decide.

Fuzz raced down the hallway, searching for Skye. He was always eager to see her. One or two days a week he'd go to work with her. His cops and her deputies fought over time with his dog, and that amused him.

Just as eager as Fuzz to find her, he followed his dog. Tomorrow was the grand opening of the Marsville UFO Museum, and they'd worked hard completing the tasks Miss Mabel kept assigning them. Tonight, though, all was done and ready for the opening, and it was just him and her and a bed. Also, she'd gotten word today that Mason's discrimination claim had been dismissed for lack of evidence, so a reason to celebrate. Not that they needed a reason.

He found her in the bedroom, on her stomach on the floor. He leaned against the doorjamb, smiling as Fuzz gave her love kisses on her chin while she giggled.

"My turn next," he said.

She smiled up at him. "I'm saving the best for the last, Chief."

"You better love me more than my dog." He glanced at the coloring book and crayons scattered in front of her. When Skye finished coloring that page, she would take the book back to Everly to color the next one. The game had started when Everly decided she needed to teach Skye about art and colors. His niece was a harsh critic but had recently declared that Skye was improving.

"I don't know. Fuzz here is a pretty good kisser. I might love him more."

"We'll just see about that. Get up."

She raised her brows at his command, but anticipation flashed in her eyes. They were still learning things about each other, but early on they'd discovered they both liked to take control at times and other times liked handing over control to the other. He decided it was his turn tonight, and from the way she was looking at him—daring him to make her get up—she was good with that.

"On your feet, Sheriff. Now." He choked down his laugh when she rolled her eyes, and then went back to coloring. "Little brat," he muttered as he walked to her. But a sexy brat. She had on her favorite at home wear. The boy cut panties and white cotton camisole never failed to get him hot and bothered. Her hair was still in her sheriff's bun because she knew how much he loved pulling those pins out of her hair, freeing those beautiful strands to fall down her back and over her shoulders.

When he was standing over her, he snapped his fingers, getting Fuzz's attention. "Bed." His dog gave him sad eyes and sighed but left his favorite girl and went to his bed. Tristan stepped one foot to the other side of her thighs, so that his feet were straddling her. Then he leaned down, put his hands on her waist, and lifted her to her feet. He pulled her to him, her back to his chest.

"You know what happens when a police officer gives an order and it's ignored?" He slipped his hands under her top, slid them up her stomach, and cupped her breasts.

"Bad things?" she said in a hopeful voice that made him smile.

"Very bad things." While he toyed with her nipples, he lowered his mouth to her neck. There was a place just below her ear that, when he nipped at it and sucked on it, made her whimper, and he did love her sexy noises. And there it was…that whimper, that sound that went straight to his groin.

When she tried to turn around, he dropped his hands to her hips, holding her in place. "Didn't give you permission to move, Sheriff." He rocked against her. "Feel what you do to me?" he whispered in her ear.

She wiggled her bottom over his arousal, making him groan. "Two can play this game, Chief."

He chuckled. "She wants to play dirty." He walked her to the wall. "You know the drill."

"Make me." She rubbed against him again.

Every single time he thought she couldn't make him any harder, she proved him wrong. This minute, he could hammer nails into concrete with his dick.

"Hands on the wall. Legs spread." He bit her earlobe. She moaned. He squeezed his eyes shut, fighting for control over his body when what he desperately wanted was to pound himself into her until they were both too sated to stand on their feet.

"Do you want me in you?"

She nodded.

"Words. Give me the words."

"Yes."

"Not good enough. Yes what?"

"Yes, please."

"Then hands on the wall and legs spread."

She slapped her hands on the wall, spread her legs, then turned her face back and gave him a disgruntled look. "So bossy."

"You're not fooling me with that sour face, sweetheart." He put his mouth to her ear again. "You love my bossy. I bet your panties are soaked right now because of my bossy. I think I should find out." He slipped his hand inside her panties and slid a finger inside her. "Oh, yeah, that's what I'm talking about."

She pushed her head back, pressing it against his shoulder. Her eyes were closed, her breaths coming faster as he slid another finger inside her while his thumb circled her clit. He would never tire of watching her face as he pleasured her, and when she came, making those damn sexy raspy sounds, he almost came with her. Just crazy that. He'd never had this much trouble staying in control of his body with another woman. But Skye made him feel like a fifteen-year-old boy again, ready to blow at the merest touch.

He wrapped his arms around her and held her until

she found her legs again. When her breaths evened out, he scooped her up. "Bed now."

She nuzzled her face against his neck. "You smell yummy."

"For you." He'd stopped at home and showered before coming over because he knew the minute they were in the same room together, this would happen.

They made short work of getting their clothes off and getting on the bed. He rolled over on his back, pulling her on top of him. "Ride me, Skye."

One of the things he loved, and there were a lot of them, about their being a couple was that they'd both gotten tested and she was on birth control, so there was no synthetic barrier between them. Making love to her bare was incredible.

He sighed when she lowered herself onto him, and his heart felt like it might burst from happiness as her eyes held his while they made love. In those beautiful blue eyes that used to turn to ice when they looked at him was now love. He was one lucky son of a bitch.

They reached the pinnacle together, and as they both fell over the cliff, he caught her in his arms and held her close, this girl who'd brought love and laughter into his life.

"Tristan," she whispered.

"I'll always catch you," he promised.

"Look, Mommy, it's spaceships!" The little boy tugged on his mother's blouse. "Look! There's three of them!"

Skye shared a smile with the boy's mother. Children had been jumping up and down and pointing to the sky all day. Hidden from view on the roof of the museum were the operators of the three drones—Kade, Cupcake, and Viper. They'd managed to get leave to come and give kids a thrill thinking they'd seen spaceships. Skye still didn't know Cupcake's and Viper's real names since they just smirked every time she asked, but she'd find out eventually.

The museum's grand opening was a success, but not overwhelmingly so, which she and Tristan were thankful for. The town couldn't handle many more visitors, but everyone was happy with the uptick in business. It had been a long day, but the museum had closed fifteen minutes ago, and a relaxing bath was in her near future.

She scanned the area, searching for her man. As if her heart knew exactly where he was, her gaze went straight to where he stood across the street. There was his beautiful face. She fluttered her fingers when he smiled at her, then she took a step to go to the parking lot to check on her deputies, who were directing departing traffic. Something struck her on the back of her legs.

"Ow." She was wearing her sheriff's uniform. Who would whack a cop and expect to get away with it? She spun, ready to have a word with the offender. Okay, Miss Mabel was the only person who could whack her without ending up in handcuffs, and that was only because, like Fuzz, the woman terrified her.

"Stay still, girl," Miss Mabel said.

"I'm just going to check on my deputies." She edged away from Miss Mabel's deadly cane.

"They're fine. Don't move." Miss Mabel looked up.

Skye looked up. All three of the drones were hovering above her head, then one lowered, stopping in front of her face. The other two floated behind it. A metal arm sprouted from the drone closest to her, and in its claw was a piece of paper that said Follow Me.

She was whacked with the cane again. "Go on, girl. Off with you."

"Off with me where?" It was disconcerting getting whacks and being called *girl* by a little old lady who was half her size.

Miss Mabel rolled her eyes. "Can't you read? Follow the spaceship."

"I'm going," she said, sidestepping the cane coming at her legs again. Jeez.

The drones led her to a black limousine parked at the side of the museum. Parker stood behind the open back door, and Everly stood in front of it, her face lighting up at seeing Skye. "Miss Skylar, here you are. You have to get in."

"Where are we going, sweetie?" Where did they get a limo, and why?

"You'll see."

Skye was more confused than ever when Parker, without saying a word, closed the door behind them, then went to the driver's side and got in.

Everly hopped to one of the other seats. "It's so big in here. Are you excited, Miss Skylar?"

"I might be if I knew where we were going."

"To—"

"Everly," Parker warned.

The little girl dramatically sighed. "It's a surprise. I want to tell you, but Uncle Tris made me promise not to. He said if I did, I couldn't have any more pickles."

"Well, don't tell me then."

Everly chatted away, jumping from one subject to another, and from one seat to the other, for the next ten minutes until Parker came to a stop in front of Fanny's shop. Apparently Fanny was expecting them, and before Skye could figure out how it happened, she was in a dressing room, putting on a dress that Fanny swore was perfect for the evening.

What evening? What was Tristan up to? She had to admit as she stared at the dress in the mirror that it was beautiful. The azure-blue wrap dress made her eyes pop, and the surplice bodice showed a hint of cleavage but not too much. She really liked the fluttery short sleeves, and the just-above-the-knees hem was the perfect length. She turned and looked over her shoulder at the back. The dress was flattering, and she loved it. But why was she trying it on?

"Come out, Miss Skylar," Everly yelled. "I want to see."

"I knew that dress had your name on it as soon as I saw it," Fanny said when Skye came out.

Everly circled her, then threw her arms wide. "It's so pretty, Miss Skylar, but you need shoes. You can't go barefoot."

"Okay, but why am I trying it on? I mean, it's beautiful, but I don't understand what's happening. And there's no price tag on it." She'd already decided she was going to buy it. It was too perfect not to, but go barefoot where?

"Oh, there's no price tag because the dress is already yours." Fanny picked up a pair of silver slingback pumps with kitten heels. "These are perfect for that dress."

"Are they already mine, too?"

The woman gave her a sly smile. "Of course." Her gaze lifted to Skye's head. "The bun is fine for work, but tonight it has to go."

"Huh?" By the time Fanny and Everly were done

with her, along with the dress and heels, she was wearing dangling silver earrings, a silver bangle bracelet, and her hair was down.

"Isn't she just beautiful, Miss Fanny?" Everly asked.

"She sure is, honey."

"Come on, Miss Skylar, we have to go now." Everly took her hand.

She was led to the Kitchen, where Parker stood outside the door. "You look lovely, Skylar." He opened the door of the restaurant. "Go on in now."

"What's going…" She glanced inside, and her question died on her lips. "Oh," she whispered.

She vaguely registered Parker's chuckle as she walked in, and the door closed behind her. The interior of the restaurant had been transformed into a fairyland. Soft music played over the speakers, fairy lights were strung from the ceiling, wildflowers in vases were on every table, and silver balloons with silver ribbons tied to their ends floated above her.

Everything was so beautiful, but it was the man standing in the middle of the room watching her that took her breath away. He wore a tux—blue bowtie and cummerbund matching her dress—and, heaven help her, it would be a miracle if she didn't melt right on the spot.

His hands were in his pockets, his eyes were on her, and a soft smile was on his face. As if entranced, she went to him. "Hi." Amazing how breathy a two-letter word could sound.

"So beautiful," he murmured.

"I could say the same about you." She glanced around. "It's not my birthday, you know."

"No, but it is a special night…well, I hope it turns out that way."

There was uncertainty in his voice, or maybe nervousness. "Just my opinion, but any night with you is special."

"Let's hope you still think that in a few minutes." He glanced down. "Fuzz has something for you."

She hadn't even noticed Fuzz was in the room; that was how mesmerizing her man was. A laugh escaped her when she saw the blue bowtie around Fuzz's neck. "Aren't you a handsome boy?" Hanging from his mouth was a silver gift bag. "For me?"

Although she still didn't understand what was happening, butterflies danced in her stomach. She took the bag from Fuzz, then glanced up at Tristan.

He nodded. "Open it."

When she pulled out a small blue velvet box, Tristan dropped to a knee, and she almost went down with him, so weak were her legs.

He took the box from her. "Skye Morgan, from the time you walked into my life, there's been only you. My heart said, 'Mine.' That never changed, even when I'd given up hope that there would ever be an us. And when I say, 'Mine,' it doesn't mean that I own you. It means that you are mine to love and cherish."

"And you're mine."

"I am. Always and forever. Will you marry me, Sheriff?" He opened the lid of the box and removed the ring, a beautiful bezel set diamond.

She'd never seen a flat diamond secured by a platinum ring instead of prongs before. It was unique, and she loved it. "It's perfect." Tears pooled in her eyes. "Yes. Oh, yes, I will marry you, Chief."

His big smile was a beautiful thing to see. He slipped the ring on her finger, then stood, wrapped his arms around her, and kissed her.

When they came up for air, he yelled, "She said yes!"

People poured out from the back and surrounded them. Parker, Everly, and Kade were front and center. Her future brothers-in-law each gave her a hug and a kiss on her cheek.

"Welcome to the family," Parker said.

"You're gonna get tired of seeing his ugly mug every day, Skylar," Kade said. "Run away with me."

She laughed. "If you'd only asked me five minutes ago, before he put this beautiful ring on my finger."

Everly grabbed her hand and stared at the ring. "I want one just like it when I get married. Are you my aunt Skylar now?"

"Yes, and you're my niece."

"She's never getting married because no boy is getting near her," Parker muttered.

Kade nodded. "Truth, because if they get past you, they'll have me to deal with."

"And I'll slap handcuffs on them and haul them off to jail," Tristan said.

Skye shared an amused glance with Katie, who was standing nearby. Poor Everly, with three badass men guarding the gate.

"Congratulations, Miss Skylar," Earl said after pushing his way past the brothers. "This means you're not gonna run off, right?"

"No, I'm here to stay." And as she scanned the room, seeing the people who were here for her and Tristan, her heart sighed with happiness. She really was home. One by one, they came and congratulated her—Fanny,

Katie, Miss Bauman, Mary Beth and Melissa, Rebecca, her deputies, Tristan's cops, and even Luther and Miss Mabel.

Champagne bottles were uncorked, popping a few of the balloons, much to Everly's delight, as the corks shot to the ceiling. A section was cleared, making a dance floor, and Miss Mabel ordered her and Tristan to dance to the first song, just the two of them.

"I was afraid you wouldn't like sharing this night with everyone," Tristan said as they danced. "But the word got out that Katie was decorating the Kitchen, and then their nosy selves learned why, and they weren't willing to be left out. I could have put a stop to it, but I wanted you to see that this is your town, too. That these people are your people. I hope it was okay."

She lost herself in his eyes, so full of love for her. "It was perfect."

And it was.

* * * * *

Acknowledgments

If you're reading this, that means you just finished reading Tristan and Skye's story. Thank you! You might have seen the meme going around on how to thank an author...wine and chocolate are never refused for sure, but the best way—and it won't cost a cent—is a review. We seriously love you for those reviews.

So much goes into writing a book, and that means there are many people to thank. I'm never sure where to start because there are a whole lot of people I want to send some love to. But really, the only place to begin is with you, the reader. Without you, there would be no reason to write my stories. Thank you for reading them, thank you for sharing your enjoyment with me... the things that made you smile or laugh or cry. I heart you all.

Next up—the members of my reader group, Sandra's Rowdies. OMG, y'all are the best! You earn your name every single day, and I love you troublemakers and your shenanigans so much! Thank you all for the love and support you give me and my books! A special thank-you for all the laughter.

Jenny Holiday and A.E. Jones, you are amazing authors and the best critique partners in the world. Thank you for helping me making my books better. Heather, beta reader extraordinaire, thank you for reading my first drafts and your great suggestions for my stories. Miranda Liasson, we started this journey at the same time, and wow, look where we are today. Who would have guessed? Our long phone calls mean the world to me.

To the book bloggers who read, review, and recommend my books, thank you, thank you, thank you! A special shout-out to Christine from ireadromancetoescape, and to Brandy, Clarissa, and Doni!

Kerri Buckley, I enjoy working with you and Carina Press more than you can know. Thank you for being awesome. Deborah Nemeth, super editor, my stories wouldn't be what they are without you. Sometimes when I first get edits and read over them, I don't like you…but it doesn't last long. Ha-ha! Seriously, you're almost always right, so thank you for showing me how to make a story shine. Also, a big thanks to everyone at Carina for being awesome great.

Courtney Miller-Callihan, what an amazing journey we've been on. Thank you for being the best agent I think I could have. Here's to many more years together!

Last, but never least, a thank-you filled with all my love to my family—Jim, the best husband in the world, Jeff, my awesome son, and DeAnna, my beautiful and wonderful daughter-in-law.

About the Author

Bestselling, award-winning author Sandra Owens lives in the beautiful Blue Ridge Mountains of North Carolina. Her family and friends often question her sanity but have ceased being surprised by what she might get up to next. She's jumped out of a plane, flown in an aerobatic plane while the pilot performed death-defying stunts, gotten into laser gunfights in air combat, and ridden a Harley motorcycle for years. She regrets nothing.

Sandra is a Romance Writers of America Honor Roll member and a 2013 Golden Heart Finalist for her contemporary romance *Crazy for Her*. In addition to her contemporary romance and romantic suspense novels, she writes Regency stories. Her books have won many awards, including the Readers' Choice and the Golden Quill.

To find out about other books by Sandra Owens or to be alerted to cover reveals, new releases, and other fun stuff, sign up for her newsletter at bit.ly/2FVUPKS.

Join Sandra's Facebook Reader Group, Sandra's Rowdies: www.Facebook.com/Groups/1827166257533001/

Website: www.Sandra-Owens.com

Connect with Sandra

Facebook: bit.ly/2ruKKPl.

Twitter: www.Twitter.com/SandyOwens1

Instagram: www.Instagram.com/SandraOwensBooks/

Everyone thinks Harper Jansen is dead.

*She is not, and she wants her life back. Delta Force
operator Kade Church will do whatever it takes to
keep the woman he's falling for safe.*

Keep reading for an excerpt from
Her Delta Force Protector, *book two in the*
K-9 Defenders *series, by Sandra Owens.*

Chapter One

"I need help."

Kade Church's heart skipped a beat at the voice he never expected to hear again, mainly because she was dead. "Harper?" The only reason he'd answered the call from a number he didn't recognize was because it could be from Talon Security, the Charlotte-based company he had an interview with in the morning.

"It's me. They found me, Kade."

"Harper, I…" Kade shook his head, this couldn't be Harper. "This isn't funny. Who is this?" He was all for practical jokes when they were good ones. This one was not good. Whoever this was had her voice down pat, and he felt the loss of his best friend all over again.

"I swear, it's me."

"Whose Celebration of Life did I attend?" Had it been only five weeks since he'd sat in the back of the base chapel and listened to her father and her friends give their eulogies of a daughter, a friend, and a woman he felt honored to know? It seemed like yesterday and at the same time, a lifetime of missing her. He stared out the kitchen window as he tried to wrap his head around hearing her very much alive voice.

"Mine."

"So this is a call from the beyond?" He'd grieved for this woman, still did. And all this time she'd been alive?

"Don't be ridiculous."

Ridiculous was getting a call from the dead. "You want to tell me what's going on?"

"I can't, not over the phone. Please, Kade. I need help. I don't know who else to call."

"Where are you?"

"Myrtle Beach."

That was why he was hearing motorcycles in the background. It was the Myrtle Beach Fall Rally Bike Week. "What kind of help?"

"Help staying alive. I have to go. I've been on this phone too long."

"Okay. Hole up in a motel and don't leave the room. Can you pay cash?"

"Yes, but I doubt there are any vacancies with all these bikers here."

"If not, lose yourself in the crowd or find a hole-in-the-wall bar that has dark corners. Can I reach you at this number?"

"I'm keeping my phone off, but if I know what time you'll call, I'll turn it on."

He glanced at his watch and did some calculations. Marsville, North Carolina, was about five hours from Myrtle Beach. "Turn your phone on at eight." He could be there tonight and get her back to his house, where she'd be safe. Although just barely, there would still be time to make it to his interview. That was one thing he didn't want to mess up. Talon Security had a stellar reputation, and he wanted that job.

"Okay. Kade?"

"Yeah?"

"Thank you."

"See ya tonight." He stared at the screen after disconnecting as his mind tried to wrap around the fact that Harper was alive. She sounded like she was fighting tears, but he wasn't ready to forgive her. Even if she had to fake her death, she could have come to him. No matter how grave the situation was, he would have been there for her. She knew that.

Duke, the dog Harper had conned him into fostering while she was in the Peace Corps, sat at his feet, wearing his goofy smile. Kade had brought the dog home for his brothers to take care of until he was back for good. The golden retriever believed humans were put on this earth for his personal pleasure. When Kade headed for his baby brother's art studio, Duke tripped over his feet in his excitement that they were going somewhere.

"You're a goofball."

Duke barked his agreement.

Parker's studio was a separate building from the house the three brothers shared, and at the door, he told Duke to sit. Duke rolled over. "Were you dropped on your head as a puppy?" He opened the door just enough to slip in and quickly closed it, keeping Duke out.

The dog had gotten into the studio once and had ended up with a coat of many colors. It had taken days to get all the paint out of his fur. Parker hadn't been happy with the mess Duke left behind or the canvas Duke had destroyed.

Parker, a famous artist known as Park C, was standing in front of a canvas, giving it the stink eye.

"What's wrong with it?" The painting—an oil of Parker's young daughter and her cat staring out a window as it rained—looked great to him.

"The colors are all wrong."

"If you say so. Listen, I have to head over to Myrtle Beach."

Parker glanced at him. "You going to bike week?"

"Only for the day." He didn't bother explaining his reason for the trip. When Parker was painting, he tended not to retain anything said to him. Parker's attention returned to the canvas, Kade's presence already forgotten.

As he headed to his rooms to exchange his running shoes for biker boots, he called his older brother. Tristan was the Marsville police chief, while Parker, along with being a famous artist, was the town's fire chief.

As a Delta Force operator for ten years, Kade's life had been one of high-stress life-and-death situations, and never knowing where he'd be tomorrow, or if he'd even live to see tomorrow. He was using his thirty days of leave time due him while he waited for his separation from the Army to become official.

His plan all along on getting out had been to chill for a month. Well, he'd had two weeks of chilling, and he was bored. Not that he'd choose for Harper to be afraid for her life, but he couldn't deny that he was amped to be on a mission.

"Hey, can you come get Duke and keep him until tomorrow?" he said when Tristan answered. If Duke was left to his own devices, the results wouldn't be good. Poor Duke. Everyone liked him, but no one wanted to deal with his craziness.

"I guess, but why?"

Kade told his brother about Harper's phone call.

"Do you know what has her afraid?"

"Not yet. I'm going to bring her back here. Figure

this is the safest place for her while I get to the bottom of it."

"You taking your bike or the Ram?"

"The bike. With bike week going on, I'll blend in better."

"Okay. Be safe. And call if you need help with anything. I'll head over now to get the goofball."

"Great. Thanks. He'll be in his crate." He didn't dare leave Duke out with no supervision, even for the ten minutes it would take Tristan to get here.

After changing his shoes, Kade slipped on his leather jacket and put his gun in one of the pockets. His wallet went in his back pocket, then he grabbed his motorcycle key. Duke wasn't happy about being left in his crate, but he'd forget that as soon as Tristan showed up to get him.

Kade headed for the garage. Now that he was opting out of the Army, he'd treated himself to two things: a Harley-Davidson Road King and a Ram 1500 TRX pickup, both black and badass. He had his brothers to thank for being able to do that. They had refused to take money from him for household expenses while he was in the military. They said it was enough that he was risking his life for his country.

Because of his art, Parker was a wealthy boy, and he paid most of the bills. He'd also covered the cost of remodeling their house after their aunt had died. Now that Kade was getting out of the military, it was time to contribute his fair share.

He emptied his saddle bags, making room for whatever Harper might have with her. What wouldn't fit in them would have to be left behind. It still hadn't sunk in that she was alive. He took a few minutes to mud the bike up, including the license plate, obscuring all but two of the plate numbers. It killed him to dirty his bike up, but the less attention it got, the better.

As he rode toward Myrtle Beach, his thoughts drifted to the first time he'd seen Harper. She'd been running down the street, chasing a dog. The dog would run, then stop and let the woman almost catch up, then he'd run again. The dog was having a blast, the woman not so much.

Kade and a teammate were doing a ten-mile run, and the dog veered their way, coming to a stop at their feet and giving them his goofy grin. He wore a collar, so Kade grabbed it and held the dog until the woman reached them.

"Lose something?" he said.

She bent over, put her hands on her knees, and gasped for breath. "Yeah. Thanks."

"No problem." He tapped the dog's nose. "And who are you?"

"This is Duke, better known as the military-dog school flunky. He thinks everything's a game, even bombs."

"My kind of guy."

She laughed as she stood. "Figures."

Kade's teammate jogged backward. "I'm going to keep going."

"Catch you later, man." Kade took the leash dangling over the woman's shoulder and hooked it to the dog's collar, then held out his hand. "Kade Church."

"Lieutenant Harper Jansen."

"Nice to meet you, LT."

He walked with her back to her house, one she shared with another woman, a civilian. After that, they'd crossed paths several times, and one day he'd invited her to a party he and his roommate were throwing.

Over time, he and the lieutenant became friends. When he learned that she loved horror and action movies, they'd started a movie night. For the next year after meeting her, they'd been best friends. Nothing more.

They were both planning to leave the Army around the same time, her a few months before him. She'd promised to come get her dog as soon as she returned home from her Peace Corps stint.

Then she'd died.

Since her promise to come get the dog ended with her death, Duke had become his. When he'd learned Harper had died, he'd wrapped his arms around her dog and cried against his fur. But she wasn't dead, as it turned out.

He wanted answers, and he was going to get them.

Don't miss Her Delta Force Protector,
book two in the K-9 Defenders series by
Sandra Owens, coming soon from Carina Press.

www.CarinaPress.com

Get 4 FREE REWARDS!
We'll send you 2 FREE Books plus 2 FREE Mystery Gifts.

FREE Value Over **$20**

Both the **Harlequin Intrigue®** and **Harlequin® Romantic Suspense** series feature compelling novels filled with heart-racing action-packed romance that will keep you on the edge of your seat.

YES! Please send me 2 FREE novels from the Harlequin Intrigue or Harlequin Romantic Suspense series and my 2 FREE gifts (gifts are worth about $10 retail). After receiving them, if I don't wish to receive any more books, I can return the shipping statement marked "cancel." If I don't cancel, I will receive 6 brand-new Harlequin Intrigue Larger-Print books every month and be billed just $6.24 each in the U.S. or $6.74 each in Canada, a savings of at least 14% off the cover price or 4 brand-new Harlequin Romantic Suspense books every month and be billed just $5.24 each in the U.S. or $5.99 each in Canada, a savings of at least 13% off the cover price. It's quite a bargain! Shipping and handling is just 50¢ per book in the U.S. and $1.25 per book in Canada.* I understand that accepting the 2 free books and gifts places me under no obligation to buy anything. I can always return a shipment and cancel at any time by calling the number below. The free books and gifts are mine to keep no matter what I decide.

Choose one: ☐ **Harlequin Intrigue Larger-Print** (199/399 HDN GRA2) ☐ **Harlequin Romantic Suspense** (240/340 HDN GRCE)

Name (please print)

Address _____ Apt. #

City _____ State/Province _____ Zip/Postal Code

Email: Please check this box ☐ if you would like to receive newsletters and promotional emails from Harlequin Enterprises ULC and its affiliates. You can unsubscribe anytime.

Mail to the **Harlequin Reader Service:**
IN U.S.A.: P.O. Box 1341, Buffalo, NY 14240-8531
IN CANADA: P.O. Box 603, Fort Erie, Ontario L2A 5X3

Want to try 2 free books from another series! Call 1-800-873-8635 or visit www.ReaderService.com.

*Terms and prices subject to change without notice. Prices do not include sales taxes, which will be charged (if applicable) based on your state or country of residence. Canadian residents will be charged applicable taxes. Offer not valid in Quebec. This offer is limited to one order per household. Books received may not be as shown. Not valid for current subscribers to the Harlequin Intrigue or Harlequin Romantic Suspense series. All orders subject to approval. Credit or debit balances in a customer's account(s) may be offset by any other outstanding balance owed by or to the customer. Please allow 4 to 6 weeks for delivery. Offer available while quantities last.

Your Privacy—Your information is being collected by Harlequin Enterprises ULC, operating as Harlequin Reader Service. For a complete summary of the information we collect, how we use this information and to whom it is disclosed, please visit our privacy notice located at corporate.harlequin.com/privacy-notice. From time to time we may also exchange your personal information with reputable third parties. If you wish to opt out of this sharing of your personal information, please visit readerservice.com/consumerschoice or call 1-800-873-8635. **Notice to California Residents**—Under California law, you have specific rights to control and access your data. For more information on these rights and how to exercise them, visit corporate.harlequin.com/california-privacy.

HIHRS22R2

Get 4 FREE REWARDS!

We'll send you 2 FREE Books plus 2 FREE Mystery Gifts.

FREE Value Over **$20**

Both the **Romance** and **Suspense** collections feature compelling novels written by many of today's bestselling authors.